Among the rush-hour crowds and abandoned levels of the London Underground, someone is pushing women under trains. In his search for the killer, Casimir, a Tube worker, is led ever deeper into this city beneath the city.

Below the bright crowds and tunnel musicians is a labyrinth of long-forgotten cross-passages, deep shelters and derelict Victorian stations. Hunting for the clues that will lead him to the killer, Casimir is also drawn back into his own past and the terrible secrets of his Polish childhood. In subterranean London, Casimir has gone to ground. But in his desperate search he discovers a chance for forgiveness and the emergence of a new life.

*Underground* is a compelling, intensely atmospheric first novel. It confirms Tobias Hill as an author who, in the words of the *Observer*, 'writes the kind of fiction that can change the way you look at the world'.

Tobias Hill was born in London in 1970. He has published three award-winning collections of poetry, has worked as a rock-music critic for the *Sunday Telegraph*, and in 1998 was the inaugural resident poet at London Zoo.

*Skin*, a collection of stories, won the 1998 PEN/Macmillan Award for Fiction and was shortlisted for the 1998 *Mail on Sunday*/John Llewellyn Rhys Prize. *The Times* compared the 'surprise and precision' of Hill's writing to that of Nabokov, while the *Independent* dubbed him 'a canny master of the uneasy and the alien, the slyly violent'.

# Underground

## TOBIAS HILL

*faber and faber*

First published in 1999
by Faber and Faber Limited
3 Queen Square London WC1N 3AU
This open market edition first published in 1999

Typeset by Faber and Faber Ltd
Printed in England by Mackays of Chatham plc, Chatham, Kent

© Tobias Hill, 1999

Tobias Hill is hereby identified as author of this work in accordance
with Section 77 of the Copyright, Designs and Patents Act 1988

A CIP record for this book
is available from the British Library

ISBN 0–571–20109–1

Quoted material from: 'All Along the Watchtower'
(Bob Dylan/Jimi Hendrix); 'Electric Ladyland' (Jimi Hendrix);
'Flash Gordon' (Queen, written by Freddie Mercury); 'Teclo' (P. J. Harvey,
written by Polly Jean Harvey, copyright Island Records Ltd); 'Down to the
River' (Bruce Springsteen); Lewis Carroll, *Alice Through the Looking-Glass*;
Zbigniew Herbert, 'Two Drops', *Selected Poems*

2 4 6 8 10 9 7 5 3 1

To my family, with much love.

The apparition of these faces in the crowd;
Petals on a wet, black bough.
Ezra Pound, 'In a Station of the Metro'

# Underground

# Electric Ladyland

*'Mind the gap. Please mind the gap. Please –'*

The echo of closing doors goes along the Underground platform. The train creaks with stress as it begins to move. Its half-empty carriages fill with the sounds of motion, tunnel air loud against the dirt-streaked windows.

In the first carriage sits a large man in station worker's clothes. He rests with his eyes shut, arms crossed heavily, shoulders down. The skin of his face is tight against the cheek-bones, smooth and reddened where he has shaved without water. The tunnel smells of car exhaust and human hair. It is familiar to him as the smell of his own rented room, which is the smell of himself.

First he is sleeping, then he is not sleeping. London passes overhead. He dreams briefly of catch pits, tunnels of white tiles, tunnels of dark grime. His hands lie twisted together in his lap, the tendons drawn clear towards the raw skin of the knuckles. Between his feet rest the black boxes of a cellular telephone, a track voltage tester and a waterproof torch. He keeps his feet and ankles touching them, like a cautious traveller in a foreign country. The groundwater on their scuffed rubber dampens his socks and working trousers.

The tunnel air sighs, open-mouthed: *Haaaah.* Where the structure widens or joins other tunnels, the sigh hollows out. Like water underground, the man thinks. He has not eaten or drunk this morning and the image of water makes him thirsty. He thinks of the city. Rain against shop windows. The smell of low tide near the river, in the plaster in the walls of his room on Lower Marsh. It makes his head hurt.

He knows the Underground line and that he will be awake when he arrives at work. It is not necessary for him to open his eyes. At each station, the rumble of the train doors cuts off fragments of platform announcements and the distant sounds of escalators in the miles of halls and concourses. Twice there is a movement of people in the carriage, their bulk blocking the light on his eyelids.

But it is early morning and there are few passengers. When he is asleep, the man still feels his hands against each other, the palm of the left slightly warmer than the heel of the right. When he is awake, he listens to the sound of the tunnel, how it deepens out at junctions and abandoned stations.

After some time he becomes aware of a voice. There is someone sitting to his right, singing. The voice rises and falls, loud for a moment and then quiet, humming against closed lips. He opens his eyes.

'There must be some kind of way out of here. Said the. Too much *confusion*. Can't get no.'

He has never liked music, the ways it changes what he feels. But the girl in the next seat is singing to her Walkman. Her voice is very young, musical even without the music. A beautiful voice, the man thinks. He tries to listen without being seen to do so. It is something to know about the girl, what music she likes.

She has her headphones turned up loud. He can hear the hiss of a beat over the Underground's roar. He listens with his head leant a little to one side, tie pulling tight against his throat. He keeps his eyes fixed on the yellowed strip lighting, the row of grey hand-grips swinging on their springs. *Cha, cha, uh-huh.* Her fingers beat on the armrest between them.

He wants to turn and look at her but does not. It is the same instinct which makes him cross the road at night if he is walking behind a woman. Because he is strong, he doesn't want to frighten people. He keeps to himself. But he has never heard a girl singing down here alone. Only the junkies. She doesn't sound junked-out. This is part of what interests him.

He looks along the carriage. This is the first up-train of the day, the 5.39 under the river and the West End, out towards the North Circular and the Green Belt. He can see two black men in tunnel-cleaner overalls, a boy dozing with a backpack on his knees, a woman reading the morning business sections.

There is no sound of people except for the girl's voice. Clear but out of tune. No one looks up at her. He watches her hand on the armrest, at the periphery of his vision.

'Have you ever been *have you ever been* to Electric Lady-land?'

She has been eating oranges while he slept. He can see the yellowish pith under her nails. Around her is a litter of peel, small bits torn off and thrown across the stained and corrugated wood floor. The sour smell of fruit mixes with those of rain and urine.

She smells of homelessness. He wonders how old she is and where she sleeps. He looks back at her hand.

There are ink marks where the prominent bones run to her index and middle fingers. A jumble of red and blue words and symbols in smudged print: UNDERWORLD, ΩHM. His eyes narrow as he tries to understand.

He looks down at her small boots. The left sole is coming away; she has tied it on with a second pair of shoelaces. He wants to tell her to use glue, glue would be better. The beat of her hand is regular as a pulse. He imagines what it would feel like, reaching out and covering that movement.

Instead he watches her in the window opposite. Against the dark of the tunnel walls, her skin and the scuts of her dreadlocks are white-blonde. The curve of the glass lengthens the angles of her cheekbones and chin. He doesn't remember seeing her on the first up-train before. But she is familiar from somewhere on the Underground. This also interests him. Her head is leant back, her eyes are closed, the eyebrows raised. She looks like she is dreaming. He wants to know if she dreams in colour.

She opens her eyes and looks back at him, first through the window's reflection and then directly, turning in her seat.

He thinks how dull they are, her eyes. Blue like blood seen through muscle. The shock of them makes him sit up. He is slow to register that she is talking to him.

'I forgot my Travelcard. I forgot it at home. It's for a month.'

Her voice is too loud, compensating for the Walkman. All the lilt of the music has gone out of her speech. When she sang she had an American accent; now she talks with the stopped-consonant voice of London or its satellite towns. For a moment he doesn't understand what she is saying. He turns to face her. She is looking at his uniform, not at him.

*She has no ticket*, he thinks. He shakes his head, tries to smile.

'I'm sorry. I'm not a ticket inspector. You don't have to –'

But she is looking away from him, eyes flickering across the windows. Outside the dirt-black tunnel gives way to a blur of posters, blue and white tiles, slowing past red-blue London Transport roundels and the station name, WARREN STREET. He turns back to her again.

She is no longer in her seat. He looks up and round, surprised at the quickness of her movement. She is by the door, staring back at him while the train brakes to a stop. He looks at her hands, balled into fists, the ink marks clear against the whitened skin.

He has a strong urge to get up and go to her, to tell her – what? That he finds it hard to look away from her or that he has seen her before? That he knows homelessness in himself, years old, still felt as if the bones are indelibly stained inside him? Instead he makes himself sit back. He wonders if he would be able to explain. The doors open and she steps out and begins to walk as they close behind her.

The train starts to move again. The man looks down at his large hands, thinking of hers. After a moment he turns quickly in his seat. The girl is walking along the platform, not hurrying. She has begun to sing again; he can see her lips moving. Her eyes are fixed ahead. She doesn't look up at him as the train carries him out of sight.

'So. Burton. Nice name. Where you from?'

'Mile End.'

'That's a way to come to Camden. What's that, thirty minutes' drive even this time of the morning, am I right?'

'Yeah.'

'Not to worry. Anyway, I'm Mick Adams. I'm Super. The bloody great foreign geezer over there, that's Cass. He's Assistant Super. You're trainee muck now, but one day all this could be yours. All you have to do is like being under six hundred square miles of London. OK? You must be a Hammers fan.'

'Oy. Don't diss my team, all right?'

'All right. I was only asking. I didn't say a word. Did I, Cass?'

He is by the escalators, down on his haunches. Something is caught in the machinery, he can hear it in the whirr and clank of parts as the steel-and-wood steps are carried round. Most likely it will be a plastic bag or a bag strap. Later he will check the maintenance chamber. The obstruction tears rhythmically, down in the works. He half-closes his eyes, trying to concentrate.

'Hey, Cass.'

For the most part he is not thinking of the escalator. He is remembering the girl on the morning train. The bones of her hands, marked with blue ink. The skin was very smooth, almost without lines, as if she might have no fingerprints.

The sense of having seen her before is still with him. He grinds his teeth gently, trying to remember.

'Casimir?'

'Yes.'

He straightens and turns. Adams is watching him, running fingertips across his side-combed scalp. A sharp, compact man, facial skin punctured with red pores and broken veins. The trainee is standing further off by the wall, very black against the white- and blue-glazed tiles. A pattern of stars is shaved into his hair.

'I was just asking him, wasn't I?'

'Of course. You are the supervisor.' He walks towards them across the tiled hall, which is also only a junction of corridors. Behind the station supervisor, dot-matrix boards begin to light up with the times of early trains to Morden and Bank.

'This is Burton. He's on Youth Training and he likes West Ham Football Club. Isn't that right, Burton?'

The younger man is looking down at his palms. Where he has touched the concourse wall tiles, a glittering grime has come away on his coat and skin. He swears, face wrinkling back from his teeth, narrowing his eyes. 'Look at this cack. It's all over everything.'

Adams tuts his tongue against his teeth. 'Force of gravity, Burton. All the dirt ends up down here. Don't knock it, though, it'll keep you in work for years. They should put it in government. Be like Cass here, he loves it. Still gets here an hour early for work, don't you, Cass?'

The younger man is looking away, up the escalator shaft. Weak dawn light reaches across the upper ceiling. Casimir thinks it will be a fine day outside. Sharp and bright. Adams goes on talking behind him.

'You're not worried by a bit of dirt, are you? A bit of hard work? No. Tell you what, since you've come all this way. Go back downstairs and tell Mister Oluwo to show you the old cross-passages. It's like the Cheddar Caves down there, all snickets and pope-holes. You can do a bit of cleaning, if you're feeling strong. All right? Remember the way?' A man in pinstripes heads past them, walking hard towards the City platform. 'Chop chop.'

Casimir watches as the trainee goes, shoulders hunched angrily, rubbing his hand on his trousers. He remembers his own first few days on the Underground. The feeling of control in the tunnels and halls, their light and air and even life rationed out; and with that, the gradual calm of finding his own life under control. The darkness out in the open, all around him, so that although it could and can still bring him out in a cold sweat, he is always ready for it. The fear never takes him by surprise. The Underground's great extent and age were things he learned later, but the sense of order has never gone away, not yet. It is something he needs, the control.

Most of all, he remembers the Tube seeming like a hiding place. It felt as if he was coming to ground here, waiting for something to catch up with him. He doesn't know what he is waiting for. Casimir does not understand where this sense comes from.

A lorry goes past overhead, the crash of its load and fittings filtered down. He turns away. He finds the distance of the sound soothing. Like rain through windows. He leans back against the wall. 'He won't be back tomorrow.'

'Of course he won't. Why should he? There's nothing for him down here.' The supervisor hawks and spits away.

They go on towards the platforms. Overhead in the city Casimir walks stooped, shy of his own height. But here in the passages he moves more naturally, the scooped curve of the tunnel leaving him scant headroom. He is always aware that people can be threatened by him, and not only because of his looming, soft-footed bulk. He is disturbing, in the way someone who has been through deep fear is disturbing. He imagines it coming off him like an odour: not fear any more, but something to be frightened of.

Along the walls, layers of old advertisements have been ripped off, strips hanging down loose where the poster hangers have left their night-work unfinished. Casimir looks up at the shots of blue sky, water beading black skin, car tracks on white sand. The slogans: 'GET DOWN AT G-SPOT SNOOKER & BEER HALL!', 'MANY WHO PLAN to seek God at the eleventh hour DIE AT 10.30'.

The floor is uneven by the next junction of tunnels, scarred by heavy machinery. He stops and takes a spray can out of his work coat, then kneels to mark round the rough tiling. Later he'll get a warning sign from the storerooms.

'What's wrong with that? Eh?' Adams waits for him, impatient. Something of him is always moving, hands or mouth or eyes.

'It could be dangerous.'

'Dangerous! Did you hear what happened on the new line? The drum diggers went through into a cave. Eighty feet deep. So what they've done is, they've concreted over the top of it and gone and laid the track. What do you think of that? All those passengers thinking they're going underground, when really they're chuffing along eighty feet above it.'

The supervisor is looking up at the NO SMOKING sign bolted to the wall, the shine of black enamelled smoke. 'No, you're right to be careful. Good lad. Christ, I need a fag.' He puts his hands in his pockets, keeping them still. 'How are you, Cass? I haven't seen you much this week.'

He shrugs. 'We were on different turns. I'm well.'

'You don't look it. You look peaky. Cash flow all right, is it? No family trouble?'

'No.' He is surprised. Family is not something he and Adams have talked about since Casimir filled in his job application. *Next of Kin*: 'none', he wrote. Which was not true, although it is how Casimir lives his life. In eight years, the relationship of Casimir and the supervisor has never gone much beyond work. Casimir tries to remember if they have ever met above ground. He thinks not. Real friendship is never something he has wanted from the supervisor. He feels no need to be understood. He stands back up, clapping his hands clean. 'No trouble. I have no family.'

'That's right, isn't it? No offence meant, eh?'

Adams slows as they reach a flight of stairs. The steps are worn down at their centres, metal and stone uneven. He goes down with one hand on the ironwork banister. Two steps behind, Casimir tries to imagine him retired, in a room of his own. All he can see is Adams in the station office, leant forward over the stained plyboard consoles, face lit with closed-circuit monitor light.

At the bottom of the stairs, the poster hangers have put up a new film advertisement. The paper is still shiny with wallpaper paste. They stop together in front of the clean, blue-white image. A single figure stumbles through a field of snow. Smaller flyers have already been stuck over the poster diagonally, like steps through the white field: HAVE YOU SEEN THIS CHILD?, a picture, a number. Adams tuts and reaches for the flyers, then lets his hand drop to his side. An indecisive, anxious movement. 'What shift were you on yesterday, Cass?'

'Middle turn. With Sammons.'

'So you were. You missed the news, then.'

'What news?'

Another commuter passes them, a young woman reading a paperback as she walks, hair blown into her face, skirt blown back against her ankles. Adams follows her with his eyes as he talks quietly. 'There was a bit of fuss yesterday. An accident. Late turn, round about afternoon rush hour.'

'Here?'

Adams nods. They begin to walk again. It has been almost a year since the last accident at their station. A failed Bank Holiday suicide, a scrawl of explanation twenty pages long stuffed into his jacket pockets. Casimir remembers the man weeping, bloody and wretched. The hum of electricity trying to earth itself.

He requires the thoughts to be gone and they are. 'A suicide?'

Adams looks back at him, half-smiling. 'A suicide wouldn't be an accident now, would it? Line Management reckons it was a fall. The platforms were crowded up to the white lines. Most likely someone got too close, pushing and shoving and that. This girl went down into the catch pit like that –' He snaps his fingers. The retort echoes along the tiled corridor.

Casimir waits for him to go on. Adams adjusts his watchstrap, then looks down towards the platform. 'Clean fall, but she tried to climb up out on the negative rail. Caught a bit of current and a bit more off the signal line. The bruises were worse than the burns and no blood to speak of. They've kept her in overnight for, you know? Just in case. It looked worse than it was. The way she fell.'

'What was her name?'

'Her name?' Adams frowns, blue eyes staring. 'Is, not was. She's not dead, for Christ's sake. Doesn't matter anyway, does it?'

Casimir shakes his head, embarrassed by the other man's sudden irritation. It comes to him that this is the edge of something in Adams, some larger anxiety or hurt. The girl matters to him. Casimir wonders why.

'S something, Sarendon, Savallas, I don't know.' The supervisor has stopped again, still frowning. 'Nice girl, she looked. Done up nice. Training to be a foot doctor.' He grins at Casimir, suddenly relieved. 'I never knew there was doctors just for feet, you know?'

They go on out on to the platform. It stretches away from them, long like a church nave. The three entranceways are Victorian mock-classical, bas-relief architraves and columns curved round the tunnel's proportions like images seen through a fish-eye lens. Casimir feels a momentary familiar sense of dislocation at the subterranean space, its scale and lack of natural light. The black platform surface is reinforced with steel chipping and edged with white. Beyond that, the four track rails shine. Under them is the deep gutter of the catch pit. Casimir thinks of the Tube workers' slang: *suicide pit.*

He sees the gutter as that; the term feels accurate. Suicides are what it's made to catch.

The news of the accident touches him, but he is also relieved. He knows how bad accidents can be on the Underground and this is not a bad accident. The electricity in the negative rail is only as strong as the current in a household socket. And there was no train collision. A minimum of blood.

He blinks once, looking back at himself, feeling his own unease. It jars with him, the way Adams has told him the news. The supervisor has always been quick-witted and quick-tempered, but the nervousness is new to Casimir, the sense of strapped-down anger. As if the accident were more serious than it is. He feels a faint current of air along his left cheek and the broken line of his nose. A train is coming, still far off in the dark.

Casimir feels shifting motion around him. Not the tangible matter of air, but a moment of dizziness, more inside him than out. A perception of change, a loss of control. It is a kind of fear he has not felt for a long time, not for years. He goes on talking, willing it away.

'Did she call for help?'

'Oh yes. Plenty of noise.'

'You don't think she jumped?'

Now the train is audible, the sound of it warbling through the tracks. Like a stone thrown across ice.

Adams looks away northwards, the direction from which the train will come. After some time he shakes his head, no.

'That doesn't make it an accident. She could have been pushed.'

The supervisor looks back up at him. His reddened face and blue eyes are cocked like the head of some bright, sharp bird. 'It's an accident until Line Management says otherwise. D'you get me?'

'Yes.'

'That's good. Right then, son.' He slaps Casimir's arm. A friendly movement but also automatic, without affection. 'We should be going. Rush hour in no time.' He has to shout a little over the roar of the oncoming train.

He wakes up in the dark. The muscles of his shoulders ache from overwork. The window is open but the room is hot, and from outside comes the sound of a car alarm, streets away.

His left hand is raised on the mattress, next to his upturned face. He can hear the tick of his watch, separating the dark into measured time. He turns to see. On his wrist, the watch-face emits its faint, definite light.

His mouth is dry and he gets up for water, asleep but not asleep. The hallway carpet is a numb fur under his feet.

He was dreaming of the girl. Already he can't remember the colour of her eyes. He tries to picture her clearly, letting nothing else fade as he wakes. The muscles of his erection are still drawn out hard and aching, warmer than his inner thigh. He clicks on the bathroom light and the bulb goes with a dull *pock*.

The flash of light stays on his eyes. He turns back into the hall. The light switch is by the staircase, away from his rented room. There are no windows, only a square of pinkish London cloud through a skylight. He gets to the switch and the bulb is dead.

He can feel a familiar, drowsy panic rising in him and he stands, waiting for it to pass. Light bulbs go together, he tells himself, because they are bought together. He tries to think rationally. It is possible to control the fear this way, he has done it many times. The dark looms over him and he arches his bare shoulders forward against it. His hands cross at the wrists, holding on to the indistinct light source of the watch-face. It is no more than five feet to the staircase. He makes himself go forward and down.

Outside the car alarm stops, long after he has ceased to hear it. The silence jolts him fully awake and he misses a step, keeling forward in the stairwell. He reaches out for the banister and swings upright, breathing badly.

At the bottom of the stairs is the first-floor kitchen. The sweet smells of frying oil and raw chicken-meat seep up from the shop below. Casimir clicks on the light and stands in its abrupt illumination, the dark pushed back outside small windows. He puts his head back, glad of the glare on his eyes.

The wall clock ticks loudly towards four-thirty. He has

another hour before he will leave for Camden Town. He turns on the radio and sits down at the Formica table. The air is warm against his bare legs. After some time he closes his eyes and sleeps with his head on his folded arms. The news whispers behind him.


He closes the scuffed side-door and stands outside on the pavement. Taking a breath, getting his bearings. The plate glass next to him is smeared with rain and grease. Above its window, the shop's name is printed in red: DON'T FRY TONIGHT PHONE CHICKEN DELITE.

Casimir looks up, shading his eyes against the dull light. The early-morning sky is grey and clear and the moon is still rising, a northern summer crescent that reminds him of Poland; the flat, cropped fields of Silesia and the moon over them at midday, unnatural in the blue sky. The eye of a fish beached in the Russian waterlands. Out of place; out of its place. He looks down and starts to walk, up Lower Marsh towards Waterloo station.

The shops he passes – Tribalize Body Piercing, Honour Exclusive Ladywear – are unlit behind chain-links. Only the cafés are already open. Market stall-holders smoke and chat outside Olympic Sandwich and Maria's. Casimir walks between their vans, the scaffolds of half-erected stalls and the crates of jogging bottoms, dusty plastic geraniums, bruised green bunches of plantain. His work clothes chaff against the skin of his neck and thighs.

He has lived in this place for eight years. The smell of the weekday market is intimate to him; diesel and fried onions, like a fairground. The soot-black brick houses have become his mental neighbourhood. It is the nearest thing he has to a sense of home. He walks with his head down, uncurious, black hair hanging forward past his temples.

Outside the Fishcoteque Bar, a man with birds tattooed on each hand is unloading painted eggs in glass boxes. One of the boxes falls as Casimir passes. He turns to watch without stopping. The man carefully picks up pieces of red eggshell, glass and black lacquer in his faded-ink hands.

Casimir knows his face and his name, Weaver. His memory is good and he knows many of the people here, sellers and buyers. But few of them know him. He likes it that way. He turns left up the incline of Spur Road, towards the high arched windows of Waterloo terminus.

At the top of the road he stops to catch his breath. Tower blocks loom overhead, nearer the Thames. Already the sky is lighter; he can feel the changing warmth of it on his face. Below him, Lower Marsh is a row of sallow net curtains, extensions built in brick the colour of new skin. The rear views make him think of city hostels in Poland, cheap back rooms with windows looking out on to nothing but other windows. Casimir would watch people eating alone at small tables, old men brushing their teeth, young women walking up and down behind blown-in curtains. Humanity crammed in together; he always liked that, except when he caught people looking back at him.

He searches for the window of his own room, but there is nothing to mark it out and after a moment he turns away.

There are steps up to the terminus and he hunches forward as he climbs, too lanky for their measure, taking them in twos and threes. A dog skitters down past him, white with pink-rimmed eyes, quiet and alert. Casimir turns right along the foot of the terminus building. The side-entrance is a brick arch, small and ordinary as the house doorways of Lower Marsh.

He goes through, into the arched concourse. Pigeons whicker around the four-faced station clock, jostling for resting space. There is a young man by the W. H. Smith, slumped against newspaper bundles. His head rests on his T-shirted chest and one inert bluish arm lies outstretched, as if asking for something. Casimir can see no one else and there is no sound of people yet, only the hushed echoes of arrival boards and cooling engines. Casimir feels a need to shout, to fill the place with the sound of voices. He smiles at himself. The expression works against the drawn lines of his features.

He walks across the white-tiled hall to a descending shaft, over-lit and loud with machinery. There is a London Underground map on the entrance wall, a knotwork of tunnel lines, purple and brown and black: Metropolitan, Bakerloo, Northern. Casimir steps on to the down-escalator and stops walking. Behind him, a telephone starts to ring, faint but insistent in the huge interior space. Casimir turns to look back at it as he is carried down.

*'All this time the guard was looking at her, first through a telescope, then through a microscope. At last he said, "You're travelling the wrong way," and shut up the window and went away.* Look. Can you see the guard in the picture?'

'No. Lie, lie. Lie-lie-lie.'

He is sitting opposite a woman, a suitcase, a dog and a child. The woman is reading to the child. The dog tugs at the worn-down seats. Behind them is his own reflection in the Tube windows. Today the seat next to him is empty. His uniform jacket is open. He does it up.

*'But the gentleman in white paper leant forwards and whispered in her ear, "Never mind what they all say, my dear, but take a return ticket every time the train stops."'*

'Lie, lie. Mum, I'm tired.'

'Are you listening to this?'

'You did a lie.'

'What lie?'

'There ain't no gentleman in white paper.'

The boy is frowning across at him, dark irises under lowered brows. Casimir smiles back. He remembers the story, the soft Polish of his mother's voice. Now the woman looks up at him quickly. Not worried, just watching. Her eyes are shadowed, the skin bruised with lack of sleep. He thinks how early it is to be down here, with a suitcase and child and a dog.

He looks away at the tunnel going by. After some distance it opens out, losing definition. Through his own reflection, Casimir watches another train go past. Faces at the window turn slowly to look back. The boy cranes round in his seat, but the other train is already gone.

At Camden Town he gets out. The train pulls away beside him as he walks down the platform. The air today smells wet and warm. Casimir guesses it will rain, and he regrets that he won't see it. It'll be ten hours before he is outside again. He has always enjoyed summer rain.

Half-way down the platform, a black sphere hangs from the tunnel ceiling. Casimir can make out the shapes of closed-circuit cameras inside the translucent plastic. He nods at them, half-raises a hand.

At the southern end of the platform he turns down a side-passage. The lighting here is poorer, less public; signs point off to other platforms and the deep well of the emergency stairs. The right wall is lined with dirt-clogged grilles, 1930s panelled wooden doors and extractor fans from the Camden take-aways. There is a thick, sweet smell of junk food in the low-ceilinged hall. Casimir feels his stomach turn over with hunger.

At the corner of the passage is a blank modern door. Off to one side is a sign:

STATION SUPERVISOR: ASSISTANCE. PLEASE ENTER.
! FIRE DOOR: KEEP SHUT.

Casimir stands for a moment, unbuttoning his jacket. He can hear the sound of static and voices through the door, faint and serious.

An old woman comes round the passage corner. Two lean grey dogs strain ahead of her, tongues lolling out in the underground humidity. The woman's mess of dull hair has become tangled with the dog leashes knotted to her belt. She stares up at Casimir, at the door and then away. She is talking under her breath and Casimir has the impression she is asking him for help. He leans forward instinctively, trying to hear.

'Why are church roofs green? Because they're eyes because they're cheese because they're grass –' She looks up at Casimir, puzzled and urgent. 'Because they're sunglasses.'

She begins to move again, keeping to the far wall, away from the figure and the door. As if they are out of place or somehow dangerous. Casimir watches her go. His face shows almost no emotion. He turns back to the door and goes in.

'Casimir! Good morning. Are you well?'

Aebanyim grins down at him. She is standing on a swivel chair by the ventilation shaft with a black rubber torch in one small hand and a screwdriver in the other. The chair wobbles and half-twists under her. Her teeth are stained bleach-white. Casimir grins back despite himself.

'Well, thank you. And you?'

'Oh, well, I am well too, of course.'

The office is a sparse, L-shaped room, cut in two by a ply-board counter. The paint on the walls was cream livery in the 1940s; now it is discoloured by decades to an uneven yellow. Casimir is always struck by the absence of windows here, the feeling of airlessness. Outside and above the walls there is nothing but water and power in pipes and shafts, and the density of London clay. The air smells of burnt coffee and the sour dirt of tunnel clothes.

Behind the counter Oluwo is leant back, watching the closed-circuit monitors. The screens flicker, as if their reception is almost lost. Oluwo's eyes are very white and unblinking in their dark sockets. Sweat silvers his face along the flat of his forehead and the angular three-scarred cheeks. He lowers his eyes to Casimir and nods once, without smiling.

From round the corner of the room, Casimir can hear Adams on the station-to-station telephone. Between bursts of static and distant conversation, his voice is harsh, losing patience. Casimir shrugs off his jacket and hangs it behind the door next to the racks of cellular phones, voltage testers and fluorescent waistcoats. He walks to the counter, opens it and edges through. Round the corner where Adams stands, the room is illuminated only by monitor screens. Adams's skin is lit the colour of newspapers.

'I don't care what they do on the Vic. Oy. Oy. Are you listening to me?' Adams is bent towards the wall phone so that his face almost touches the wall. One hand is leant out to support himself, the other grips the receiver. His face is screwed up with emotion. To Casimir he looks like a man in pain. He doesn't notice as Casimir finds a plastic chair and sits down.

'I don't care what they do on the fucking Vic or the fucking Pic. On this line you get your men off the track by switching-on time, all right? Because it's not even seven now and already the trains are ten minutes late because you and your lot were still fucking around in the tunnels at five-thirty. All right? Have I made myself clear? That's good then, and you fuck off too.'

He shoves himself off the wall and back upright. For a moment he rocks on his heels, staring up into space. Casimir watches the anger going out of him or back into him.

'Adams.'

The supervisor flinches and turns. 'Cass.' He rubs his eyes with the knuckles of one hand. Smiling, tired. 'You're early.'

'So are you.'

'So I am, yes. We catch the worms. Who else is on today?'

'Sievwright and Leynes. Oluwo is on double shift.'

'Is Aebanyim leaving?'

'No. She is also early.'

He knows all this, Casimir thinks. He is just talking for the sake of it. It is not like him. Casimir watches as the supervisor eases himself into a seat.

'Really.' He looks over at Oluwo, then smiles at Casimir again. 'What you got for breakfast, Mister Oluwo?'

The black man stares balefully at Adams, clicks his tongue and looks away.

'No, really, what is it today? Pork pies? Jam tarts?'

Casimir shifts uncomfortably. Everybody knows about Oluwo's superstitions. He remembers the man's slow voice. *You eat underground, you stay underground.* Casimir has seen him drink black tea, and nothing else. The man consumes nothing here, as if being underground, the food will grow roots in his stomach.

Still, this is a delicate matter. He is surprised by Adams's teasing. After all, there are other beliefs about the Tubes. They all have superstitions. The supervisor is smiling, trying to catch Casimir's eye. He meets the man's gaze and tries not to frown. 'What needs doing?'

Adams sighs, reaches for a clipboard schedule. 'All right, all right. Take your pick. There's water getting into the sub-station again, the monitors have been on the blink all day, you could get on to Thames Water.' He leafs through pages of scrawled notes. 'What else? The vendor deliverers are coming with eight hundred units of Wispa, whatever that means; they'll need keys and that. There was a whacking great Rasta-farian fellow around yesterday, nearly as big as you – Leynes caught him painting coloured stripes on the platforms, he said it was to make the doors open. So if the station starts turning green and gold, that'll be why. And there's blue graffiti all over the old cross-tunnels. The stuff's like fucking mushrooms, it comes up by itself overnight. A couple of the new lads are down there cleaning up. Unsupervised. So if you've got a minute –'

'Of course.'

'Good. No hurry. Aebanyim!' His voice rises to a yell as he looks past Casimir.

'Yes, I am up here.' There is a clang of grille metal on concrete. 'No mice.'

'I heard them. Look again.' Adams has put the clipboard down. He is picking through a pile of *Traffic Circular* magazines, timetables and large photographs. Arranging them on the counter. His head is turned down to one side; Casimir can no longer see his face. Only the forehead, the deep frown lines. 'If I'm going to sit a hundred feet under the ground all day, I'm not going to breathe mouse shit too. Do you see them now?'

His voice is quick and sure but also flat, lacking the intonation of emotion. He has been drinking, thinks Casimir, and the thought surprises him. He has never seen Adams drunk. If he had been asked, Casimir would have guessed the supervisor drank often and alone. But not here. Not where he is seen and matters, on the Underground.

He runs his nails down the undersides of his thumbs. A small pain, to help him consider.

'No, I don't. No mice. I do not see no mice.'

'Bloody Jesus.'

Adams is on his feet quickly, pushing past Casimir and Oluwo. The black man follows Adams with his eyes. Then he looks back at Casimir, his head cocked, questioning. From beyond them comes the sound of Adams and Aebanyim arguing, the shrill clang of the ventilation-shaft cover as Adams climbs up on the chair and reaches out.

Casimir shakes his head and turns away. He hears the office door slam back as more workers come in, Sievwright and Leynes. Their London accents echo loudly, the sound trapped in the small room.

He leans forward on the counter. With his head down, the

sound of voices is diminished, cut off by the angle of walls. In this position he has some sense of privacy; the feeling of crowding is not so bad. The in-house circulars and papers are scattered where Adams left them. Casimir gathers them together, sorts them. After some time he stops. The photographs are in his hands. He remains bent forward while he looks.

There are only two shots. The first shows one of the four platforms at the station, Casimir can't be sure which. The other is of a woman in a street photo booth. He looks at the woman first.

She is leaning her head against the booth's orange background curtain. Light comes through the curtain and the pale weight of her hair. Her eyes are looking away from the camera and her smile is slight, distracted. She is wearing a man's pinstriped shirt. The collar is too big for her; it emphasizes the leanness of her throat. Everything is grainy and just out of focus, as if the image has been enlarged from a much smaller print. Written across the woman's shirt collar is a name in white developer's ink: REBECCA SAVILLE.

He puts down the picture of the woman. The other photo is a still from the station's closed-circuit cameras. Casimir recognizes the high angle of the black sphere, the slight curve of the tracks. Next to him, he knows, Oluwo will be looking at the same basic image. The freeze-framed tunnel is crowded with people, the tops of their heads packed up to the white edge of the platform. The still is grey-white, the quality too poor to enlarge.

A figure is falling from the crowd. Its arms reach out, instinctive, to stop the fall. The action is distant, sixty feet away or more; there is little facial detail, only the mouth's dark smudge. Hair spreads from the turning head, blurred by movement. In the camera's monotone it has become a startling white.

Something else extends from the mass of people at the platform's edge. It is hard to make out and Casimir narrows his eyes. The smudged shape resolves itself as his eyes adjust. There is a black sleeve, white skin, the suggestion of a hand behind the falling figure. Reaching out from the crowd.

'Cass. Casimir? Are you not gone yet? What's keeping you?'

The supervisor's voice jerks him back guiltily, as if he has pried into something private or illicit. With the sense of guilt comes an opposing impulse to go to Adams with the photographs, to ask him what they mean. The confusion of emotions disturbs him. He puts the photographs down where Adams left them, arranged on the dimly lit counter. Pushing the thoughts away.

'Nothing is keeping me.'

He stands up to go, and when he turns Oluwo is watching him, head still cocked a little to one side. In the other man's face Casimir sees how he must look himself. His threatening, looming tension. He makes himself smile, forces his shoulders down.

Oluwo smiles back. All his teeth are white metal, silver or cheap alloy. He has the shy grin of a child. Then the smile passes and the lines of his face settle back into their mask. Casimir steps behind him and past. When he blinks there is the image of the woman falling. The hand behind her, reaching out for her white-lit hair.


The graffiti are angular and intricate, like some violently debased Arabic script. Blue knotworks of writing have been sprayed on the yellowing tiles of the disused platform-to-platform tunnel. The tunnel itself is cluttered with stored materials. Boxes of pearl light bulbs, canvas-covered lengths of shining steel track. Casimir picks up a spray-paint can from a broken box of neon tubing. He turns it in his hands. Behind him, the two trainees work at the far wall with chemical sprays and sheets of green scouring fibre.

'Do you understand it, sir?'

Casimir looks round. One of the trainees is leering back at him. Hair the colour of rust, skin reddened with freckles. He nods at the graffiti. Casimir shakes his head.

The trainee puts down his scouring sheet and moves across the tunnel. He traces out the spray-painted writing without letting his fingers touch the waxy dirt of the wall tiles. Ian something, Casimir remembers. Weaver. Like the painted-egg man. He doubts they are related; London is too big for that. It is one of the reasons he likes cities. In this preference he is unlike most small-town Poles, he knows, with their sense of inferiority, suspicious of an order in the big cities beyond their comprehension.

'Look, see? That's an S. Then P, little I –'

The young man traces out a signature name. For a moment all Casimir sees are the shapes of snarling teeth, smiling faces, formed out of the lines like the ideograms in Chinese characters. Then the letters resolve themselves, curved backwards and into each other. Huddled together until it's difficult to tell them apart. Like the homeless, thinks Casimir. The canvas covering at his feet has been disturbed, pressed down. Casimir can see the indentation of a body, perhaps more than one. He looks around, narrowing his eyes to make out the graffitied names: SPIDER, JACK UNION, MISTER LEATHERS.

'What do they mean?'

'Mean?' The trainee shrugs, still grinning.

A rush of stale air and dust goes past them as a train arrives or leaves, somewhere up on the working platforms. The second trainee swears and covers his eyes, hunched over.

Weaver looks back at him, distracted. 'Nothing. They're just names.'

The second trainee stands upright, tall and angry. 'What are we cleaning down here for anyway? It's all locked up and that. No one comes down here.'

'It needs cleaning. We clean it. That's our job.' A length of rail has fallen off the stack near Casimir. He squats down and lifts the end back on to the pile. Quickly and easily, hand closed around the damp steel. The metal is cold and very heavy. There is the slight, good pain of work in the muscles of his arm. 'And you are wrong. Someone has been down here.'

He pulls the tarpaulin back over the stack of rails. The impression of a sleeping body vanishes as the canvas is straightened out. He stands up, puts the spray can in his jacket pocket, claps the tunnel dust clean from his hands.

# 2

# Red is the Colour

Here. I am here. I am. My mother's voice comes calling, dipping through the trees.

There are my high places and this is my special place and his too with the black wet town road, horse carts, coal trucks, mud sleighs, a blue car coming to meet me with the flats over it like stone sky. I can see my flat with my head right back on my shoulders, I count up, eight nine ten floors and the winter coat collar wet against my hair. From here I can see almost everything.

My flat has green curtains, not orange. When I hide inside them they have green bits but also blue. I want blue cars and red meat so I am not hungry. I will eat fast to get it while I have the chance. I touch my face with my hands and my hands are colder. My face is nothing, I do not know it.

I can run away under the trees, which are white with the snow and blue with the snow in shadow and green and red-skinned and orange where the bark is broken, they are all the colours of traffic lights. I can run down my Strug C Block steps like flying, I go faster than snow when it falls from the wings of trees, I roll and laugh under it. I can press the snow in my hands and it shows I am here. There is proof of me in its shaped blue shadow.

Look at my hands! The cut short nails dig into the snow. The more you press snow the harder it gets. The skin is going red like meat but meat is only my outside. Inside I am Kazimierz Ariel Kazimierski. If I could choose I would be like the snow.

I have secret lists. There is the list of names and of frightening things, the list of loves and of trees. All are in my head except for the list of names. Today Piotr has written the names for me on thick dark rough ripped sack-paper from the farm.

For nothing he does this for me. It is because I am his friend. We do anything for each other.

This is my list of secret words:

People – *Ariel* my middle name is *Roman* it is Piotr's *Monika* who is a girl but with a rabbit's mouth *Tomek* who is Militia and the father of *Wladislaw* who has been into the burnt flat *Karol* whose brother found a German shell in the old coal mine. Something happened to him like to my balloon at the factory parade which went up into the sky and disappeared. *Boniek Lato Denya* they are footballers. I am the goalkeeper. As far as I can remember, I have only let in seven goals.

Places – *Poland Silesia Gliwice*, which is here. *America Russia Germany The English* we have beaten them all except the Yanks.

Machines – *Ursus* it is a tractor *Leyland* an engine *Berliet* the buses *Jones* the cranes in the shipyard, Father teaches me these names with his finger on the metal letters. *Polski Fiat* which Father will buy when he gets the big deal.

*Kraut Cholera Blood Cock Gyp Damn Shit Fucking Devil Piss Yid Yank Balls Cunt Whore Slut Jew Arse Bastard Runt.* All these were my father's. I have no words from my mother. It is because she speaks less. I list the sound of her voice but Piotr says that it isn't a name. *Black Market. Speculator. Underground.*

There are other names but they are not so important. I never forget because I have lists, it is the reason. I learn fast. I see everything.

In my fist the snow drips. All the colour has gone from it, even the white, it is no-colour. It takes time to run away. My hand hurts but I do not let go. I last, nothing of me has gone. I am stronger than the snow.

I listen. It is now that Mother is calling, her voice dipping through the trees. She does not know what I am doing. She does not call for me to stop. No one can see me, so no one will stop me. I breathe deep when I smile.


In the beginning there is Father and I remember he is happy.

My father travels for money. Now he is back and when he swings me up I watch him, to remember. He is frowning and laughing. As if he doesn't understand me but he is happy to see me anyway. As if I am a pleasant surprise.

There are people waving around us. What are they waving? I watch and it is arms, hands, footballs, bottles, woolly hats, scarves, kitchen pots and radios. The room is full of noise. Outside the moon is out. I watch the words come out of my father's mouth.

'Poland beat the English. Poland beat the English! *Poland beat the English!*'

This was a while ago now but I remember it. It is the first thing.

My father has a gun from the war. It is small and has no bullets left. He shows it to me at the kitchen table. It comes apart like all machines.

'Russian guns are best. One day I'll get you a Russian gun, Kazio. When I get a big deal. Only the best for the best.'

I am four now. Not so small that I like being called Kazio. My real name is Kazimierz. Father doesn't smile when he puts the gun back together.

'Always shoot the German before the Russian. Remember that too. Business before pleasure.'

The Russians shot my father's mother. It was in the war and her name was Kasia. I love my father but he scares me. Only sometimes. My life is not ordinary, not good or bad. Sometimes he smiles with his mouth open and you can see his tongue. It is like watching a dog in June heat. It is when he smiles that I keep away from him.

Another time when I was very small, I was in a field of flowers with my mother and father. The flowers are yellow and white, scrambled together, spring flowers.

'Cut-upped egg,' I say. 'Like cut-upped egg.'

They laugh and laugh.

There is a sound above me. I look up and see an aeroplane and understand what it is. Father lifts me up on his shoulders. His hands are harder than my mother's. He is harder than her.

They are still laughing together. I put my head back. The aeroplane's shadow goes over us and is gone.

I ask Mother about the curtains. She does not tell me. I ask Piotr.

'Piotr, why do I have green curtains, not orange?'

He puts down the coal and wipes his fingers on the steps. Even so his hands stay black as if they are burnt. Our old flat was burnt; Mother did it. She cooked duck eggs and forgot about them. They split open as if they were hatching and out flew the flames. The smell was terrible, so we came here to Strug C Block. I don't remember this at all, but people tell me.

Piotr gives up cleaning his hands. 'I think it is to do with money. Green is in the middle. White net curtains mean they have less cash, and brown means they are old and rich. Red is for the people with Polski Fiats.'

'What colour do you have?'

He picks up the coal again. 'Mostly yellow. Yellow is for farms.'

He is writing on the steps of Strug C Block with the coal, I don't know what. I say, 'Black is for when there are dead people.'

I like it better when he draws. Sometimes he does tanks and we fight with them. Poland against the Germans and Russians, the Americans and English. Poland against the world. Most times I am Poland, so I win.

'Blue is for dirty Yids.'

I stand up and push him over. I am taller than Piotr, who is a year older than me. Now he looks at me and stays down.

'Why did you do that?'

I don't tell him. It makes me confused and angry, so I shout at him, 'Don't write when I don't like it. Now you must do drawings.'

'All right.'

He starts to draw something. I sit down to see. It is a ship with guns. There are people with hats and people with cats. There are black chimneys and flags. Some people are playing football.

'Does it go on canals?'

'Yes, it does.'

He draws the Gliwice canals. I keep quiet now. I do not tell him about my curtains, which are blue when I am close to them. I feel something like fear and it is shame.


Vodka hurts when you smell it. There are three bottles at home. One is in the guest room and it is Russian. One is in the kitchen on the high shelves with the glass doors and it is Father's. The third bottle is behind the stove. It's empty and flat, like it was made to be hidden. I think Mother forgot where she hid it.

When my mother was four she went to France. She told me there were fields of sunflowers, all in rows, all facing the sun. Only one sunflower was looking away from the sun and her father picked it for her.

Later she didn't remember that any more. I had to tell it to her. She forgets lots of things.


No one is here. I go into Mother's room. The beds are higher than mine and between them is a table made of glass. If you put your ear to the clock you can hear it tick. Like seeds falling.

There are wooden drawers painted white and I open the bottom one. My father's clothes are here, brown shirts and checked ones and socks. They smell of church, which is the mothballs. Of being dried on the balcony window in the sun and dust. Of Father. I press my face against the smell of him. When I am done with it I go.


Me and Piotr and Wladislaw, we go to the burnt flat. Everything is black, it looks like a picture Piotr has drawn with his coal. Sometimes there are other pictures in the black, just shapes. Wladislaw says it is from the fire moving. I can hear the loud-hailer cars, they are outside in the rain, they go round near and far loud-hailing about food.

'Dare you to go into the last room.'

'No.'

'Chicken.'

'You're chicken. Do the Choosing Song.'

Piotr does it, between the three of us. 'Ana Dua Likka Fakka Torba Borba Usmussmakka Deus Deus Cosmateus Imorella *Bugs*. It's you.'

It's me. I go into the last room, where there are no windows. The floor's burnt through to black wooden planks. I walk lightly. Piotr and Wladislaw stay in the first room, waiting for me to fall.

Me and Piotr, we have not been in the burnt flat before. It is a new thing. Before now there were Jews here, a man and a woman and three babies, two boy babies and a girl baby. I never talked to them or anything. I don't know where they have gone now.

There is black glass in the last room. It is round at the edges and quite smooth. Black for dead people. I put it in my pockets and go back to the first room.

'What's in there?'

'Nothing. Just the burning.'

I don't show them the black glass. It is my secret. I deserve it because I didn't fall. Later I will look at it again, when I am alone, and see how beautiful it is.


Today Father is home and with him there is blood.

It is dark like cod liver on the floor then red on the white bowl. Red for people with cars. The iron smell of it fills the kitchen. I stand away from him across the table.

I stop breathing to keep the smell of him out of me. I can make it so I am not breathing at all.

'We've no iodine. I'll go and ask the Sommers to –'

'Stay here.'

'But, love, it needs to be clean.'

'Make do. We can look after ourselves.'

She brings hot water in a white bowl. He smiles when his hands go under the water and smiles again when he takes them out. It is nothing to smile about because he is still bleeding. His teeth are yellow in the kitchen light. Quickly Mother cleans all the blood off his hands. She has white cloth and she

[29]

puts it round and round. First the blood comes through a lot then a little then not at all.

We all go quiet, waiting to see if the blood is gone. It is. I can hear Monika who lives next door, she is singing play songs. I hear her through the wall.

'I'm not going back down. The shipyard was better than this.'

'We need the money.'

'Eh?'

'We need the money, love.'

'Money again! Money is all you think about. And why should I be surprised?'

My mother moves around the kitchen and says nothing. Her dress has flowers the colour of new leaves. It makes her look pale. It is usual, her not talking, Father talking. This is an ordinary night. My life is not good, not bad.

'As if you've got nothing stashed away. Such a good little miser. I know, *love*, we'll get you a job, how about that? How would it be if you got your hands bloody for a change? Your precious white hands. I'd like to see that. *Blood!* I need more cigarettes.'

Father looks at me and he sees me. *Blood* is the worst curse, the most secret. Sometimes he looks at me and doesn't see but now he smiles again. I take a step back, nearer the door.

'Where's your grandfather, son?'

'In his room.'

'See if he's got any cigarettes.'

'OK.'

I go out. In the hall I sit down like I am playing and I listen. It is not hard.

'They won't have me back anyway. The Black Trout Shaft foreman said so. Says I'm a danger with the machinery, so that's that. I'll travel again.'

'No.'

'What's wrong with you? Didn't you hear about Latek? Three months ago all he could buy was soap, now he's selling leather jackets. Do you know what he gets on those?'

'You could find other work.'

'And the Party worker in Katowice, didn't you hear that? A

million dollars from nothing worse than tractors, and now he's disappeared to Cuba! Cuba. It drives me mad, Anna, watching them. I feel stuck here.'

'Don't go.'

'I didn't say that.'

'Don't leave us.'

'I didn't say that, did I? Why, would you miss me?'

'Yes. I don't know. I don't.'

'Ah. You look so much better when you're sad. Say it again. Nicely.'

'Don't.'

They stop talking. Now there is only sound and movement. It is stupid and I am bored. I can hear Monika in the hall now. If I tell her about her mouth she will run away. I think I will do it. I run.


Karol has a red Brando. Monika has a green one. They click them in their mouths. *Clickety-click*. I have no Brando but I see everything, I watch the day happen. The Chorzelski brothers have a motorbike but there are four of them so they take turns. The sky is yellow at the ends and blue on the top and the grassy dust is warm. It's a good day. It would be better with a Brando.


This is the list of frightening things. It is still in my head. I am not scared of so much as Piotr or Monika but more than Wladislaw.

Piotr doesn't write the list for me. He is at school now. I am alone.

- The statues at the Hall of Local Government which are devils, they have horns and no cocks and their knees go backwards.
- Wallpaper flowers.
- Lighting cigarettes from candles because it means you'll die at sea.
- My father's blood.
- Writing.
- Meat tokens. Mother got liver for a month.

- Wax dropped in water which tells fortunes.
- Turning lights.
- The burnt flat.

It happened at night and we went down and stood on the steps in rows, all of the neighbours in Strug C Block, hundreds all big and small and fat in coats and blankets and pyjamas and sometimes nothing, just pink. The firemen's ladder went up five floors and they waved.

I never saw this myself but Mother tells me it was so. I was mostly asleep. I only remember stairs and turning lights.

My father drinks winiak brandy at breakfast. It is to thin his blood. He went on an aeroplane and brought me back three lemon wipes. I keep them wrapped up in brown paper with red writing on it. The first wipe stopped smelling, so now I'm on the second wipe. It smells better than real lemons.

Games are good. I play the Anywhere Game with my mother. We do it on the bicycle.

'Now where?'

'Left.'

'Here?'

'Yes. Faster.'

'All right. There, this is pretty. And now?'

'Left. No. Right. *Right*.'

'Leave the – Sit back! Back. Or we stop.'

One time we came to a road with no other roads at the end, only sunlight striped down a wall and big crows eating from rubbish bins. In the wall was a door and we went through and there was a garden. It was beautiful. There were trees and water.

'Can I play here?'

'Of course. It's for everyone.'

Her face was all ripply with light from the water. I laughed back at her like an echo. I ran into the trees, where I could be her echo.

Or there were riddles. They can be done anywhere.

In the cheese and shoes shop: 'Why are birches white?'

'Because they're whitewashed, like apple trees?'

'No.'

'Because they're hiding in the snow?'

'Yes.' She's quite good at riddles. In the bath: 'What is red the colour of?'

'I don't know. Mind your eyes. Here it comes.'

'People with cars. Why does Dad go away from us?'

'I'm not sure.'

'To get money?'

'Maybe he just likes going away. Careful. Ariel –'

My mother sneezes when she gets wet. Three times, then a breath, then the fourth. She always sneezes the same way.

When she cries it is like coughing, like something breaking. It is small sticks breaking under the trees when I run. When I dream of running under the trees I know this, that Mother has been crying while I sleep.


I hate music. It gets in the way of thinking. There is a hole in the radio's back where a button came off and I get a little stone and push it inside to stop the music but it doesn't.

I go to the road where the new flats are going up, high and hollow. There are loads of little orange stones and I take them home. I put more little stones in through the hole in the radio. It takes 226 stones to stop the music. I go and smell my lemon wipes. It is quiet in my room and the sun comes in through the open window, bright and sharp like the smell of lemons.

Now Father is at the kitchen table with the radio and a winiak brandy and Grandfather's tool box. There is nothing to show it was me with the stones. I stay with him anyway. I stand close and talk fast.

'Did you eat food on the aeroplane?'

'Sure. Food, drink, cigarettes.' He frowns. When he lifts up the radio, the stones go shuffling around inside.

'Can you fix it?' Mother comes in with her hands up to her blue-black hair, winding it around itself.

'Damn thing sounds like a concrete mixer. I don't know what's wrong with it.' Now he opens out Grandfather's tool kit. I play the Question Game to slow him down even more.

'Did everyone have lemon wipes?'

'Eh? Everyone did, yes.'

'Why?'

'To clean their hands with. There –' He notches the driver into a screw. The first one comes out straight away.

'Why?'

'Mm? I don't know. Because they were dirty people.' There are only three screws. The second one is in hard. Father grunts through his teeth and it gets loose.

'Why?'

He swings his face round at me and away. The third screw rolls off and he catches it in his hand and grins. 'Why? Because they were on dirty business, that's why.' He takes the back off the radio and lifts it up to look inside.

'*Borja!*'

Little orange stones come rattling out over Father and the kitchen table. He drops the radio and jumps backwards. The glass of winiak cracks like ice on a waterbutt. I watch it drip gold before I run.


We went to Krakow to see soldiers. It was the first time. On the train there was a tunnel and my father said we had to hold our breath, it is the Breathing Game. I held my breath as long as I could, but when I opened my eyes we were still under the ground. My father held his breath right out into the light.

When I came back my town was different because I could smell it. The smell of my town is of coal. I like it. Coal smells like under the pine trees in summer, but sweeter.


We are making supper but I am thinking of the names of trees I have learned. Birch, larch, sycamore. I stand on the stool and she is behind me. We are four hands. Our hands clean the potatoes. Our hands take them out of the sink. The potato skins are grey and shiny, like aluminium.

'You're quiet.'

'Yes. I'm making secret lists.'

I can feel my mother laugh through my back. Laughing is a feeling.

'Are they good secrets or bad?'

It's not a clever question. How can I tell her? If I did I wouldn't have secrets any more. We go on cleaning. The big windows are open and the blue-green curtains are open and the net curtains belly inwards, full of light. Outside children are screaming. I wonder if they are hurt or playing.

'Do you have secrets?'

'Yes.'

'Do you make lists with them?'

'No.'

'What do you do with them?'

She lifts out the potatoes. They are drained and almost dry but they still shine.

'What do you do with them?'

'I try never to think of them, or say them. That way I forget. Then I have no secrets. Arms out.'

She dries our hands on the blue towel. Next I will go and play.

'Like middle names.'

Her hands stop drying. Her arms go hard round me. I look up with my head right back.

'Like Ariel. No one says it so they forget.'

Her face is upside-down and I smile at it. I can't work out if she smiles back. She puts her wet hands on the sides of my face and she leans down to me.

'That's right. It was your grandfather's name.'

'No, it isn't.' Grandfather's name is Pavel. I heard him say it to a Militia man.

'Your other grandfather. Mine. Now it's our secret, yes? It belongs to both of us.'

'Yes. And to Father. Your hands are wet.'

'Not to Father. Just us.'

She kisses my face. Breathes in my ear, *Shhhh*. It feels nice.

'Do it again.'

Laughter. *Shhhh*.

'Again.'
She bends low. Darkness. *Haaaah*.


Winter. I am watching at my window. The world is black and white with snow. Down there I see my mother. Her footsteps go small and black down the centre of the white path. In the distance she stops. She has forgotten which way she is going. For a long time she stops. Then she goes on again.


I turn back from the high place. The trees are all quiet and listening. One, I put my head right back on the flat of my shoulders. Two, I open my mouth back over the teeth to shout and, three, I breathe right in. It will be so loud this shout, it will be like the whole trees breaking. Here it comes.

# 3

# Roses

It is a day before he sees her again and then it is twice in the space of hours. As if she is a new word in his life, something he has never known and so never seen. He catches sight of her bent by a platform drinks machine through a crocodile of day-trip schoolchildren, gone when the crowd separates. Then again, that afternoon.

He recognizes her before he has seen her face. It's the end of middle turn, three o'clock. Sievwright's cracked voice echoes through from the office toilets, singing one line of pop music again and again over the hiss of a basin tap. Casimir looks up absently at the monitor screens. Smile lines crease around his eyes. The irises are near black, red-black only in the strongest light. Now they stop, pupils narrowing to focus.

'Flash! Ah-hah. Save every one of us. Flash! Ah-hah –'

The Underground girl is walking down the platform, quick among the loose mid-afternoon crowd. A train pulls away next to her, black roof curving close to the fish-eye camera. Casimir can't see her face and she is wearing different clothes – a man's chinos and a pale cord jacket. It is the way she moves that he recognizes. Faster than the crowd but not pushing. Just faster, as if her blood is circulating at a different rate.

He sees that her hair has changed, the dreadlocks washed out. She still has her headphones on. Once she turns and he sees her face smiling, lips moving. Then she is taken in by the crowd and he can't see her face any more.

'Ah-hah. Flash! –'

The screen blinks with interference, then clears again. Casimir wonders how many times he has seen her before, or looked at her without seeing. How long can it have it taken him to notice her? He tries to place the earlier sense of familiarity, but there are so many people and places on the Underground. The grey thickness of the monitor screens, slow parades of rush-hour crowds. Solitary figures in the halls or wells, shafts or concourses.

Even so, he is surprised to have seen her twice in a day. She has not been commuting, he thinks. Not in transit, but here in a less temporary way. Again, he wonders where she sleeps.

'Flash! – Hello, Cass. You look like the cat what got the Mogadon.' Sievwright peers past him at the screens. 'What's up?'

'Nothing. I saw someone I knew.'

The pace of the crowd slows as they reach the exit. Casimir narrows his eyes, trying to keep track of the Underground girl, but it's impossible. She is becoming lost in the crowd. He is losing her for a third time.

'I didn't know you knew anyone. Who was it, comrade, Mikhail Gorbachov? Your mum, was it? Oy –'

He is on his feet, the swivel chair clanking back against the control-room wall. Weaver and Aebanyim are by the door, shrugging off orange visibility vests. Casimir pushes past and out into the Underground, Sievwright's laughter echoing after him.

The passage is still crowded with people. Casimir stands back, waiting, his eyes going from face to face. He sees a man built like a darts player, the nails of one hand broken down past the quicks. A woman with blue-rinse hair and matching blue jogging shorts. A tall Chinese man, shirt loose over his hollow ribcage. Children kick up against wall posters as they run by.

He waits until they are almost gone, checking that the girl is not among them. Then he turns up the empty passage towards the southbound platform, quick but not yet breaking into a run. There are two side-passages before the platform entrance and he stops at each, listening. There is no sound except the whirr of ventilation outlets and the sound of a busker's music from one of the distant tunnels; the engine growl of a didgeridoo, becoming indistinct against the subterranean roar of trains.

Casimir tries to think what he will say if he catches up with her. The English in his head seems to condense, becoming inexpressively hard. He thinks of what he felt when he saw her on the morning train, the sense of shared experience and the physical desire: simple things. But he knows he'll say none of this. If he tells her anything it will be to remind her of the train, of her own song. He remembers the words of it. *Have you ever been to Electric Ladyland?* He wonders if she will remember him at all.

At the point where the passage opens on to the southbound platform he stops. The crowd has thinned out, filtering up to the surface or through to other platforms. On the nearest bench an old couple are eating white-bread sandwiches, greaseproof paper spread on their knees. They don't look up at Casimir.

He turns back. Twenty feet down the corridor a figure is turning into the first side-tunnel. Small steps and a woman's fine long hair, blown back bright. Moving fast, already out of sight.

'Wait! Miss, I need –'

He doesn't know what he needs. He begins to run fast, too fast to speak. Air filling his mouth, the sound of his own feet clattering around him. There is a sign on the side-tunnel wall, NUMBER OF STEPS TO EXIT 100, the enamel lettering dull with dirt. Casimir swings into the emergency stairwell and goes up the spiral of steps, taking them three at a time.

'Wait! Please –'

It is hard to make out the footsteps ahead of him, but they are there. Casimir gauges they are not far ahead, but quickening. He feels a momentary shame, that the girl should be running from him.

He goes up fast, large but carrying his bulk easily. In his mind the Underground's levels and rooms are laid out, clear and certain. He feels a trembling in his arms which has nothing to do with exhaustion, which is instead the adrenalin brought on by excitement. He visualizes the emergency stairwell, its spiralled length. There are no exits except those at the top and base. There is time, he thinks. I have time to catch her.

The metal stairway smells of dry shit and dust around him. He is near to the top before his heart rate starts to quicken. He remembers a church tower in Poland; Pentecost, laughter, the bell-tower floor strewn with blue irises. In the sides of the shaft are painted-over doors, entrances to bricked-off levels and storerooms, wartime tunnels and deep shelters.

He comes out into the surface concourse and stops, not understanding. The Underground girl is gone. Up ahead he can see one of the trainees on the ticket barriers, bored and inattentive as the passengers mill around him.

Casimir pushes past, out of the eastern exit into the Kentish Town Road. On the pavement the crowd is thick and slow, spilling into the gutters, where a hot-dog salesman has set up his stall. Steam rises in the warm air. Bike couriers brake and hoot at the market jaywalkers. For some minutes he looks around, knowing it is useless. His breath tastes of iron and he gulps it back, breathing slower now.

I was wrong, he thinks. With the thought comes the dizziness he felt yesterday, the sensation of the Underground shifting around him. As if he is losing control. He pictures the staircase again, going over his mental blueprint, trying to imagine if any of the old doors could have been unsealed. He tries to remember which lead to storerooms, and the blueprint in his mind fades and falters. Casimir realizes he does not know where all the doorways go. The feeling of dizziness rises in him again and he groans softly, clenching his teeth.

A double-decker bus goes past, a wall of red metal briefly cutting off the light. Then it changes gears, accelerating north towards Kentish Town and Holloway. The afternoon glare catches Casimir full in the face. He frowns against it, raises a hand to shade his eyes. A stubborn man, still looking, still looking although he knows that she is gone.


'Do you want a Neon Nerd?'

The shop is full of children and the smell of chip vats. Mrs Navratil is behind the scoured-chrome counter, ruddy-faced as she shovels out fried meat. She sees Casimir as the door swings shut behind him. Calls to him without looking up, 'It's Friday. Your rent is late again. Help me with these.'

He looks down. There is a small black girl beside him, her hair braided, the braids curled flat with red ladybird ties. She is cradling a paper parcel of chips in one hand. With the other she is holding out a packet of sweets. Casimir shakes his head. 'No. You must not offer sweets to strangers.'

'Mister Casimir?'

He looks up. Mrs Navratil stares at him. Eyes wide, brows raised, almost aggressive. 'I need these portions served now.'

'Yes.' He nods and tries to make his way to the counter. Something is holding him back. The girl with the sweets is tugging his uniform jacket. He looks down at her again.

'Are you an Underground man?'

He smiles. It makes him look older, the skin at the ends of his eyes creasing. 'Yes. Yes, I am.' He pulls gently and moves through to the counter.

There are six chicken parts on the hotplate, their skins yellowed and thickened with oil. He scrubs the grime from his hands with green soap, then works with an efficient minimum of movement, folding the thighs and breasts on clean squares of newspaper. Wrapping the corners in, rolling the paper tight.

'There was a letter for you.'

'What did you do with it?'

She snorts laughter, leaning one shoulder down as she lifts a metal basket of fish from the oil. 'You think I do what? Fry them up and sell them?'

She looks over at him, still smiling. He is not embarrassed. He looks away because it is not possible to meet her stare. He would have to leave, and he cannot afford to leave. Navratil's rooms are cheaper than the hostels. The extra work he does here is not unpleasant, is easier than paying more. These are the facts of their relationship.

'It's in your room. Under the door. I didn't go in.'

He wraps the final portion of chicken. Gives it to the stretched-out hands of the last two children. A tall boy with a scar denting the skin of his forehead. A smaller boy with the same eyes, angry and eager. The shop is almost empty. He looks round at Mrs Navratil. 'Thank you.'

She is already turned away, wetting a cleaning cloth in the sink. 'I need the rent by tomorrow, please.'

'Yes.'

He wipes his hands, drops the kitchen paper into the bin

and then takes out the black rubbish sack, knotting it as he holds it up.

Outside in the street someone screams, high-pitched. He looks round quickly.

Through the plate window he can see the children fighting. One of them is hunched in the gutter between two cars. Lightly built, younger or just smaller than the children bunched round it.

There is a bag of fish and chips split open on the pavement. One of the bigger children picks up a piece of fish, lobs it at the child between the cars. The window is frosted with condensation, Casimir can't make out faces or details. He can hear other children, jeering and swearing. One of them pushes forward to kick at the smaller child.

It sprawls against a car and the alarm goes off. The sound is loud and panicky in the narrow street. The children scatter. After a moment the child in the gutter stands up. It wipes its face once, steps out between the cars and begins to run.

He turns away. Mrs Navratil is doubled over the hotplates, scrubbing at the chrome. She stops to wring out the cloth over the sink, her teeth bared with the effort. The door to the back rooms is unlocked and he goes through and closes it behind him.


His room is not tidy or cluttered, just bare. There is a grey metal bed with a plastic-covered mattress. A wardrobe hanging open and half-empty, a mirror on the inside of the door reflecting back the room's darkness and linoleum. On the wall beside the wardrobe are the thick, black lumps of gas and electricity meters. There is the small click of their mechanisms, and the faint sound of radio music from the tenants on the floor below.

There is no desk, no chair. On the floor by the bed are three books piled together: the London A—Z, a book of Zbigniew Herbert's poetry in Polish and a copy of the same book translated into English. There are other belongings in the room, but not many. Casimir does not lose things here because there is little to lose. He likes it that way. He has lived here for eight years.

The letter is against the wall, pushed back by the open door.

He shuts the door, picks up the letter, walks to the window.

The net curtains are closed and he opens them and sits down on the floor with his back against the wall. The feel of a day's work is good in his shoulders. The last daylight filters in across his hands.

The envelope is small and cheap, the blue-grey colour of soap and water. The light air-mail paper has been sealed tight, there is no room to open it with a nail or knife. The postmark has been stamped twice, each black circle skewed across the Polish three-zloty stamps. Casimir can make out the town name 'Gliwice' only because it is what he expects.

The handwritten address is unsteady but not difficult to read. An effort has been made to make it legible. It is the way people write on the Underground, when the train is moving around them. Or when they are old or weak, hands travelling uneasily across the paper. Casimir taps the contents down, tears the envelope across the top.

There is a note and a Polaroid photograph, the colours run where someone has touched the surface too soon after exposure. Casimir turns the snapshot over in his hands, looking for a date or time. But there is nothing except the familiar image, a view of the Labedy steelworks far off towards Gliwice town. Factory smoke rises in the distance, straight lines of it in a windless sky. Nearer in are trees, a back road. Meadow scrub, the rough weeds that grow quickly over wasteland.

In the foreground an old man is smiling hard into the camera. He looks anxious, as if he is trying to say something. He is drunk; Casimir recognizes it in the way he stands. Arms folded, holding himself together.

The man is wearing a quilted check shirt, a cardigan and dark trousers, all discoloured by the Polaroid's over-exposure. His hair is almost gone now, the last white strands combed across the reddened scalp. Nothing in him shows that he is a cruel man, or that he has killed. That he makes money from death. In this sense his appearance lies. This is how Casimir thinks of it.

He leans forward, hand supporting head, fingers combed under his own black hair. There is very little expression on his face. The anger he feels is internal, a private thing. He opens the note and reads it once, his eyes moving quickly along the uneven lines:

*Wittlin Farm, 22 August 1996*

*Happy Birthday – Happy returns.*

*Twenty-eight you are now. Good for you! Like you are, I am learning English. Can you read this? I want to know. Now it is the Wittlins go into Gliwice – Tomek and small Eliza and Zofia. Eliza and Zofia to the watering place. Tomek to the Laboratory of Haematology. And then to the post. When will you come home? Here is Piotr. For you he has taken this photo of me.*

*Yours sincerely,*
*Father*

When he has finished, Casimir puts the note and the photograph back in the envelope. He stands up, opens the window and looks out. The daylight is fading quickly as the sun goes down behind the glasswork of Waterloo station. From here Casimir can see the Houses of Parliament upriver. In the low light, the stonework of St Steven's Tower is the colour of rust.

Below his window are the Lower Marsh backyards. Oil drums and piles of rubbish, white in the deep shadow. The sound of radio music is clearer now, coming up from the first-floor rooms. It is like the music the Underground girl was singing on the train. Like, but not the same.

He leans out, forearms crossed on the windowsill. The letter is in his hands. He tears it in half again and again. Then he opens his hands. The pieces catch the sun as they turn and separate. He loses sight of them as they fall below the level of light.

He closes the window, goes to the bed and sits down. The room is almost dark now. He picks up the books of poetry and opens them. The rough pages hiss against his fingers as he reads, head down, not minding the dark. First the Polish, his old language, then the English. Making the words his own.

> *People ran to the shelters —*
> *he said his wife had hair*
> *in whose depths one could hide.*

\*

'Will the passenger who's lost a five-litre container of salad cream please come to the ticket office? Customers are advised to take care of their belongings. This is a platform announcement.'

Overhead the tannoy is distorted, as a voice heard through water. Casimir moves in a low ape-slouch down the platform crawl-space. A yard above him is a thick glass manhole cover, set flush into the southbound platform. Light flits across his face as passengers walk above him.

He is checking for signs of trespass – graffiti, the smell of urine. There is nothing except the stench of lime and clay. Cave-like, as if the concrete is reverting to natural stone. His radio phone coughs and stutters as he shifts sacks of Blue Diamond concrete, set hard into their slumped, bent shapes.

Somewhere down here, people have lived, he thinks. Not people in transit, but people sleeping and eating. Living. The idea disturbs Casimir and he stops, frowning, trying to work out why.

He thinks of people hiding in the station, from the cold or the police. Casimir can sympathize with that. What disturbs him is what the Underground will do to people. It is where Casimir has come to ground, but he knows it can be an unsafe hiding place. Things are less mundane down here, more precarious. There is always the way the Underground can contain things, trapping them in its corners, hiding them, making them stronger.

Adam's voice comes through on the cellular. 'Anything, Cass?'

He unclips the receiver, holds it nearer his face. 'Nothing. No one has been here. There are more chambers to check.'

'You check them then. You do that.'

He frowns. The supervisor's voice comes through again. Faint, weakened. 'Always careful, that's the ticket. Good lad.'

'Adams? Is anything wrong?'

'I'm out of fags, Cass, that's what's wrong. Look after the office for me, will you? I'm just going upstairs.'

There is a clunk as Adams's transmitter is laid down. The line is left open and Casimir waits, only curious, listening for the sound of Adams's voice or movements. There is nothing except the manic chatter of the other workers, a shriek of laughter. He can hear Sievwright and Weaver, their voices tinny and childlike with distance. The frown eases from his face as he goes forward again, listening as he checks the last yards of crawl-space.

'I'm telling you, it's the dog's bollocks. All bikes, no dykes. Five minutes in Bar Rumba and you're sorted. We should get up there tonight. Have an interfere.'

'What are you like? Dykes and bikes. You sad old man.'

'I'm not sad. I'm not sad, mate. 'Cos tonight I'm getting my ride, you know what I mean?'

Wires spill from the wall next to him, a tangle of colour like a map of the Underground itself. Casimir touches them carefully with the tips of his fingers, wary of loose current. He reaches down for the radio again.

'Sievwright. Mister Sievwright?' His raised voice ricochets along the narrow space. There is a clatter of movement from the far end of the line.

'Depends who's asking.'

'Casimir. There is loose wiring in the crawl-space under platform three.'

'Is there? Blow me.' Sievwright's voice is amused, barely tolerant.

'Yes. Do you know why?'

'Maybe it felt uptight, you know? I reckon it just wanted to loosen up a bit. You should try it.'

'Sievwright, I need to know if people have been down here.'

'No one's been down there in months, mate.' The worker's amusement is already fading to boredom. A hint of aggression. 'Anything else you want to know? Football score, price of fish?'

'No.'

'Good.'

The line clicks shut. Casimir looks over the wiring one more time, then clambers on to the chamber's far end. There is a second manhole cover here, old hobnailed wood, and Casimir opens it and goes up into a room full of ranked fuse boxes, power switches and bulbous glass insulators. He opens the fuse-room door and walks out along the public platform.

It is nearly noon and the air from the ventilation shafts is sweet and damp like old leaves, the smell of surface weather carried down through the intervening clay. People turn to look at him as he passes. Their expressions are startled and guilty, or half-smiling as if with recognition. He knows it is the uniform they see, not him. A kind of invisibility. *Are you an Underground man?* he remembers, and he smiles as he reaches the control-room door.

Adams is no longer there. Sievwright and Weaver the trainee are still arguing, leaning by the rack of orange visibility suits, the suits leaning back towards them like an audience. Casimir nods to them, goes past, sits down. Beside him at the counter Oluwo is bent over paperwork, face lined with concentration.

He looks up at the monitor screens. Two cameras cover each of the four platforms, the crossroads of northbound and southbound lines. There are elevated shots of the escalator shaft, the cross-tunnels, the surface and subterranean concourses. The monitors are the office's windows, full of flickering light.

Crowds pass from screen to screen. A tattooed man with no shirt, belly huge and mottled in the camera's abrupt light. A group of Japanese girls, black-haired, walking close. Travellers, not commuters.

Casimir is almost certain he will never see them again. He likes that about London, the way it keeps people apart. It simplifies things, like a room bare of belongings. Except there is the girl, he thinks. The Underground girl. Sievwright and Weaver chatter behind him.

'How much is it then, Bar Rumba?'

'Don't worry about it.'

'Are you sure?'

'No problem. First Saturday of the month, isn't it? I'm well wedged. All I need now is Claudia Schiffer and five pints of Grolsch. Two double shifts I did this week. You weren't in on Tuesday, were you?'

'I only started Wednesday.'

'You're lucky. You missed the accident. It's been nine, ten years since we got one that bad. Some Care in the Community bloke pushing people off platforms. Ten years at least. It's the worst thing about the job. The accidents.'

The crowds are like water, Casimir thinks. Huge and quick and mindless. They collect along the platforms and then empty out into trains and cross-tunnels. He tries to imagine what would happen if the momentum went wrong somehow, the crowd failing to drain away. He thinks of how many people have travelled through the station since it was dug, a hundred years ago. Whole populations hardly touching in the Tube's huge interior, its warren of halls and stairwells. It seems like a fragile apparatus. One accident could break it.

He checks each screen in turn, half-listening to the other men. Workers in ash-grey suits are crammed in on the Moorgate line, running late for their Saturday overtime. By the platform telephones there is an area of space, as if the crowd is pressing against some invisible obstruction. At the centre of the vacuum stands a woman dressed completely in white.

Casimir sighs and sits back as he recognizes her. The woman's black face and hair are whitened with flour or paint. Her hands are covered in long pale gloves. Her mouth is moving, but even from this distance Casimir can see she is mumbling, not really talking. On the monotone screen she shines, surreally bright.

Casimir raises his voice, loud enough for Oluwo to hear, not loud enough for the other workers. 'Rose is back.'

Oluwo's chair creaks as he stands up, comes over. 'She looks older. Shall I go to her?'

'No.' Casimir watches the woman. It has been a year since he has seen Rose in the station. Then she was on the platforms every day. Leaner, more threatening. Eating on the platform benches; white meats, white milk. He wonders where she has been for a year, to make her look so old. 'No, leave her. She is doing no harm.'

He looks up at Oluwo, smiles. He remembers the worker carrying Rose out of the station, his scarred face emotionless. Then, Rose had trapped two Asian children in a deserted sidepassage. She had covered them with white flour. Rubbing it into their hands and faces.

Oluwo nods at Casimir, not smiling, already turning away.

He looks back at the Moorgate screen. Blocked out behind Rose is another figure. Now Rose begins to move away, Casimir can make out a fat man in a logo T-shirt, jeans and backpack. One person at least who is not scared of the woman in white.

'Cheers anyway, for the club entry. We should get a crowd together, like an Underground night out. Oy, Olly! Casimir! Are you up for a bit of clubbing tonight? Cass – What's his other name?'

Laughter. Sievwright's voice is quiet, jeering. 'Mikhail, probably. Rasputin or something. I don't know. No one uses it anyway.'

The fat man is smoothing something out against the telephones with one hand; political posters, Casimir guesses, *Keep Britain White With Dynamite* or worse. There will be time to go down there later and take them down. He looks back at Rose. She is still singing as she moves away, staring people down. Avid but furtive, like the Underground trainspotters and the platform missionaries – Jews for Jesus, Nation of Islam. The Underground is full of Roses, Casimir thinks. Anyone with enough to hide from. Like me.

The poster hanger turns away from the kiosks and moves through the nearest commuters, suddenly graceful. Casimir thinks how fast he is. Big in the bone but muscular, the weight seeming to count for nothing. Already he is almost out of sight. Taken back into the crowd.

'Hey, Casimir. You coming to Bar Rumba tonight?' Weaver jostles against Casimir's chair as he moves past.

'No.' He looks down from the screens, sits back.

Weaver's shadow flickers and looms against the yellowed office walls. 'It's Saturday night, man. Come on.'

Casimir doesn't reply.

The trainee's voice is childlike, disappointed and enthusiastic at the same time. There is the track noise of tap-water as he fills the kettle, plugs it in. 'Saturday night. Olly's going to come, aren't you, Oll? What's your first name, Cass?'

'Casimir.'

'Eh? What's your last name?'

'Casimir.'

'Piss off. What, Casimir Casimir?'

'My name is Kazimierz Ariel Kazimierski. You can call me Cass. It is easier.'

'Fair enough. *Ariel?*'

'Yes.'

'What, like the washing powder?'

The station-to-station telephone rings once and Casimir leans back, ignoring Weaver, reaching for the receiver. The trainee mutters behind him.

'Camden Town.'

'Who is this?'

He doesn't recognize the voice. It seems to him over-measured, as if English is not the speaker's first language. He can hear no accent.

'This is Assistant Station Supervisor Casimir.'

'Where is Adams?'

'He's working. Can I help?'

'This is Line Management.'

The voice makes Casimir think of teachers and politicians. Low-pitched, made calm. Deceptive. Immediately he is on edge, not wanting to say more than he has to. He tries to place the voice as masculine or feminine. It is hard to be certain.

From round the corner comes Sievwright's loud voice and laughter. The voice on the line is still talking. Casimir cranes over the receiver.

'I'm sorry. I couldn't hear what you were saying.'

There is a pause. Not long, patient but suggesting impatience. 'I know Adams is working this shift. It is very important that I talk to him.'

The accident, he thinks. He remembers Adams's voice on the radio. The ashen tone and broken sentences. *I'm just going out for a minute.*

'The station is a big place. He may be working anywhere. I can give him a message as soon as I talk to him.'

'Can you see him on the monitors?'

There is an edge to the voice, almost musical. Feminine. She knows the control room and where I am sitting, Casimir thinks, and then: be careful. There is more than you understand here. Be careful if you lie.

He turns round, looks up at the screens. The crowds thicken and come apart. Monotone sunlight comes in through the east–west entrances of the surface concourse. Two children run along one of the platforms with a kite, racing to get it airborne in the tunnel wind. It batters along the ground behind them.

'Assistant Casimir –'

'I can't see him. I can give him a message. By radio or when I see him.'

The line goes quiet again. Casimir can hear no background office noise, no breathing. When the Line Manager's voice cuts in again it is more tentative, less sure of itself.

'This is confidential. It is about Rebecca Saville. The accident. It is unfortunate.'

He waits, not saying anything. He remembers the photographs. The woman's neck exposed, lean and beautiful. Her hands reaching out towards the track.

'Adams may not have told you. The doctors say she was born with a heart defect. She had a pacemaker. Any large electric shock would –'

'Is she dead?'

'Yes.' The Line Manager sounds surprised. As if Casimir should have known all along. 'She died late last night. The police are coming to talk to Adams this afternoon. Between two and three. Just for the facts. It was an accident, of course. We just want him to give the facts. Can you tell him to be ready?'

'Yes, I can do that.'

He puts the phone down. Stops with his hand out, head down. He doesn't want to hear any more. After some time he looks round at the monitors.

He can see Adams now. He is in the surface concourse, leaning by the east exit, the noon light slanting in around him. Almost lost in the public crowd. He might have been standing there all the time, Casimir can't be sure. He is quite still, looking out across the streets and midday traffic. As if he's waiting for something.

His jacket is hanging on the wall and he takes it down, looks up.

On the monitor screen Adams is watching the Camden

streets. The light coming in parches his features and simplifies them. From here it looks as if he is grinning.

He walks through the late summer rain to the river and sits, a lone figure under the trees, while the embankment pavement begins to darken and shine with water. He is hunched forward on the iron bench with his elbows on his knees, supporting himself. His head is bent and his hands are clasped loosely together, so that from a distance it looks as if he is praying. The rain plasters rat's-tails of hair against his scalp and runs down his cheeks and back.

He is not praying, only thinking. He thinks of how scared Rebecca Saville must have been as she fell, knowing the weakness of her own heart. He thinks of the Underground girl, the smell of rain on her and the acid odour of oranges on her hands. The vividness of her being alive.

A cyclist goes past and he looks up at the hiss of tyres on the wet ground. The shadows under Casimir's eyes and the hollows of his cheekbones make his face look bruised. He will not sleep until morning tomorrow as he prepares for the night shifts. But he is surprised at how alert he feels, as if the closeness of death has shaken him awake. He looks down at his watch, stands up quickly and begins to walk back up past Westminster Bridge and the grey hulk of County Hall, shoulders raised against the rain.

By the time he reaches Lower Marsh the sky is already lightening, the afternoon sun breaking through as it falls below the level of clouds. Mrs Navratil's shop is crowded with people, their jacketed shoulders pressed against the steamed-up window as they queue for Saturday night fish. Casimir can see Navratil's weekend workers behind the vats, Den and Merrick, their faces shiny with sweat and oil just as his own is slicked with rain.

He opens the door and edges through the crowd to the chrome and glass counter. The smell of cooking meat makes him hungry and he tries to remember how long it is since he's eaten. Den nods at him from the cash till, hands still working while he smiles.

'All right? How's the Tube?'

Casimir shakes his head, tries to smile back. He doesn't know how to answer. He opens the counter, goes through and locks it behind him. The vats hiss and spit as Merrick drops in fishcakes one by one.

'Cushty little job, that is. Isn't it, Merrick?' The younger man laughs and nods. 'All those strikes, feet up on the picket lines. Cushty. Desk work, is it? You're not down in the tunnels, are you?'

'Not today.' He opens the rear door. 'Is Mrs Navratil here?'

'Upstairs with her loverboy, heh. Laters, yeah?'

'Yes.' He closes the door behind him.

The rear staircase is narrow and walled-off between shop floor and storerooms. Casimir has to turn his shoulders to walk up, the bare steps creaking under him. On the first floor is the lodgers' kitchen, four o'clock light streaming in across the empty surfaces. The hallway light bulb has still not been replaced and Casimir goes on up carefully, past his own second-floor room to a last flight of stairs at the back of the building.

There is a small door at the top, thickly repainted, the yellow gloss already chipped in layered patterns of brown and red. Through the door Casimir can hear the low monologue of a radio or television. He knocks and waits, knocks again.

'Who is that?' Mrs Navratil's voice is close to the door, waiting before opening. Casimir takes a step back down before he answers.

'It's me. I have the rent.'

He is looking down, reaching into his jacket as the landlady opens the door. He hands the money up to her and waits while she counts the notes. Her hair is down and she is wearing good clothes: a long skirt and blue-grey silk blouse, old-fashioned but well kept. Casimir hasn't noticed Mrs Navratil's hair before. It is tarnished like old silver.

'Good.' She is looking at him again. 'You seem tired.'

'There was an accident at work.'

'A bad one?'

He nods. 'A death. It has never happened before at my station, in my time.' When he looks up to meet her eyes, Mrs

Navratil is already glancing away, back into her room. 'I'm sorry, you're busy –'

'Yes. Can you work the chicken vats tonight?'

'I have to go out first. I can try and be –'

'No. It doesn't matter.'

She is already closing the door. He turns and goes back down the stairs, thinking of the lodgers' stories of Mrs Navratil: that she loves a television newsreader; that she sits in her best clothes, waiting for him to notice her. Behind him the television monologue is turned up, a deadpan masculine voice against a background of theme music.

He goes into his room and locks the door. The net curtains are drawn and he opens them and then the window, letting in light and air. He sits down on the bed and then lies back on the cheap mattress.

He is still wearing his uniform jacket and he takes out the rest of his month's pay, smooth brown and blue banknotes in a white packet. The pocket is full of material, neatly folded and arranged: a notebook, a staff list, a dozen International Registered envelopes, stamps and pen. Sitting up, he unfolds £250 and puts the money in an envelope, then tears a page from the notebook.

The *London A—Z* is on the floor beside him and he picks it up, flattens the notepaper against it, holding the book's spine to keep it taut. He writes quickly. Each letter is joined but distinct.

*131b Lower Marsh*
*London SE1 7AD, England*
*Saturday 7 Sept.*

*Dear Piotr*

*Here is money for September. Write to me if Tomek's treatment becomes more expensive.*

*I hope you are all well. Summer is almost finished here. Tonight is not so warm and the leaves are falling. Even in London there are trees.*

*I do not want my father to write to me. Please do not post his letters again.*

*Love,*
*Ariel*

When he is finished he goes to the window, closes and locks it. Upriver, the faces of Big Ben read ten to five. He goes out of the room and downstairs to the lodgers' side-door. The queue for fish has lengthened into the street. Casimir walks without hurrying. Taking long steps, covering the ground.

He looks up at the railway bridges and high-rises, enjoying the feel of sun on his face where the clouds have broken. High up the nearest high-rise an office has been burnt out. He slows as he passses its blackened, hollow space. The windows above it have been dulled and warped by the fire's intensity.

The road ends at the south bank of the Thames, three streets of all-day rush-hour traffic meeting at Waterloo Bridge. At the hub of the crossroads is the Bull Ring, subways opening into its half-underground space. Casimir can see the tops of lamp-posts and a warning sign on the far concrete wall, FIRES ARE PROHIBITED. In the mouth of the northern underpass he can make out figures moving and the bare, skewed shapes of card-board shelters. Signs are already up, warning of new construction work: a multiplex. Casimir wonders where the homeless will go, forced out of the old shanty town.

The post office on the corner of Stamford Street is still open and he hands in the registered letter and leaves quickly, head-ing towards an empty phone box, crossing the street between grid-locked cars. He swings open the phone-box door and picks up the receiver. It has been smashed open, the mouth-piece trailing like a lid from a nest of red and yellow wires. Casimir holds the receiver to his ear. There is still a dial tone, only slightly muffled by the parts twisted out of alignment.

He takes the staff list out of his jacket, folds it out on the wall and leafs through the pages of names – Weaver, Sievwright, Aebanyim. Under Adams's name are a telephone number and address: 215 Coppermill Lane, an Outer London area code. Casimir feeds in a pound and dials the number. He leans back against the booth door as he waits. The smell of urine in the box is overpowering. The windows are scrawled with graffiti, purple and green ciphers like those in the Under-ground cross-tunnel.

Casimir closes his eyes while the telephone rings and rings. He is trespassing here already. He has no place in Adams's private life, knows nothing about it. He imagines the supervisor drinking alone in a dark room. Thinking of the day.

The connection clicks open. For a moment there is no voice, only a sense of distance. Casimir can hear gulls.

'Hello?'

'It's Casimir.' He waits uncomfortably. The breathing on the other end of the line is Adams but not Adams. Hoarse and weak, like an old man. 'Casimir from the Underground.'

Again there is the sound of seagulls. Now he cannot hear Adams at all, not even his breathing. The gulls and the silence make him think of waterlands, or the sea. 'Adams, are you there?'

'Yes. What do you – What can I do for you?' There is irritation in the other man's voice.

'The girl who fell, Rebecca Saville. I want to talk about it.'

'There's nothing to say. She's dead.'

He feels anger start up in himself at the quickness of Adams's answer. He waits, letting himself become calm again. 'You knew about her heart.'

'Not to start with, no. Not when I told you.'

'But you knew she was pushed. You had the photographs.'

There is no reply. An ambulance goes past outside, siren loud in the built-up streets, moving slowly through the five o'clock traffic. Casimir leans forward, trying to hear his own voice or Adams's.

'You must have –'

'Yes, I knew.'

He remembers Adams telling him about the fall, three days ago. The half-smile. *A suicide wouldn't be an accident now, would it?* Now he holds the receiver carefully against his ear and mouth, trying not to loosen the smashed parts.

'What did you tell the police?'

'I left them the photos.'

'You didn't see them?'

'I don't know anything, Cass. Nothing to speak of. They've got the photos, they can make up their own minds. I don't want nothing to do with it.'

He is surprised at the levelness of the other man's voice. Not deadpan, only tired.

'I'm on sick-leave from today, for two months. That's my notice. I'm not going back down there again. I've had done with it, Cass, and if you've sense you'll do the same.'

'Who pushed her?'

'How the fuck should I know?'

Adams's shout is distorted by the telephone. Casimir pulls his ear away from the harsh, ragged sound. The supervisor is still talking, fast and loud. Casimir puts his ear back against the broken mechanism, holding it together with both hands.

'– rotten about this whole business. Something brewing. You're a careful lad, Cass, why don't you just take care of yourself? That's all I'm doing, taking care. Looking out for myself, it's what I've always done. When I'm down there now, I keep wanting to look over my shoulder and I don't, but the feeling's that strong. I trust my feelings. I've been down there a long time, you should remember that –'

'How long?'

'Eh?'

'You know more than me. About the Underground and about Rebecca Saville. I want to know. I only want to have things clear, to understand. All you have to do is talk. Then I will leave you alone.'

When Adams speaks again his voice is softer. As if the feeling has been allowed back into it. 'Leave it, Casimir. You can't help her now. Just let it be.'

The line goes dead in his hands.


He needs to walk, and London is good for walking. Casimir crosses Waterloo Bridge with his head down, then loses himself in a mare's-nest of back streets and hotel service entrances with their smell of kitchens and clean, steaming laundry. His thoughts feel packed tight, as if the day with its death leaves him no room to think of anything else.

When he looks up again he is by Embankment station. He climbs the steps to the Hungerford footbridge, heading back south. Night trains clank past him, moving slowly over the river, out towards the suburban stations of Eden Park, Clock House and Summer Hill.

He stops to lean on the metal railing, breathing easily. The anger towards Adams is dull, walked out. Downriver the city lights are laid out along the curves of roads and the lines of towers. They remind Casimir of the bright watch-work mechanisms on his grandfather's black repairer's cloth. Cogs and teeth and springs. The dome of St Paul's is lit up, grey against the brighter illumination of Docklands. He goes on towards Lower Marsh, down concrete steps, under railway arches to the Waterloo subways.

This is a different kind of underground – more open to the sky and weather, less enclosed in itself. Unlit where the Tube station passages would be barred with light. There are graffiti on the concrete walls, high rambling letters. Casimir can read them only where there is light from staircases and entrance ramps: HOT WIRES. LITTLE LEGS LOVES MIDGET.

There are figures sitting against the walls, on damp mats of cardboard or newspaper. Casimir looks at faces as he walks carefully between their hunched forms. It is an old habit, the looking for someone familiar in these lost places. Casimir has done it for as long as people have been lost to him. It is longer than he cares to remember.

The subway opens out into the concrete arena of the Bull Ring. The place is empty except for a ring of metal benches at its centre, arranged like a barricade around one tall halogen lamppost. A small child is standing on the benches, peering downwards, her back to Casimir. From her height he guesses her to be no more than three years old; an inhabitant of the cardboard city. From overhead, he can hear the evening traffic on the roundabout, the slow groan of lorries and the late rush-hour tailback.

It comes to him that she could have been here, the Underground girl. In the dark he is almost convinced that he remembers seeing her here. She sits cross-legged in one of the subways, pulling the white dreadlocks back from her profiled face. The bones of her cheeks and the small, neat hook of her nose.

He walks towards the benches, trying to remember more. But already the vividness is gone and he is unsure. He has walked home this way many times, and the images of the homeless are dulled by familiarity. The memory seems uncertain now, or imagined. The face of the girl becomes blurred with that of Rebecca Saville. For a moment he thinks of going up to the child standing on the benches, asking her – what? She would have nothing to say to him.

He is nearer to the benches now. The child is still standing, pale and unmoving. From here Casimir can see there is something wrong with her neck, the shoulders hunched forward. He steps towards her. A gentle man, needing to help.

The child's neck stretches out as it turns to look at him, white and long as an arm. In the gloom Casimir stops, the fear jerking him back before he can understand what he sees. The figure is a heron, not a child. It angles its head away again and bends at the knees and leaps, opening out, colourless in the half-light. Casimir watches the slow beat of its wings, eastwards along the river.

He waits for the fear to pass. Then he turns towards the southern exit, away from the subway. In his pocket he can feel the watch on his wrist, small and hard and certain. He walks on towards Waterloo Road.


'Casimir. It's a nice name. Is it Polish?'

'It's just a name.'

Crunch of boots on ballast stones. Echo of voices in miles of tunnels, a city under the city. Casimir makes himself go on talking. It is good to talk, in the tunnels at night.

'My middle name is Ariel. It means Lion.'

'Polish lions?'

'No. Hebrew.'

'You don't look Jewish.'

'No.'

'Are there many Jews in Poland?'

Aebanyim walks ahead of him, bulky in her bright orange overalls. Between the rough gravel are track sleepers, wood flush with the tunnel floor. There is the smell of damp and creosote. The white bowls of track insulators gleam in the linelights.

'No. It's not a good place to be Jewish.'

The tunnel walls are riveted plates of iron, crusted with

grime. Their raised edges arch overhead, like ribs, and the grime itself is creased and ridged, layer on layer of coal dust, exhaust and limestone glittering black. Cables run along the wall at shoulder height, thick as Casimir's arms. Parallel to the cables are two thin lengths of copper, clean and bright: the old clip-on telephone wires, still kept live for emergencies. On Casimir's belt his cellular coughs and mutters on its open radio line. Garbled snatches of conversation. Interference from other lines and works.

'You must miss it. Poland.'

'Sometimes.' He thinks of zúr soup, its taste of hot rye bread and soured cream and garlic. The forest, pine trees intersecting like helices. Birches, their pattern repeated again and again; spindles of some pale and cold organism. The forest's dark, which he almost loved. 'Not often.'

'Oh, there's always something. Not your family?'

'No.' Watered light against his mother's drawn features. Just the two of them, playing. He tries to recall where and cannot. 'Aebanyim is also a good name. Where is it from?'

'Nigeria. But my first name is Sarah, you know? You forgot. I told you before.'

Her voice is full of gentle laughter. They trudge on, measuring distance by the ten-foot space between light brackets. What colour there is down here stands out, vibrant against the coal-pit background. There is a single apple-green wall cable, spiralling between grey wires. The red headlines of a tabloid front page, blowing from station to station.

'What is it like? Nigeria.'

'Oh –' She laughs. 'Well. There are lions there.'

'What about Oluwo? Where is he from?'

'Nigeria.'

'The same? Did you come here together?'

Short laughter between closed teeth. 'No. Nigeria is big. Not like Great Britain.'

Casimir thinks of the staff list, the eclectic muddle of names from Africa and East Europe. The Underground has always been a place for immigrant workers. There are never enough people willing to work the tunnels. It is part of the reason he is here himself.

'Oluwo is Yoruba.'

'What are you?'

'Not Yoruba.'

He smiles. The air is warm and stale under the weight of earth, streets and buildings. Between the harsh illumination of line-lights are bands of dark, curving around the ceiling and walls. There is always darkness waiting, underground. He tries not to think of it, to concentrate on their talk. Their voices are a thread of sound against the background hush of air.

'Just a moment.'

Aebanyim stops by a track join, squinting in the bad light. She kneels, reaching out with her hands. The long lines of metal are eroded where they meet. She reaches into her jacket, takes out a can, shakes it to loosen the spray paint. The can hisses as she marks the fault for the engineers. A circle of fluorescent yellow on the discoloured steel. They walk on.

'Are you married, Casimir?'

'No.'

'Why not?'

The tunnel walls shine with water. The cell phones crackle again, in unison. Casimir slows to turn his receiver down. Taking careful steps even now, when the track is dead. The black box of the voltage tester bangs against his thigh.

'Why aren't you married, Casimir? I am. Don't you want to be with someone?'

'Yes, I want to.'

He can hear the care in his own voice. A careful man, the way his mother took care. He tries to say something, a real answer, but it is impossible. He shakes his head, three steps behind Aebanyim. The next line light shines up ahead. The runners curve away north-west, four gleaming steel parallels.

It is what he likes best about night shifts, the tunnel-walking. If he can, he comes down here alone. Not because the proximity of the dark doesn't scare him. Once, he has been here when the lights have gone for less than a minute. The fear was so strong it felt as if his breath no longer reached to his brain. Then, he stopped, bent double, taking in great ragged lungfuls of the black air. But only if he is alone; sometimes it's better for him to be alone here.

He walks in the tunnels because he can. They are the place he has taken on the dark. He has been trying for eight years and the fear is still with him. But he has learned to manage it. Now he walks against it, leaning slightly, as if into a slight gradient.

It is why he came here, to the Underground; one of the reasons. Not because he needed a job – there was other work he might have done, on building sites, or the seasonal farm work undertaken by many immigrants. He remembers the first time he travelled on the Underground, in from the Heathrow air terminals. Besides the spread-map view from the aeroplane, the train was his first image of Britain. The suburban surface stations, plant-pots hung in a grey mizzle of rain. Then the shock of descent, under Hammersmith and the West End. He couldn't take his eyes away from the windows. The pressure of air rattling against them, the tunnel roaring past outside.

For Casimir the dark is the Underground. It is a place where light has no real place. He is here because the dark is here, because he will not run away from it. He has never turned away from what scares him. Because the fear is too great for him to ever turn his back.

'Listen. Can you hear?'

He stops. From up ahead comes the sound of voices. Laughter, raucous and high-pitched.

He shrugs. 'Cleaners. Or the Camden engineers. Maybe they are lost.'

'Yes.'

Aebanyim's voice sounds uncertain. Down here the laughter sounds eerie, hollowed out by the tunnels' acoustics. He thinks of children's stories in Poland, the frightening ones. The Ohyn, babies stillborn with cauls and teeth, who came back at night to eat their grieving parents. Voices speaking from underground.

They wait by the track side, listening as the sounds come closer. Casimir can make out a female voice, an Australasian accent.

'So I told him New Zealand, and he said, Oh, sheep country, ha ha. I said, Right, ha ha. And then I said, Actually I do have a sheep, and he said, Really? I said, Yeah, it's like a house-pet sheep, lots of folks back home have them. He says, *Really?*'

Four figures appear around the next corner, bent double under giant plastic sacks. A cleaning team, Casimir thinks. Aebanyim looks back at him, smiles. He sees her teeth catch the light, their bleached whiteness.

'I said, Yeah, they're kind of like dogs back home. People walk them around the city centres. And the guy keeps nodding and going, Oh right, right. I mean, Jesus, I felt sorry for him. Hello, who's that? Is that gorgeous Mick Adams from Camden?'

'No. Mick Adams is absent tonight.'

The cleaners stop talking at the sound of Aebanyim's voice. The odd choice of words, textbook English spoken out loud. Casimir can see them properly now. Four women, none of them young. Their hands and forearms are covered by thick rubber gloves. He recognizes the New Zealander, a stocky woman, her frizz of red hair tied back with a metal hair-grip. Her name is Muir, Anne or Anna. She doesn't recognize him.

'Mick? He's never off. What's wrong with him?'

The cleaner is looking past Aebanyim at Casimir. As if the black woman isn't there. After a moment he answers, not stepping forward, 'Adams is not well. Supervisor Leynes will be on his shifts for a few months.'

'A few months? Shit. Tell him to get well, will you?'

'Of course.'

The cleaners move past, stepping across the track to make room. The last woman's rubbish sack bumps against her side, half-open. Inside Casimir can see the mass of tunnel refuse. Neon-yellow crisp packets, bundles of human hair, torn scratchcards, golden credit cards.

As she passes him, the woman grins and thrusts her hand out. Something clacks between her fingers and Casimir steps back. She is holding a pair of false teeth, yellowed and dusty.

'Look what I found!' She turns away, small and anxious. The other cleaners have already gone on southwards. She grins again and then hurries after them.

They walk on. Now there is no sound except the crunch of their feet. Two rhythms, not quite in time.

The wall beside him gives way to space. Casimir steps sideways, ducking under the loops of cables and the line-telephone wires. Beyond is another track, an adjoining tunnel curling away. He looks up and down, checking for damage to the walls, track, signals. Moisture shines on the tunnel's curvature, so that it looks like a giant sewer.

'Why was Mick Adams sick? Was it because of the woman who fell?'

*The woman who fell.* He turns back to Aebanyim, frowning at her choice of words. Not an accident, or a suicide. Just the woman, falling out from the crowd. He shakes his head.

'I don't know. Does it matter?'

'Maybe.' She turns to walk on northwards and Casimir follows, two steps behind. 'He is a careful man. Maybe it matters, if he leaves. Once I was with him down here. The line was not working, because there was water coming in from the big sewers, the old rivers. We came to the break – I was in front. I saw black things moving in the water. They were – fish like snakes.'

'Eels.'

'Yes. From the underground rivers. Like snakes. I wanted to move them but Mick said they bite. He said they were dirty inside, like rats. He was very careful of them. We went back to the station, and cleared the lines, and he turned the power on –'

There is a rattle of loose stones as Aebanyim stumbles. She falls over towards the track, her hands going out, twisting down. Casimir bends and reaches out, instinctively quick, so that she falls into his arms. She is heavy but surprisingly thin, the uniform flapping around her torso. Casimir lifts her upright, stands back.

'Are you hurt?'

'No, thank you.'

He watches the worker feeling her hands and left arm, checking for blood or broken skin.

'Not another accident.' She smiles up at Casimir, teeth very white in the dark between lights. 'Thank you.' Then she turns away, walking on more slowly. She doesn't talk again.

Casimir follows her, moving carefully on the wet ballast stones. They come to another junction, their northbound tunnel opening briefly into a southbound. The line-light has shorted out here. There is the sound of water everywhere in the near-dark. Casimir listens to its musical drip-drop, trying to place the source of the leak.

'I was working when it happened. The accident.'

He stops and looks round. It is impossible to make out the other worker's face properly, to see what she is thinking.

'In the control room?'

'Yes.'

'You saw it on the monitors? When Rebecca Saville fell?'

'Yes.' Aebanyim steps closer. Now Casimir can see her eyes, their whites, staring. She talks quickly, the accent making it hard for Casimir to understand. 'They are video cameras. So it is all recorded.'

'Photographs. I saw.'

'No. Not photographs. They are video cameras.' She is nodding, as if agreeing with Casimir.

'There are videos, of course. Where are they kept?'

'The police took them.'

Casimir feels the urgency go out of him. 'The ones who tried to talk to Adams?'

'Yes. One police. A policewoman. She took all the tapes from that day.'

He swears in Polish: *Cholera*. Aebanyim's cellular crackles into life and she unclips it from her belt, talking into it between bursts of static.

'Yes? Aebanyim. Yes. I will come back. Casimir . . . I will come now.' She clicks off the radio, looks up.

'Go. I can manage here.'

The black woman smiles. 'See you soon.'

Casimir watches her walk back along the tunnel towards the Camden Town platforms. Long after she is out of sight there is the sound of her footsteps, echoing back along the empty line.

He looks down at his watch. It is past three-thirty, less than an hour before he has to be clear of the track. He can hear the soft tick of the mechanism as the watch-hands move imperceptibly, thin and black against the luminous dial.

He holds the small light up ahead of him briefly, like a beacon. Then he lowers it, curls up his hand. The next line-light is close; he can see illumination diffused around the gradual north-east curve. He is almost at the midpoint between stations now. Somewhere ahead are the disused platforms of South Kentish Town, where he can turn back towards Camden. He knows the distance in line-lights; there are a hundred more. His radio volume is turned down and he switches it back up before he starts to walk.

When he reaches the next light he stops in its bluish illumination, breathing a little fast. It is very warm here; he can feel sweat running down the sides of his torso. There is the sound of water too, the drip and echo of it.

The line is straight here and he keeps his eyes on the patches of illumination, measuring off the steps. The ballast stones have been scattered away and his rubber-soled boots slap on the bare concrete.

He has been hearing the music for some time before he registers it. It is very faint – a voice, guitars, echoes. Out of place among the hushed sounds of the tunnel. Casimir feels for his radio, lifts it to his ear. There is no sound from the receiver now except the soft hiss of static.

The sound is coming from up ahead. Turned down low or played softly or simply distant, echoing back along the tunnel. They are playing music at the next station, Casimir thinks, but as the idea comes to him he already knows it is wrong. The Kentish Town platforms are nearly half a mile away. If I am hearing music from there, he thinks, I should be hearing the engineers working at Camden.

He starts walking again, trying to tread without sound. He is closer now and the music is perceptibly louder. He frowns, trying to remember if there are any ventilation shafts from the surface here, anything that might carry the sound of music down from an all-night restaurant or dance hall.

It is at South Kentish Town, he thinks. There is someone at the abandoned station. Briefly he can make out sung words and a female voice, clear and low.

'Let me ride . . . Let me . . . ride on your grace for a while . . .'

Then the sound is carried away again. He moves forward and immediately there are ballast stones under his boots. He is not ready for them. Gravel clacks and skitters against the track metal. There is an echo of movement ahead and then the music stops abruptly. Another sound, regular, almost too soft for footsteps.

Casimir breaks into a run, through the last barred sections of light and dark. Then the tunnel walls widen around him and he is at South Kentish Town. The derelict platform is almost chest high beside him. Rows of tiny stalactites are forming from the platform's lip, gleaming grey. Broken equipment is piled against the far wall. Sixty feet away a single light bulb shines in the platform's only side-tunnel, swinging slightly on its flex.

He puts his hands out on to the platform, vaults up and stops still, listening, dirt cool on his palms. There is no sound now except his own breathing. The light from the side-tunnel fans out across the platform, filtering away between the crates of equipment.

The smell of limestone is strong here. Sweet and damp, like church stone. Casimir tries to remember how long ago the station was abandoned; seventy or eighty years, sometime between the wars. Now it feels more like a great natural cave than a place dug and built. He kneels down, looking away across the black platform grime. Deposited in thick ridges, it is too uneven to keep much sign of movement.

He moves forward along the platform, stopping to look between teetering stacks of wrought-iron benches, fourteen cracked-faced platform clocks, enamelled cigarette sand-trays, great rotting scrolls of posters for THE UNDERGROUND: ALWAYS WARM AND BRIGHT and MASKELYNE'S MYSTERIES – ST GEORGE'S HALL. Letting his eyes adjust to the empty dark between objects.

At the side-tunnel he stops. The bare bulb shines off the tiled walls. Casimir can make out old serif lettering, EXIT THIS WAY, the words defaced by graffiti. Down the passage he knows there must be other platforms and tunnels, staircases, an old cage-lift. He remembers that a worker was once trapped in the lift shaft for three days; he wonders if there is still a surface exit. On the floor by the corner of the wall, something catches the light.

He stoops down. Against the platform wall are metal electricity cables and emergency power points. Pushed back against them is a small square of glass. Casimir picks it up, turns it in both hands, wipes it clean.

It is the lid of a box, chipped but not cracked. Small enough to lie flat in the palm of his hand. There is a faded picture on the glass. A man in military uniform next to a burning match. Casimir narrows his eyes. 'LIGHT A LIGHT FOR IKE!' is written under the picture in curving script.

He smiles. Around him the deserted platform and the memory of music suddenly seem fantastical, half-imagined. He closes his fingers on the box lid and tucks it carefully into his jacket pocket.

There is a cough of static from his cellular and then an alarm tone. He looks at his watch. It is four-thirty; already he should be out of the tunnels. In an hour the track current will be switched back on. The alarm tone blares again. Once, twice.

He looks up. The graffiti are directly in front of him, stark black on the cracked tiles. The pattern of letters is familiar. He can resolve the shapes into words: JACK UNION. The spray paint shines and he reaches out, touching the motif.

His fingers come away clean. The cellular repeats its warning. He stares back up at the graffiti for a moment longer, as if he is waiting for something to happen. Then he turns back towards the tunnel mouth.

# 4

# After the Candle

'*Either the well was very deep or she fell very slowly, because she had plenty of time as she went down to look around her, and to wonder what was going to happen next.*'

'I know what happens.'

'Because you're so smart.' The page chuffs like a kitchen match. '*She tried to look down and make out what she was coming to, but it was too dark to see anything.*'

This is mother reading to me. Before she came in I was in the mirror. In the mirror I was the second-shortest thing. The tallest was the wardrobe, then the picture of London Piccadilly England from a magazine, the white CaPamoB Russian refrigerator, the black Singer in its hood, the desk with the green candle on it, then me. Then the bed. Over the bed is Jesus Christ. He is nailed to the wallpaper with its greenish flowers which used to frighten me and now they're ordinary. The nail only goes through his cross. Altogether there are four nails.

'*She found herself in a long, low hall, which was lit by a row of lamps hanging from the roof.* Go on then, what happens next?'

'There were doors.'

'*There were doors all round the hall, but they were locked.*'

I waved at the mirror. It was my left hand but the mirror's right. It was my west hand and the mirror's west too. I know why it happens. Left and right are inside, like blood and liver. West is outside, like London Piccadilly England. West is the best. It stays still.

'"*Oh, how I wish I could shut up like a telescope! I think I could, if I only knew how to begin –*"'

Outside will be dark soon. The town is already dark because the lights have gone down. My candle is square and green, and in the mirror my skin was green in its light. I felt my chest, knuckly ribs, belly, cock. My cock is much smaller than Dad's in the swimming changing rooms, but my belly is pretty big. It's all because we had zakashka blood sausage for breakfast and there was one left in the CaPamoB on a white plate with blue spots and I ate it. I was hungry. My dad swore and put down his mug so hard the handle broke off. He didn't touch me, but I am going to bed without supper.

Supper was only liver anyway and I still get a story. I lie with my eyes shut. I can taste the oiled spiced sweetness of zakashka in my mouth.

*'And she tried to fancy what the flame of a candle looks like after the candle is blown out, for she could not remember ever having seen such a thing.* Have you ever seen that?'

'No.'

'There, enough. Tomorrow we'll do Pippi Longstocking.'

'No. More Alice now.'

'Not tonight. Only when you're good.'

'One page.'

'No.'

'Up to the next picture.'

'*No.*'

I don't mind so much. My eyes are shut. The candlelight is green through my eyelids. Sometimes I am awake and then not. I dream something about water, light on it and under it. I hear Mother shuffle around. She is looking for the cigarettes, which are on the desk. In a minute she'll find them.

'Listen, Casimir. Ariel, love. I'm sorry if you're hungry, but you mustn't steal food, not ever. I know it's hard.'

'Why?' I'll play the Question Game to keep her here. I try to open my eyes but it's difficult, part of me is not trying hard enough.

'Why? Because things are hard for us.'

'Why?'

'Just because. Because life is hard. We have to learn to find ways through. Sometimes they are the right ways. If we are good rats.'

The bed creaks as she leans away. Everything is quiet and slow because I am asleep, and then the cigarette crackles. I open my eyes and Mother is leant over the candle and her face lit up green and white like a face under water. Her breath hisses, *sss*, through the cigarette. I jump up shrieking.

'Mum – Mum, *no! Mum!*'

I pull the cigarette out of her mouth and throw it across the bedroom. It hits the dark blue of the window and scatters red. Mother pulls away from me.

'Oh, *Borja!*' She stamps around and shakes the curtains, putting out bits of cigarette. I sit on the bed with my knees up, hard on my hard ribs. The air is cold on my skin. In a dream it wouldn't be so cold. I don't cry yet, not on my face.

She stops. 'What the hell were you doing? What's wrong with you tonight?'

'You lit it from the candle. You'll die at sea.'

My voice is small. It makes her sit down. It is the smallest thing in the room.

'Ariel! It's just a story. A stupid story, like Alice. Don't cry. Shh.'

Later she blows out the candle and goes. I look for the flame but there is only the smoke. It twirls up for a bit and then stops.

Alice is right about the flame. She is right. The story is right, it is not stupid. I cry without making noise. In the morning I open my eyes and I can still smell candlewax and burning.


Now and from now there is school. The steps are clever. They have wavy thin iron up over them to keep the rain off; it is like an umbrella. The walls have little patterns in them like biscuit. I have seen it all before.

It is the Strug Estate school, with the blocks all around it like a great stone fence. I am surprised because I do not recognize the children, even though they are from my home.

Mother goes. It is like usual. I am all here in my arms, legs, heart, teeth which taste of breakfast, it was oiled salt herrings; I run my tongue against them to get the taste of it. I put my hands in my coat pockets to be together and strong.

Someone screams but it is just girls. I am ready for it. There is sand and a slide and the sun is out.

In the classroom I am next to a girl and her hair is red. I do not know her or anyone. Piotr, Monika, Wladislaw and Karol are all in other classrooms. All the children have their own friends here, so they can talk.

It is a bit worrying, so I keep looking down. I have a desk; it is grey metal like an Ursus. I try and wrap my legs around its legs. The legs of the desk are very much colder than mine.

If I were not in school I could play with the desk. I would drive to Russia with it. Already I want to be out of here. I make the desk move with my legs and it bangs on the next desk. The girl with red hair looks at me. She has a little case with lots of long pencils. I have only one pencil and it is not so long.

A woman walks in. I look up quick to see how big she is. She is quite big and she has a black shiny necklace; it is very pretty. Everyone stands up, so I stand up, and then everyone sits down again.

I am left standing up. It is so strange, now I am swaying, I don't know why. Someone laughs and then I can make myself sit. I hate them already. I will be careful. They will not laugh at me again.

The woman doesn't say anything; she turns her back on us. She is writing with chalk and suddenly everyone is writing too, but with pencils. How do they know what to do? I know. Their mothers and fathers have told them. I am angry that Mother did not tell me this.

There is my small pencil on my desk. Next to me the girl with red hair is writing. I copy her with my small pencil. It is not so hard.

I am writing! It is this: MY NAME IS MRS NALKOWSKA. YOU ARE CLASS 1C. TODAY IS MONDAY 4 AUGUST 1974. THE TIME IS 09.06. THIS IS POLAND. WELCOME.

It looks clever.


Wedel bonbons are good. With three you can make a door. With four you can make a wall. With two you can do nothing but eat them. If you only have two it's best if you can get red and green. Together they taste like blood. The taste is exact.


Only once. My father hurt me only once. It was because of the little bottles. My life is not good, not bad. We are ordinary, like anyone.

Once he was in a fight at the shipyard. He hit a Czech with a long hammer. It was because of foreigners, expecting us to roll out the bloody red carpet. The Militia men came and talked with him. There was no blood on him that time. They all bowed and clicked heels and the Militia went away.

Once he was home from travelling. I went into the room where he sleeps with my mother. His suitcase was empty on the floor, a big loose mouth with small bright teeth. I went to the white drawers, to touch his clothes.

In his winter coat were two bottles full of powder. They were small and glass, white and green. They had labels with writing, like the bottles in the story of Alice: *Drink Me*. Mother bought the story of Alice from France. Every time she drinks from a bottle, the whole world changes. Caterpillars as big as cows.

I took the bottles out. They were small, like things made for children. You could tell they were for booze from the labels, all gold and great colours. On one was a smiling man in a red suit and red hat, and on the other two dogs, black and white. There was English but my father had written over it, to show what was inside.

I held the bottles up. It took me a long time to read the words right. The first one said *Water*. I unscrewed the top but there was nothing to drink, just the white powder. It had almost no smell, like water. Maybe it was powdered water though. Afterwards snot came out of my nose and I couldn't stop it, and the blacks of my eyes went small as millimetres. I could pinch my nose and cheeks and not feel them, it was pretty good.

The second bottle said *Flour*. It was the same inside, only green glass. I opened it to make sure the powder was flour, but it was different. It hurt my eyes, so I closed the bottle again. I touched the bottles together, a toast: *To the name of Jozef Stalin, Na zdrowie, Na zdrowie*. The bottle glass clicked; a clean, fine sound. I did it again, then harder, *clack*. It echoed in my mother's room and I laughed.

Then I was hit. I dropped the bottles and above me was my

father's voice, roaring and swearing. I never heard him come in because of the noise of the bottles clacking. He tried to get me but I ran out around him and out, out of the room and the apartment, down the concrete stair flights, to my special places. Later I came back and he was OK, he hugged me and told me never to look in his things. I asked him about the little bottles but he said they were gone. He asked me if I touched the powders and I said no.

I don't know what he did with the little bottles. Maybe he made bread. Flour and water make bread. I don't know.

It hurt when he hit me. I didn't cry at all. It only hurt because he is so strong. When I am as strong as my father, I will never hit anyone.


When I grow up I will make time.

'The wheels have teeth, you see? They bite together. And here I wind the spring, the spring turns the little wheels, the little wheels turn the big wheels and the big wheels turn the hands, so we make time! All because of the little wheels.'

When Grandfather speaks, it sounds like the new houses where the road ends. It is the noise of machines mixing concrete and it means he will die. He spits snot the way Wladislaw can do it. Christ knows it is the cigarettes. Sometimes I don't understand what he says, it is bad as foreigners on the radio.

He is eighty-three years old and that is the second oldest on the list of ages. Father is fifty-one, Mother is forty-six, Piotr's father is thirty-one and his mother is thirty-one and Monika is almost seven, Piotr and Wladislaw are six and as for me, I am five. King Casimir the Great is 365. I have no grandfather from Mother, no grandmother and no uncles and no aunts. They all died in the war.

First he lived a way away and then he lived in Butcher's Square, but for most of the time he has lived with me. This is Grandfather. He smells like Father except more and older. Older cigarettes, older meat. His room smells of it and even the carpet in the hall outside his room all the way down to the kitchen.

Sometimes I stay with him. Only to watch the watch-works.

'There. And the face, so.'

He holds it up next to his big grey brown white face. The hands of the watch make a V. Two faces smiling. 'What time is it, Casimir?'

I don't know. There are lots of things I don't know; it is quite worrying. However, I can lie.

'It is too late.'

Grandfather laughs. 'Too late for what?'

I hate him laughing. It makes me speak up loud. 'Too late for old people. Too late to kill the Germans because they killed us first. Too late because we did the pleasure before the business. Too late to kill all the Yids because they went away –'

'Enough, Kazio. Quiet now.'

He is not laughing any more. His big face turns away, looking out of the window. 'Remember that every man is a variation of yourself.' What he says makes no sense. Now he is not moving at all. It is like the watch when it is not put together right.

While he is still not looking I touch the watch-works. With my fingertips I stroke the cloth, which is soft and black like cat skin. I pick up the wheels and put them down quickly.

They are so precious. Shiny and sharp bits of time.


I can lie. It is good; sometimes I believe it myself.

I tell Monika that Grandfather is dead. Blood came out of his mouth because of the cigarettes. She cries. I cry too.

Now I don't let Monika come to play in my flat. If she does she will see Grandfather and how alive he is, coughing snot and smelling up the carpet.

I wish he would die and then Monika cannot believe I am a liar. If he dies I won't cry. I will have his cloth, which is like black cat skin.


Me and Father, we go into town in a taxi. We are going to find Mother, who is queuing for meat, and we have things to give her: presents. They belong to us now but soon they will belong to her. Father will give her cigarettes and me, I have sweet tea in a thermos. It is big on the outside but it only makes one cup.

The taxi driver has a flat hat on backwards. You can feel the engine through your legs. It is a Fiat of course. Outside it is late and everything is the same dark colour as the sky, first fir trees then flats then houses. Only the birch trees are not dark; they are cold, white, thin. It makes me tired and I sleep a bit until Father speaks.

'What will you say to her?'

'Dad's sorry. Will you forgive him?'

It is because she was crying in the night. I heard her crying and his shouting. It doesn't happen so often, not so often. Sometimes she has to stay in bed afterwards. I always say sorry for him.

It is Zwyciestwa Street and there are light bulbs on strings between the houses. One of the light bulbs is dead; I watch it as it goes over. The shops are still open, Kapelusze the clothes shop and the grocery which only sells stockings and canned ham and the queues of people, all women standing in the dark. There are nuns there too, queuing for stockings.

The Fiat taxi stops and we get out and Father doesn't pay; the taxi man owes him. Outside the air is freezing, tasting of firs. I wake up fast. I look around for Mother but it is hard to see, there are so many women here.

'Casimir!'

It is her. We go. She gathers me up and she whispers my other name, *Ariel*, our secret. Her face is hot and red raw. It isn't just the cold. I think of Dad's face, grinning. Soon he will go away again. It is ordinary, his going; both good and bad.

'Dad's sorry.'

'Shh.'

She has two pairs of Miss Marilyn and all the meat she had tokens for. Father takes out the cigarettes. I give her the one cup of tea.

'Will you forgive him?'

'What for?' Father lights the cigarette for her and she smokes it, watching him, smiling at him. 'I've forgotten already.' We pass round the tea. The nuns go off into the dark. All you can see is their white headscarves floating away.

On the register I'm Kazimierz Kazimierski. The middle name stays mine. My favourite class is Military Studies. We do the Nazis. I am the youngest in 1c and the second biggest. Wladislaw is bigger. He is a different Wladislaw. He has eighty-four stitches; they are in his belly. He shows them to his friends. I have not seen them. He is older than me so he will die first.

The girl with red hair is clever in class. Everyone knows it's a stupid thing to do. Whoever shows they are smartest is the one everybody hates, and it is her. Her name is Hanna.

I push her up against the wall of school, which is grey like the wall of home. She hits me in the mouth and I feel her knuckles get wet on my teeth. I am bigger than her so she only does it once. Instead of hitting she talks and her voice is strange.

'Please leave me alone.'

When she says the words they sound wrong. It is because she does not come from here.

'*Leave me alone.*' I copy the way she says it and she starts to cry.

I pull up her dress. Her pants are dirty and baggy, like mine. I hold them by the edge and pull them down.

It's true what Piotr said. She has no cock, just the skin and a hole. It's terrible. I shout and let go because I'm surprised to see it.

When I start shouting, she stops crying; now she is just looking at me. Something has happened and I cannot understand. I go away from her three steps. She's putting her dress down straight, not even looking at me; she isn't scared of me now. I turn back from her and run.

I look for her again. She is sitting on the ground. She has little stones from the asphalt. She is making patterns of black stones on the white sand.

Will I talk to her? Yes, I will.

'Do you forgive me?' She says nothing. I sit down. 'Do you have a Polski Fiat? Because your hair is red. Red is for people with cars.'

Hanna looks up at me very quick, with her eyes and nose screwed up.

'You're stupid, Casimir. Red is for Communists.'

I don't hit her when she calls me stupid. Everybody hates her so I don't bother. I ask her, 'What is Communists?'

She shrugs. 'Communists have cars. Like my father.'

Now she goes back to her stones. She is making words, black on white. I can read it pretty well now. She showed me how to do it. The stones make HANNA.


It is Mother's birthday and so we go to the Restaurant Diamont. There are red curtains, red carpets, red walls, red cloths on the tables. There is a piano but it isn't red. A restaurant man comes with a list of food. He has a red tie clipped on his white collar.

It can only mean two things. Either the Restaurant Diamont is all Communists or the restaurant man has brilliant cars. I ask him when he brings the food but everyone is talking and he doesn't hear me. I get cherry soup with stones in it and then pork. Father asks for steak tartare, but they don't have it, and caviare, but they don't have it either; the man's list is quite wrong.

Mother drinks vodka with bison grass. They have that. Her dress is made in London and the buttons shine. It's so beautiful, it makes her look tired. Father never looks tired.

He puts his food away fast and I do too. When it's all gone, he wipes his mouth three times on a red napkin. 'Heh. Why not play the piano?'

'Michal. No.'

'Go on. Play. Play!' He's smiling. She is too.

Mother goes to the piano. Everyone looks at her but she looks at no one. The waiter opens it for her but she doesn't notice. What is she doing? She just sits there with her hands on her knees and her head down. Then all at the same time she breathes out and looks up and starts to play.

She makes beautiful music. I didn't know she could do that. When she has finished, everyone claps for her. When Mother smiles her lips stop against her teeth. Not like Father. When he smiles you can see his gums and the insides of his mouth and the gold dog teeth.

Once I had lots of lists but now there is only one. It's the list of trees. Some is from the radio programme *Poland: Forest, Lake & Mountain* and some is mine. I keep it all in my head. I say it to myself before sleep.

*Larch.* Interestingly, in the coldest climes it is the deciduous trees that flourish. Take the larch. Tall and handsome, it conserves water by shedding its leaves, and so it thrives where evergreens cannot.

Larches look dead. They go near death and trick it. It takes patience.

*Poplar.* They are twisted and black like balcony metal. When you break branches they're the colour of rust.

*Firs* go up in green heaps. The biggest heap at the bottom. At Christmas we put lights on one while we wait for the first evening star, when we can eat. Last Christmas the Gypsies came with a thing blown up and we jumped on it.

*Pines.* From the Krakow train they are all one green height, like soldiers. Inside they are like a cage. The cage has no inside or outside. It moves with you.

*Birch.* Snow goes blue in shadow but birches don't, so birches are whiter than snow. You can peel the skin off like white sunburn. On Piotr's farm there are fat old birches and we peeled one and wrapped up Monika and she looked like an Extra Mocne cigarette.

They are white against the sky. All other trees are dark. Inside birch forests the darkness is broken up with white lines. Ice weighs down the saplings and they make doorways in and out.

At night they are so white and clear, straight and arched and leaning, it must mean something. It looks like writing. If it was English I would never know. I look hard to read the language of trees.

I walk to the forest. The land goes away in lines: a picket fence, a long dirt path, then railway rusted up orange. A woman is on the path, walking balanced with buckets of potatoes.

Now the forest. The soft ground smells sweet as coal. The orange railway goes on, east towards Oswiecim. Sometimes there are pylons like tall grey climbing frames. There is nothing else, nothing made. Only me. The forest is dark and safe and in it I know everything.


'Casimir's got a Yid girl!'

Wladislaw says it. We are in class and waiting for Mrs Nalkowska. He is smiling and his eyes shine, as if he has found out a wonderful joke.

No one laughs, not yet. As for me, I say nothing. I don't look at Hanna for the whole lesson, not at anything, I just sit here with my eyes on the desk. Grey metal, like Russian guns. Hanna keeps looking at me; I see her doing it. I hate her for it. I wish she would look away.

I wait until the lesson is over and we are in the playground. Out here it is just children and for the moment it is better like this. Wladislaw is with all his friends by the back wall and I am alone.

I go up to him. They're eating Nuscaat bars from the Strug Estate shop. I knew that one day I would have to fight Wladislaw anyway. My pockets are heavy because they are full of sand from the pit. His friends all lean around against the wall.

'Why did you say that lie about me?' I meant my voice to be loud, but it comes out soft. It's still clear, though. Wladislaw takes his hands out of his pockets.

'Piss off, Casimir. You've got no friends round here.' His eyes are narrow and blue. It makes him look worried, even though he is bigger than me. It is not so good always having friends, because now he can't run away.

He comes up to me, close. I can smell candy in his mouth. Brandos, warm and sweet like animals breathing. 'Go fuck your Jewish girl.' He smiles around the candy and starts to say something else.

I push the sand up into his face, into his eyes and mouth with the heel of my hand. He groans and bends over. Green drool and sand come out between his teeth but I keep pushing. I am good with my hands, like my father. I hold on to his hair with one hand and his face with the other. Then I throw his head back into the wall. It makes a noise like a hoofbeat on cobbles.

After the fight no one talks to me much. I stay away from Hanna. She plays by herself at the edge of the yard, making words with stones.

Me and Mother and Father, we are listening to the radio. It is the Thirtieth Anniversary of the People's Republic. Even the music is better than this. I look at Mother's hands on the kitchen table. Her fingers are big, red, hard on the sides of them. The nails are dotty with old bits of red paint. I turn the hands in my hands. Back, front, back.

'What are you doing?'

Nothing. There is nothing wrong with them. They are just my mother's hands.

'What's your name, son?'

'Casimir Ariel.'

'Ariel? Ariel what?' This is the Militia man who is talking. He has a big moustache. I am by the Ikarus Street cheese shop, waiting for my mum to come out. Why did I tell him my other name? It just came out. But he is Militia, he must know all my names.

'Kazimierski.' He is looking at me hard and straight.

'Kazimierski. What does your father do, Ariel?'

I shrug. 'Lots of things.' I wish he wouldn't look at me so hard. He smiles.

'What is his job?'

I can't remember. My dad goes to Russia for money. I shrug again; I try and hide down between my shoulders. 'He's my dad. That's all.'

'Where is he from, your father?'

'Casimir?'

The Militia man and me look round. It is my mum.

'Mum!'

It's great to see her. She gives the Militia man a hell of a look. He stands up straight and tries to say something but it comes out soft and jumbled; it is half one thing and half the other. He clicks his heels and bows and goes. I sit close to Mum on the tram home. I would hold her hand if I could, but people are there.

He is my dad. That's all.


It's the night of St Andrew's Day. In my grandad's room there are:

Eight big cans of Russian fish with pictures on.

Two boxes of Russian vodka. There were three until tonight.

The gun of a cosmonaut in a wooden box.

Fish eggs in little jars. Lots of them.

Furs. Smooth black and grey curly. The smell of them is so strong I can't smell Grandfather any more. I don't know how he stands it. The gun is small and ordinary with Russian on it. Dad says it was in case the cosmonaut came down in a jungle. It was a present to Dad from colleagues. It has a red star on it too.

St Andrew's Day. The guest room is full of people. I go round counting cigarettes. Elzbieta and Eva smoke Carmen. Mr Wittlin and Mr Chorzelski smoke Caro. Grandfather smokes Extra Mocne and coughs black spit. My father smokes the fastest and it is Marlboro. Once he offers them round. Everybody takes one except Mother.

'Casimir! Oh, sweet little big child. Come here. Hup.' It is Eva. She is Father's friend, like everyone. She is old and her hair is purple. 'Look what your Auntie Elzbieta is doing, see?'

Elzbieta isn't my aunt. I look anyway. On the table she has my green candle, our door key and the washing-up bowl. The bowl is purple plastic with black bits and full of water. Wax drips from the candle, through the key's hole, into the bowl.

'You see? She's telling her fortune.'

'I know what she's doing.' Eva's breath feels wet against my ear. I don't like her breath or the fortune-telling either. It is better not to know. I try to get down but Eva holds me tight. 'I'm tired.'

'Poor little big boy. Look, look! It's a palace!'

Everyone looks. There is wax on the water and Eva says it looks like a palace, so Elzbieta will get rich. I lean over the bowl to see, but there is no palace; the wax is just wax. Dad comes round with more vodka. His face is red with drinking, burnt with it around the eyes. His eyes are shiny and clear, like the vodka. He shouts and waves to Mother.

'You see what Elzbieta has got? Palaces. Palaces, Anna, wife. Come here and we'll find our future, eh? Maybe we'll find my big deal.'

My mother shakes her head. She is standing in the guest room doorway. The air comes in cold behind her.

'Dear wife, come.'

My mother turns back, out of the doorway. She didn't smile.

Eva shouts after her, 'Anna! What are you afraid of, eh? An unhappy marriage?'

Everyone goes quiet. I get away from Eva and go. Mother is in the kitchen, making beetroot soup and cabbage pasties. The stove flame makes her face blue and calm. She is singing to herself, words I can't understand. Sometimes she does that. When she sees me she smiles but not until.

'Hello, love. Are you having a good time?'

'Yes. Are you?'

She laughs in the stove light. 'Me?' She picks me up. She is thin but strong, my mother. 'Thank you for asking, Casimir. Sometimes I worry about your father, that's all. About what he plans to do for work. Bedtime, yes? I'll ask them to be quieter.'

'And get my candle back.'

'And the candle.'

I try to sleep. The light comes in, long flowers of it through the net curtains. Gold from the streets and grey from the moon.

I know why my mother is afraid. It is not because of my dad. I go to the window and stand. There is a coal train going east. I count the trucks up to thirty-one. Past the train are the railway's blue lights. Then birch forest, the line of its edge like writing. I screw up my eyes to read what it says. My mother will die at sea, but if there is a way to save her I'll find it. Like a good rat, finding the way.

# 5

# Alice on the Underground

He is woken by the flash of sunlight between houses. The Underground carriage has come out of the dark, on to the surface tracks north of Tottenham. Casimir looks out at the rows of pebbledash houses, disoriented for a moment. Terraces stop dead where the railway runs through them.

At Blackhorse Road he gets off, takes Adams's address from his pocket, then walks towards Coppermill Lane. After a few blocks the buildings begin to separate out. High metal fences run on towards the Walthamstow marshes. The wind comes in over open country, whining in the razor wire. The air smells of water and Casimir feels something shift inside him, a sense of loneliness as he looks at the last houses, their peeling clapboard and isolation.

Number 215 is the last before the road ends. There is a sign on the fence behind Adams's house: DANGER DEEP WATER. RESERVOIR NO. 5. Through the fencing Casimir can see electricity pylons marching off eastwards between colossal stretches of water, railway sidings and dump-hills of sand and gravel. Miles away is the pyramid summit of Canary Wharf tower, already illuminated in the early evening light.

The windows of the house are dark and uncurtained. Casimir walks up towards them between soft white beds of pansy and cyclamen. From the door he can see Adams, hunched forward in a front-room armchair.

He rings the bell and the supervisor turns his head. His face is round and moon-like in the dark room. He raises a hand to Casimir and stands, supporting himself on the arms of the chair. Casimir turns and looks out across the reservoirs while he waits. A flock of birds is settling over the water, silhouetted against the sky.

'I told you not to come.'

'I'm sorry. I need to –' he searches for the English phrase – 'to sort things out. About what is happening, underground. It's important to me.'

'I'm not even talking to the police. Why d'you think I'll see you?'

'I'm sorry.'

'Why? You haven't done anything yet. Come in.' The supervisor goes back into the front room and Casimir follows him through.

'I can do you tea or coffee, if you like.'

He sees that he was wrong; the room is not dark but full of mobile light. It is reflected from the water outside, then again off the polished wooden surfaces of furniture, so that the room is filled with an oddly beautiful lucidity. There is the tick of a carriage clock from the mantelpiece. Photographs of smiling faces. The sweet musty smell of old cigarettes and English food.

He goes to an armchair, sits down. 'I would prefer alcohol.'

'I don't drink.'

Adams is still standing, so that Casimir can't make out his face. Only his voice, the tightening of it. The edge of what might be anger or a lie. But he has seen Adams angry before and his anger is not quiet like this. He waits, head slightly to one side, not looking at the other man or away.

After a moment the supervisor walks towards the mantelpiece. In the half-dark there is the sound of a screw-top on the lip of a bottle, the clink of tumblers and liquid. He turns back without speaking, hands a glass to Casimir. Then he sits down in the second armchair with his back to the window, takes a drink, bares his teeth as he swallows. Casimir can smell the whisky in his own glass, cheap and harsh.

'You have a nice home. Close to the water.'

'Tell me what you want, Casimir.'

'What do you think happened?'

'To the girl?' Adams barks laughter. A nervous, unhappy sound, without humour. 'She fell, that's all. It might be she was pushed or it might not. If it's an accident it's bad, if it wasn't it's worse than bad. I don't think it was an accident. I think there's someone down there who gives me the frights. I can't tell you anything you haven't thought for yourself.'

Casimir sits forward in the armchair, the glass held in both hands. He waits patiently for the supervisor to go on. A car goes past outside, high beams wheeling light across the far wall. Adams looks up at the window, eyes narrow. When he talks again his voice is soft, an amazed whisper.

'Thirty-seven years I worked down there. Quite a time.'

'You think she was pushed.' He watches Adams's slight nod. 'Sievwright was talking about another killing. Someone else who was pushed, years ago.'

'Was he now? Sievwright doesn't half talk, eh? It wasn't just one person pushed. Three died. The last one was at my station. Ours, Camden. That was the first time I thought, maybe I don't like it down here any more. Underground. Maybe it's changing down here, I thought. And I was right.' Adams screws up his eyes, presses his fingers gently against the eyelids. 'It was a few years before you came. One day after the general election, so I remember it – 12 June 1987. That's when they caught him. His name was Thomas Gray. They kicked him out of hospital, so he was living down in side-passages. Got away with it for months, staying down there all night, out of the way of the cameras. Not that we watch, half the time, or know half the tunnels there are any more.'

'Where did he hide?'

'I don't know, do I? Maybe he was in the old cross-tunnels, like you thought someone was the other day. There's all kinds of places down there. Snickets and pope-holes, you know that. He probably knew it better than we did. You'll not guess how we caught him. All the men he pushed looked just like him. Only men, spitting images. He just waited in the crowds for someone to come along. Six million people a day. All he had to do was wait.'

Adams's voice has gone soft and rapid. Private, no longer meant for Casimir. 'I caught him, as it happens. I was the one who recognized him. I thought I was stopping something then, I really did, but he wasn't the only one. You see? He was just the first one I noticed. And this one's going to be the last, because I've fucking well had it up to here.'

Casimir hears the chink of ice. As if the older man is

swirling his glass, or as if his hands are shaking.

'I used to love it down there, really I did. It has been my life. I've had precious little enough of it up here. I loved being inside the system, like being in the pipes of a whacking great engine. It scares me now – enough to leave. And I trust myself on that. I dreamed about the Tube the other night, and it was like Joe Stalin's railway, where one bloody worker died for each sleeper. That's how it was in the dream: dead bodies and sleepers. What gets me is the line between it happening and not. What does it take for somebody to push someone? And all I can think is, it could be anything. Anything at all. Who's to say what? In a place the size of London, there's somebody pushing all the time.'

'What about this time?'

'Eh?'

He looks up, distracted. Even in the bad light, Casimir can see how grey the skin of Adams's cheeks and forehead has become. This is not the face of a well man. He wonders if the supervisor's sick-leave is necessary or if it will become so. How Adams will look out for himself, alone in the last house by the water.

'How do you know Saville was pushed?'

'There's the photograph. Anyway, she told me. She said it. She wasn't talking to me by then.'

Casimir drinks. The alcohol settles in his gut, warm and oily. 'You knew her?'

Adams stands up, goes back to the mantelpiece. 'No. I went to see her, in hospital. Just to see how she was doing. They took her up to the Royal Free. She was full of pipes and junk. Past noticing.' There is the chink of glass as he refills his tumbler. 'But she was muttering all the time. This was Wednesday night. I went back the next day and she'd gone quiet. The doctors couldn't keep her going long.'

'What else did she say?'

'She didn't know him – she kept asking who he was. Like the men who Gray pushed, they wouldn't have known him either. Strangers in the night, eh?' Adams sits back down. 'I thought I might get him then. She might have said something then. But she didn't really, and I was getting the frights. I wanted to keep off it, even then. I only went to see how she was doing.'

'It was a man?'

'It was.'

'Will you help me find him?'

'No.' Adams knocks back his drink. Bares his teeth again, hisses against the burn of it.

'Don't you want to find him?'

'I want to be left alone.' He stands up. Puts down his empty glass. 'And I want you to do me a favour. Keep the police away from me. Will you do that?'

Casimir stands. He shakes his head. 'I can't. I want him found.'

'I know.' For a moment they stand in the dark, watching each other. Then Adams moves past, into the hall. 'It's time you were leaving.'

Casimir hears the front door click open. His glass is still half-full. He puts it down and turns to go.


It is the third day of night shifts. There is time to kill before work begins. He walks up Spur Road in the early evening, through Waterloo terminus, down towards the Thames embankment. An elderly busker sits on a fishing stool by the Hungerford foot-bridge, playing ragtime clarinet into an echoey amplifier. Casimir goes past him up the steps, over the river.

The tide is strong today. He watches it as he crosses, the way the sea currents churn the green river water back against itself, forcing it upstream. He enjoys walking in London, the simple rhythm of movement. The way his thoughts become clear and deep, skimmed of consciousness.

Near the north bank a small man in a grey winter coat stands by the footbridge railing, an oversized spool of kite string in both hands. Casimir follows the cord with his eyes, out and up over Cleopatra's Needle and the white stone of the Inns of Court. The kite is a glittering silver edge in the dusk, almost imperceptible above the Thames mud flats.

'Nice evening for it.'

It takes Casimir a moment to register that he is being spoken to. The kite man is talking to him.

'Nice evening. You work round here?' The man doesn't look away from the sky.

'No. Not so near.'

His own voice is still sleep-rough and he coughs to clear his throat, leaning forward. When he straightens, the kite man has turned to look at him. His eyes are keen and intensely blue. It makes Casimir think of the sky from the aeroplane when he came to Britain, the colour of sky light at high altitude. Beautiful eyes in a wrecked grey face.

'Office?'

'No. Underground.' The man looks at him, expressionless, as if not understanding. 'The Underground. I am a Tube worker.'

The kite man turns away. 'You poor cunt.' His voice has gone quiet. Casimir can still see his eyes as he looks back up, the pupils narrowing to pinpoints. He steps back and walks on.

The footbridge goes on overland, a raised walkway above Embankment station and the left-hand side of Villiers Street. The riverside plane trees are already beginning to lose their leaves, late seed-balls hanging from the bare branches like winter decorations. There is the smell of frying food from the take-away cafés below, sweet and rank and familiar.

He is following the Underground line northwards and as he realizes this he smiles, looks down. There is nothing to see, although he can track the direction of the tunnels with his eyes. The Tube system is like the city's bricked-over tributary rivers, he thinks; the Tyburn and Fleet, other names he has never learned. A network hidden under the surface and visible only sometimes, like the blue of veins where they lie near the skin.

By the entrance to Charing Cross terminus a small market has been set up. The stall-holders stand hunched forward, hands shoved in pockets while they wait for custom. Casimir goes on between the trestles of second-hand books, cheap cut-glass figurines and used telephone cards.

The station concourse is crowded with people, faces upturned as they wait for the departure boards to change. Casimir finds his way through the commuters and out across the Strand. A car blares past on the red light and he moves forward out of its way. His reactions are quick and he is in control of the instinct. Not falling. Not like Rebecca Saville.

The thought of Saville has been with him for days now; since before he knew she was dead, he realizes. Since Adams told him about the accident, the day he saw the Underground girl.

He thinks of the supervisor, his fear. *Keep the police away from me.* He has never spoken to the British police before. He keeps away from authorities, when he can. In Poland he would do the same; even in his own town, Gliwice, with its canals and looming garrison church. It is the way he is with control. He doesn't like to be authorized or unauthorized. Still, he thinks of going to them, to tell them he can help. That he knows the Tube, the ways people think and behave underground. The ones who feel trapped and those who feel hidden.

There is a Chinese pharmacy at the top of Adelaide Street, windows full of ginseng roots and medicine jars. Casimir ducks through an arch next to it, then down into the passage of Brydge's Place. Security lights click on over the back doors of pubs and concert halls. The grime-black walls are high and narrowing towards their end, creating a trick of perspective, the vertical line of yellowing sky seeming far distant. Casimir's jacketed shoulders scrape against the bricks as he steps out on to the busy pavement of St Martin's Lane.

There are taxis double-parked outside the London Coliseum, the traffic hardly moving around them. The road is filled with the smell and light and noise of traffic brought to a standstill. Casimir crosses carefully between two orange-striped *Evening Standard* vans, then goes on down the paved side-streets towards Leicester Square.

He walks almost without looking where he is going, a large man alone, passing easily through the crowds. There is no one thing that makes him look not English, only the combination of details. The colours of his clothes, they way they hang on his prominent bones. The bones themselves, the angular cut of his cheeks and hands that suggests an experience of hunger. The black of his hair and eyes, which is revealed as red-black only in the strongest light.

His face is slackened and set in its natural half-frown. His thoughts are disconnected but also seamless, passing from thought to thoughtlessness and back without intention.

He is thinking of his home. Of his and Piotr's mothers on the canal bridge, selling fruit and herbs. Fennel laid out on newspaper like pale green ox-hearts. Bilberries measured out in a chipped white enamel mug. Then later, in the curtained dark of the kitchen, his father's hands cupping his mother's face, holding up its heart shape. His father's voice, its undercurrent of laughter cold and dangerous. *Better. You look so much better when you're sad.*

He is thinking of the platform photograph. The hand in the crowd, stretching out from the mass of bodies. He cannot tell if it is pushing Rebecca Saville away or reaching to save her.

Then he is thinking of nothing again. He looks up to find he is in Piccadilly Circus. He has walked more than a mile from his lodgings. Electric light twinkles cleanly on the high circle of buildings. He remembers a picture of exactly this scene in his childhood bedroom, something his mother cut out of a magazine. The memory is painfully sharp. Tourists mill around the statue of Eros, posing for photographs. The fountain is blocked with rubbish and water spills over on to the steps, staining the grey stone black.

A neon hoarding flashes up Coca-Cola slogans, the temperature and time. It is past nine o'clock. Casimir turns away. Tomorrow night he has a double shift, three in the afternoon until seven the next morning. Then for fifty-six hours he will be free, on his own time. The entrance to Piccadilly station is yards from where he stands, steps curving out of sight between wrought-iron palings.

He takes a last breath of the stale city air, then goes down to the underground concourse. The ticket barriers at this station are mechanized, filling the hall with the clank of their opening and closure. Entrances lead off like spokes from a wheel, some of them continuing on into underground shopping malls. Casimir takes the escalator down to the Piccadilly Line platforms, an anonymous figure in his everyday clothes, work bag slung over one shoulder.

The train is hot and packed with people. There are no seats

and Casimir stands, head touching the curved carriage roof, held motionless by the crowd. At the next stop he gets out and walks across to the Northern Line platforms. The tiled cross-passage becomes yellowed and uneven as he passes into the Tube's oldest excavations. Across each wall poster someone has stencilled SUBCIRCUS in crimson or bright green. It is senseless to Casimir, just another thing he doesn't understand about the Tube. He wonders how much he has ever understood of the system. What proportion of it he still has to learn.

The northbound train is half-empty. The windows between carriages are open, and the air is warm and damp, as if the weather underground has no relation to that above. Casimir watches the passengers around him. A Rasta girl with silver platform shoes and blue sunglasses, an old Asian man reading a worn Koran, lips moving silently, stations passing behind him. The Rastafarian makes him think of Adams again. *If the station starts turning green and gold, that'll be why*. He realizes he misses the supervisor and is surprised.

The stations give Casimir a sense of motionlessness. Each platform is the same blur of crowds, tiles and hoardings under London's great squares and malls. A woman sits down next to him. Tweed jacket, wire spectacles. She picks a magazine off the carriage's wooden floor, snaps it flat, folds it and begins to read. Casimir can see fragments of headlines like incoherent snatches of conversation: 'BLIP GIRL', 'MAD COW', 'ANY MINUTE I'LL JUST START SINGING'.

When he looks up again, the Camden Town roundels are flashing past the windows opposite. He stands up as the train slows, reaching for a hand-grip. The woman looks up at him. Smiles widely, too wide, light opaque against her spectacles. It blinds him and he looks away.


'Cass! All right?'

'Cass, you're early, ain't you?'

'Casimir, come here. Look at this.'

The control room is crowded with the last of the late-turn crew and the first of the night-shift workers. It takes a moment for Casimir to get through to the counter. Supervisor Leynes,

Sievwright and Weaver are standing under the monitor screens, staring up at them. Casimir ducks through, looks up.

'There. You see her?' Leynes is pointing up at one of the southbound platforms.

Casimir frowns, eyes moving quickly. A train is just pulling away towards the camera, under it. The evening crowd moves slowly along the platform, making its way out towards Camden's bars and restaurants.

He watches the passengers. They are wearing night clothes now, the colours and cuts of fabrics darker and more varied than in the daytime. On the train in, Casimir could smell the make-up and perfumes on women, sometimes on men. Now he can see the shine of jewellery and accessories in the stark light of neon tubing.

The current of the crowd is uniform, moving towards the exit. A few people stand still, waiting for the next train southbound. Now he sees that there is only one figure walking against the current, down towards the side-tunnel passage. The woman stoops down, one hand moving out of sight. It is a moment before Casimir makes sense of the scene. As she moves on the woman's hand comes back up, out of the shoulder bag of the person next to her.

It is an old woman, hair long and frayed, a great grey rope of it down her back. She walks with a sluggish wide-shouldered roll, one hand tugged ahead of her by dog leashes, the dogs themselves out of sight in the crowd. The woman's other hand is stuffed in her coat pocket as she turns back down the platform. Behind her a tall, elderly woman in black reaches into her handbag. Stops walking, looks down at the platform floor.

'I have seen her before. The woman with the dogs.'

'I was just saying that. Didn't I say that? I seen her hanging around weeks ago. Did she talk to you? She's ape, man.'

'Obviously not that ape, Mister Sievwright.' Leynes turns away and snaps the counter back, raising his voice. 'Weaver? Call the Transport Police – no, ring Kentish Town Met, they'll get here faster – then get up to the barriers. Casimir, wait down by the side-tunnel. Apeman will be with me. We'll come on to the platform from the escalators in two minutes, then shepherd her down to you. All right? Let's go.'

Casimir runs out after the others, into the public tunnels. Weaver is already going up the emergency stairs, the echo of his footsteps pounding back. Leynes and Sievwright turn left, running hard. Casimir goes right, stopping at the mouth of the southbound platform.

There is a circular mirror on the corner wall, a convex metal plate placed so as to make the platform visible. Reflected in it, Casimir can see the crowd emptying out, the dog woman left behind. She is not coming towards him. Instead she sits down on a bench near the public telephones, clicking her tongue at the lean grey dogs until they have curled up at her feet. She stretches her legs out straight, sighs with satisfaction. The platform starts to fill up again with new passengers, waiting for a West End late train.

The dog woman goes still, head cocked sideways. Casimir follows her gaze. Leynes is at the main concourse entrance, looking up and down the platform. The woman has seen him long before he notices her. Sievwright appears behind the supervisor, still slowing down from a running pace.

She turns her face away from them. Casimir can see her features creasing up into habitual lines. Bitterness and disappointment, but also something harder, tougher. She keeps her head turned like that while the men in uniform walk quickly down the platform towards her. They are yards away when she yells out in her cracked voice.

'Kill'm, girls!' She stands up and begins to run.

Behind her the dogs uncoil with their heads raised, skin peeling back from the teeth as they bark. The sound is savagely loud and rapid in the enclosed space. Casimir hears Sievwright shout out in pain, his voice high-pitched, almost a scream. Other screams, passengers moving away from the scene. The woman looms up fast in the metal mirror, not looking back.

He catches her as she comes around the corner, then he holds on tight. She cries out once and tries to bite him, but her face is against his chest and her hands are trapped between them, pushing to get free.

She begins to kick out at his legs. Taking her time, the blows slow and hard with her weight behind them. He listens to her boots thudding off his bones. For a moment he is detached, waiting for the pain to come.

It is bearable. He staggers back at the force of one kick, feeling blood on his legs, hot and then quickly cold. She struggles again, heavy-built but not muscular under the layers of coats and shirts. He tries to keep her still, his face against her hair. She smells of dogs, sweaty and sweet.

She goes loose in his arms, then he feels her begin to cry, the sobs rocking through her. He waits a few seconds longer to be sure, then stands back. Immediately she begins to slump against the passage wall and he catches her, holds her up.

'Ah, you bastards. Why can't you never just leave me alone?'

'It is our job.'

She looks up at him, calm and sad. 'What will you do with my lurching girls?'

He shakes his head, not understanding. Leynes comes round the corner, his eyes jittering from the woman to Casimir, taking everything in. He nods at Casimir as he takes half the woman's weight. His voice when he talks to her is smooth and fast. Part-parent and part-interrogator.

'There we go. Easy. OK? This way, please.'

The woman looks round at Leynes, eyes wide. 'Will you give me back my lurching girls?'

The supervisor grins. A cold expression, bone-hard. 'Your dogs? Lurchers, are they? Well, we'll see about them a little later. Right now we're going to sit you down in the ticket office. See the stairs? Off we go.'

By the time they reach the surface concourse the dog woman is a dead weight between them. They carry her out to the ticket office, but at the door she wails and pulls back. 'No! I'm not sitting in a room. I never sit in rooms.'

'It's all right, love. Mister Casimir here's going to wait with you, and I'm going to get you a chair. All right?'

It is a cold night. The concourse is crowded with people, waiting in the light and the warmth until the station closes. Casimir can feel them watching the woman, their interest and detachment.

The dog woman begins to pull things out of her coat, piling

the objects in her lap. A green canvas wallet and a black leather purse. A Knickerbox plastic bag, small and unrumpled. A full hip bottle of Rebel Yell bourbon. A necklace of garnets, tiny and bright and blood-black.

'Tell me something.'

He looks up. The dog woman is leaning towards him. Hissing, owl-eyed. 'What's behind the doors? All the doors underground. They all go somewhere. There's something on the other side. You know, don't you?'

'The doors?'

She picks up the Knickerbox bag, distracted. Smiles, sweet-faced. 'The last time I wore these, I was invisible for six months.'

Blue light flashes in across the oxblood tiles of the concourse walls. The dog woman stands unsteadily. Two policewomen come in from the western entrance. They nod at Casimir and he steps back.

'Right then. Are you coming with us?'

'Yes, I am.' The dog woman looks back at Casimir, still smiling. 'Goodbye, then, Abyssinia.'

'Goodbye.'

He watches them go, the voices of the police hushed, the crackle of their radios loud as they hustle through the crowd. He feels a sudden sense of regret and guilt, wishing that he had let the woman go.

'You're bleeding.'

He turns round. The Underground girl is standing by the emergency stairs, against the wall. Watching him.

He looks down. The uniform trousers are short on him, and the skin of his ankles is bare and startlingly red. His feet are cold. He realizes his socks are soaked through with blood. But the Underground girl is talking to him again. He stares back up.

'I said I've seen you before. What's your name?'

'Casimir.'

She meets his eyes without blinking. Not aggressive, just considering. 'I saw you on the train.'

'Yes.'

'You're very tall. How tall are you?'

'I don't know. I haven't –'

'Do you work here?' Her eyes stare through him, making their own private calculations.

'At the station, yes. I've worked here for years.'

'I thought you were a ticket man.'

'No.'

'Because you were watching me on the train.'

He stops. Her gaze stops him. It is the way crowds sometimes look at those outside themselves: without expression, with no need to communicate. He thinks of it as almost inhuman and, briefly, he wonders what she wants from him.

She is waiting for him to answer. He moves a hand inexpresssively. 'Yes. I thought you were beautiful. I think I have also seen you here before.'

'Maybe.'

She is wearing the same clothes he saw her in last week, chinos and jacket. They look clean and he wonders where she washes them. There are ink marks on the back of her hands, like the first time. Her hair is loose except for two rat's-tail braids, tucked back behind her ears.

'It makes me think of blood, "Casimir".'

'Why?'

She shrugs. 'It just does. What's your first name?'

He sees that her skin is freckled. Even now, in autumn, when the sun is weak. 'How do you know Casimir isn't my first name?'

She shrugs again. It comes to him that she looks a little like Rebecca Saville. There is a similarity in the leanness of her neck and cheeks. Her skin is paler than Saville's, even her lips lacking redness; a face without colour, except for the freckles and eyes. It makes her look cold.

'My first names are Casimir Ariel.'

'Ariel.' She repeats it carefully, the first vowel long and open. *Ah*, like a sigh. It shocks him, a physical feeling like static; the sound of her voice, saying his name. He sees that there is expression in her eyes, but that it is kept back; the way she smiles without it going beyond her eyes.

He takes one step towards her. She doesn't move.

'Casimir! You there?'

'Yes.' He looks round. Leynes is at the door of the ticket office, silhouetted in the bright light.

'There's an ambulance coming for Sievwright and a van for the dogs.'

'Is he in pain?'

'He's not in pleasure anyway. He needs shots and stitches. The police are coming back for a statement. You OK talking to them?'

'Of course.'

He expects her to be gone when he turns back, but she is still there, waiting for him. He tries to think of something else to say. Anything that will keep her there. It is hard, knowing so little about her.

'You have writing on your hands.'

She looks down, then back up at him. 'From clubs. Don't you know?'

When he shakes his head, she smiles properly. Eyes narrowing, head cocked fractionally to one side. It brings warmth to her face, he thinks. A car goes past outside, stereo bass echoing through the concourse. The girl looks away towards it and then at the western entrance, where the police came from. He can see her thinking, the alertness of her.

The smile is already gone when she looks back at Casimir. 'Nightclubs, concerts, parties. Sometimes they stamp your hand, it's like a ticket. If I know people, I get in free. It's somewhere to go at nights. To keep warm.'

'What's your name?'

'Alice. Jacqueline. Lin.'

'All of them?'

'Yes. I use them all, and others too. You can choose, if you like. I have trouble with names.'

*Trouble with names.* He turns the phrase over in his mind. 'Jacqueline is your family name?'

'I don't have a family.'

She doesn't smile. He wants to apologize, or to make her smile again. He feels so slow, and speechless, as if English is a new language again and every sentence an effort.

She squints up at the lights and the station clock. It is almost twelve o'clock, closing time. 'I have to go now.'

'Why now?'

She shrugs. 'Places to go, people to see.' Already she is distracted, buttoning up her jacket. 'You should clean up the blood. Get some antiseptic.'

'I would like to see you again.'

'I know. Here.' She holds something out to him. It is a glass tray, smaller than her palm, cracked and dusty. 'You forgot this.'

He takes it, turns it in his own hands. There is a ridge around the top, where a lid would fit. On the bottom a brand-name is embossed in tiny letters: VICTORY SULPHUR MATCHES.

'I'll see you there.'

'Wait –'

He looks up. Alice is walking down the emergency stairs, out of sight. She doesn't look back. Casimir thinks of the abandoned station, the echo of singing. JACK UNION on the age-cracked walls. He stands quite still, waiting until she is gone.

'Mister Kazimierski, is it?'

'Casimir. I prefer Casimir.'

They are in the back of the ticket office, pressed together on rickety Formica chairs. The policewoman is almost large as Casimir himself, broad-shouldered and masculine. She sits with a notepad open on her nyloned knees.

'That's not the name on your Polish passport. At least according to London Transport.' He sees that her eyes are grey and quite beautiful. She doesn't seem to blink, although she looks away from him often. Down at her pen, up at the clock. 'Have you anglicized your name recently?'

'This is irrelevant.'

'Fine. Mister Casimir. My name is Detective Inspector Phelps.' She frowns, not offering her hand. 'Is this a bad time to talk? You look busy.'

'No.'

He shifts on the small chair. In his jacket pocket he can feel the glass matchbox, cool against his chest but becoming warmer. He thinks of her eyes, the smile held in. Alice, or Jacqueline. Jack Union. Watching him from some corner of the derelict station, with its preserved glitter of antique equipment and tiny stalactites. He shakes his head, trying to concentrate.

'Yes. I am busy, of course. It isn't a problem. You want to talk about the woman with the dogs.'

She stops writing, puts down her notebook. 'Actually, no. I know what happened tonight. It's a dangerous job, working on the Tube, isn't it? I hear about attacks on staff all the time.'

Casimir nods. 'All the time.'

'What happened last week was more unusual. The accident.'

He looks at her again, gauging her. Waits for her to go on. She smiles. It is a hard, bright expression, without humour.

'I haven't been able to meet the supervisor who was on duty that night, Michael Adams. So until I get hold of him, I was wondering if I might talk to some of the other senior staff here. A bit of a surprise visit, in case you all turn out to be as reluctant as Adams. I've talked to Leynes and Sanusi already tonight. Do you mind?'

'No.'

'Good. Why won't Adams meet me?'

Casimir sits back. Taking a breath, trying to focus his mind. He is caught off guard by the policewoman's sharpness.

'Because he doesn't want to talk about it.' Now it is Phelps who waits until he goes on. 'Adams thought the woman was pushed. Rebecca Saville. He believed it could happen again. He didn't want to be here when it does.'

From outside comes the rattle of the entrance grilles closing. The main concourse lights go out, darkening the ticket windows. The policewoman sits thinking, watching Casimir as she does so, not registering his gaze.

'I see.' She sits up, puts her pen down. 'Were you on duty that night?' He shakes his head. 'How do you know her name? The woman who fell.'

'There were photographs. I saw them.'

'You shouldn't have. What do you think?'

'I think the platform photograph shows she was –'

She interrupts. 'Your general feelings. I've seen the photographs.'

He makes himself think before he speaks. 'The Underground attracts strange people. Even ordinary people are different. Less social, more isolated. It only takes one person to push her. It happened before, about ten years ago.'

'Yes, I know.' Phelps is writing again, the chrome pen delicate in her large hand.

'I don't want it to happen again. I could help. I could look at the security videos you have from that day.'

'Could you?' The policewoman stops and looks at him again, thin eyebrows pulled together in a slight frown. 'You know a lot about this, don't you? Why is that?'

He sits forward, searching for words. 'I don't think it was an accident. I feel the same as Adams.' I can feel it in the Underground, he wants to say. In the tension of crowds and empty platforms. He doesn't say this. 'I think a woman has been killed.'

Phelps is still frowning. 'I'm afraid that's my job.'

'I know the Underground. You don't. Let me help.'

'No.' Phelps sits back. Now the eyebrows are raised, in surprise or regret. 'I'm sorry. The videos are police property now. Was there anything else?'

He feels anger building up in him and he pauses, requiring himself to be calm. 'Yes. There are signs that people have been in the station at night. Maybe the homeless –'

'Yes, Mister Leynes told me. Fine. Call me if you think of anything else.' Phelps stands, puts out her hand. 'Thank you for your help. Will you show me out?'

After she is gone he locks the grille behind her then stops still in the empty hall, listening. The sounds of his station are different at night. During the day there is the repetition of footsteps, layer on layer of echoes, a kind of human white noise. Hundreds of millions of people a year; a city under the city. He remembers his first night shift. Hearing the station by itself, the hollowness of it. There are less than a hundred people in the complex now. The tunnels magnify every noise, like a cave or a shell. Some nights, Casimir can hear the trapped air sigh against his ears: *Aaah*. Like the trains. Like his name.

There is work to be done. He digs in his pockets for keys as he crosses to the far side of the concourse. There is a single metal door at the top of a short flight of steps. He opens it and steps through into the storerooms. Feels along the wall, clicks on a switch. Dusty fluorescent light gutters over stacks of boxes. Yellow paint peels off the walls in yard-long skeins. At the far side of the room steps lead down to other levels of storerooms, and from there to stairwells, locked rooms and offices. Further, blacked-out platforms and lines. Down to deep shelters and abandoned stations. Dozens of them, under the capital. He thinks of their names, beautiful and redundant. Down Street and Waterloo Necropolis. Snow Hill and British Museum. South Kentish Town.

Outside a police car goes by and Casimir stops, listening to the howl of its siren. He closes the door, cutting off the sound. Locks it behind him.

He lies still in the rented room. Waiting for morning to come, when he can let himself sleep properly before the next long night shift. There is nothing to see except the bare bulb's light on the damp-stained ceiling. The sky outside, square and black against the window.

He is too long for the bed, so that even lying diagonally his head is tilted back on the pillow. He takes it out and lays it on the floor. Lies back flat on the sheets. Their fabric is worn soft as down.

There is pain in the muscles of his legs, where the skin has been broken. Sleep comes at him in soft waves, natural as the ache of physical exhaustion in his limbs. Usually even the action of thinking helps him sleep, but not tonight. The day runs through his mind, uneasy and uncalled for. He thinks of Adams and the falling woman. The disused station and the Underground girl. Alice. Already he wants to see her again, just to hear her voice. He listens to the sounds in the small room. There is the sigh of his own breathing, harsh against his teeth. The tick of the electricity meter in its black box. The echoed clank of goods trains from the terminus.

The electricity meter runs out. He has no more money to feed it. The dark is solid, set like amber. When he looks at the window, the sky outside has altered by comparison. Now he can see the reflected illumination of the city; a fantastic orange glow, as if the whole of London is on fire. After a while, he can make out the faintest hint of first light.

The disused station. He recollects the echo of music and the graffiti, JACK UNION. A strange name, he thinks. Political, the

British flag reversed. Rhythmical, like something from a children's story. Tomorrow he will go and ask Alice why she chose it. Tomorrow he can go to her, at the abandoned station. *I'll see you there.* The Underground girl with freckled skin and the eyes that shock him out of himself.

Sleep nags at him. He thinks of amber. His mother's voice. Clear, as if he is dreaming it. *The green ones are the rarest, see? Green, from the pine.*

She is laying out objects on a checked tablecloth. He is very small and the objects look like congealed honey, clear and dark and opaque. His mouth fills with saliva.

Baltic ambers. He remembers them with the vividness of early childhood. The way his mother laid them out, like a story. Always the smallest droplet first. It was yellow with ancient pollen, the rich colour of calving cream. Then others, a small red amber from Persia. The one which was flat, like his tongue. The yellow pebble he once found which wasn't amber at all, just a stone he gave his mother, valued only for that. Last of all the largest, green like canal water the day he fell through the ice. Bigger than his father's fist, bigger than a duck egg. Charred and cracked along one side. It was full of trapped things: round stress-cracks like little coins, prehistoric seeds, an insect crushed in on itself by the resin's dead weight.

*There were more before the war. My father had to sell them.*

*What for?*

*For me. I was so hungry. For potatoes.*

And he remembers not understanding, only turning the ambers against his fingers, the refined smoothness of them. His mother's hands are larger than his, and red from work. She is the woman who chooses to forget her past. And Casimir is the one who remembers for her, even when the remembering hunts him down. Catches him in the dark, presses over him like the weight of London clay.

He is a child again and it is five years before she leaves him. She smiles and holds the last amber for him, up to the light. A window of sky wobbles through it. It is summer, early morning, and quite warm.

He wakes. Outside there are pigeons roosting around the vents and guttering. The sound of their crooning is vivid as memories. Of his mother sobbing softly in a nearby room. Of lovemaking, and the faces of women. The shock of Alice's eyes meeting his. Waking dreams muddled together.

The room is full of grey dawn light. For a moment he thinks he is back in Poland, that there is snow on the way. Then he realizes he is thinking in English and he remembers everything.

# 6

# Squirrel Cage

'Now?'

'Wait.'

'*Cholera*, this is a bad idea. Now?'

'No. I'll tell you when.'

It's the end of spring. The sky is all blue except for five puffs of factory smoke, orange like clouds at sunset. St Barbary and the Garrison Church and the Cathedral are all ringing for Pentecost, and in the streets are stalls with Pentecost irises. In Old Square is Mr Susicka's stall with its long green tables and tall white pots and the pavement dark where Susicka has washed it down. He's got tattery bunches of yellow broom and willow buds, but most of the stall is irises. A high deep blue wall of flowers.

We have no money to buy Pentecost irises. Until Dad comes back we have no money. Mother said so, on the telephone to the telephone man. I heard it. She said other things too, about money. It was just after Piotr's birthday. He is nine now. I'm still eight, but I've got more muscles. On the classroom door my mark is the highest.

'We could get flax. That's blue too. There's still a field of them over near the state pig farm. Casimir? Casimir?'

Piotr reaches out for my arm. It still hurts from when Dad went away. He held me so hard the skin has gone blue and yellow. Like irises. He has got a big deal now. It makes him smile more. I shake Piotr off.

'It's Pentecost. You can't use flax. It has to be irises.'

'Why bother? Only old people have the irises now. Broom is much prettier. I know where there's wild broom –'

'Shh!' Two old women are at Susicka's stall. He wraps their flowers slowly because of his stumpy hand, with the bouquets on his knee. He did the hand in the Memory of Jozef Stalin steel factory and now he sells flowers. He can drive too, even going fast.

Now the old women are going off down Zwyciestwa Street with their arms full of irises. There are only the three of us in the square. It's quiet except for the churches.

'Now!'

I push Piotr out. He goes because he's my friend. I'd do the same for him. The colonnades are flat arches of sun between shadow. I run through them as Piotr walks across the open.

'Hello, Mister Susicka.'

'Hello. It's cold weather, isn't it?'

Susicka always says that. It's not cold. His big soft face is always smiling except when he drinks; then he never smiles. I come round into the southern colonnade. The stall is up against the far end. There are collared doves in the square, they sing *coal, coal*. I run in the shadows so they won't fly away.

'Yes, sir. Can I have some irises? Just three of them.'

'Just three? You know, it's only sixty for a bouquet. Don't you have sixty? Three's no use.'

I come in close and low. Susicka is wrapping the three irises, holding them lengthways on his knee. I'm so close I can smell him, like two-days-old milk. I crawl between the green tables. Susicka's shoes are home-made and rimmed black where water has stained them. His socks are worn thin between their ribs. I can see the skin of his fat ankles. It is blue-grey, like the insides of raw fish.

'All done! I put in one extra for you. Three's no use.'

'Thanks. Could I have them unwrapped?'

'Unwrapped?' He laughs from his belly. 'Unwrapped flowers are for lovers. Have you got a lover already?'

'No. I do. Yes, sir.'

He goes on laughing and unwrapping. A soft, slow man. I come up behind him, diving upwards from the push of my arms, lifting the irises out of two white pots. They squeak together, wet in my arms and smelling of onions.

'All done!'

All done. I jump back between the tables, light and strong, down through the sun and shadow. The excitement fizzes in me like bottled Fanta, bubbling up sweet. I try to laugh but the flowers keep hitting me in the face. The air is full of sweetness and church bells. I run until I have to stop and then I stop.

Piotr comes belting up. He's laughing too now, his red face happy under the grey-brown hair. He still has the four unwrapped irises. We go on towards the Strug flats, up to my place. The stairwell lights have gone and we hold the irises up ahead, the yellows of them like candles. It seems like they make the dark lighter. Piotr says they can't but it seems they do.

For Pentecost you cover the floor with irises. We do it in the kitchen and Mother's room. There are plenty of flowers and two left for Mother's bed and Dad's. It takes ages; our hands go yellow with iris dust. When we're done, the sunlight is still coming in the windows. It falls on the flowers and takes their colour, like light off water. The stove and refrigerator and white kitchen cupboards take their colour. The rooms have all gone blue and golden.

We go and wait in my room. We play with my AH-18 Combat Helicopter. Piotr is the secret police and I'm the speculator with Russian vodka and American cigarettes.

'Casimir?' It's Mum. We jump up, remembering. What do we do now? She goes into the kitchen and cries out, so we run into the kitchen.

'We got them! Do you like them? It was me and Piotr together.' Mother is smiling with both hands to her mouth. It makes her look young. Then the smile begins to go.

'Where did you get them? Casimir?'

I shrug. 'We got them. For Pentecost.' I'm still smiling. I can't make it go. It starts to hurt. 'For you. We both got them.' Her eyes are hurt. It's the same look as when Dad has hurt her. The shame begins. It's a shaking in my belly and legs, then my chest. 'For you. For Pentecost.'

I turn and run. I go into the trees and don't come out until Piotr stops calling and goes home.

I open the door and the house smells of flowers, but the irises have gone. The rooms are back to their ordinary colours. Even the golden dust is dusted away. We have chopped-ham salad and beetroot soup and cabbage pasties for supper. We don't talk because the radio is on.

She said other things, my mother. Not to the telephone man but to herself. She has no friends, my mother, no one to talk to. It was night and she was drinking, alone in the kitchen. I heard her rattling the glass and cursing, I heard her say blood. She was arguing about blood money. She wouldn't have it in her home. It sounded like she was arguing and that scared me, because it was just her there, and me listening. It was my father she was talking about. His mother, who was killed by the Russians. And blood money.

I got them without any money. And I liked the rooms being blue and gold; I never saw rooms like that before. It made me feel empty and good inside. But blue is the colour of shame.


'Ariel? Have you done your Human Philosophy?'

'Don't call me that.'

'I knew you didn't. How do you like my hair?'

'It's OK.'

'It's only hair anyway. What's wrong with it?'

'It's OK. I said it was. It's fine.'

'I don't care. It's not important. Yours is much more manageable. I can help you with your homework, you know.'

We walk home. I like it better when she doesn't talk. Once she taught me to write and I wrote my middle name and now she uses it all the time. She knows what my name means and she won't tell me. She could be lying though. She makes me nervous.

'My parents have new jobs in Warsaw. Party jobs.'

'I heard.'

'We'll move soon. In Warsaw no one knows anyone. What do you want to do when you grow up?'

It's a stupid question. I wish I hadn't told her my middle name. I try and look at her without her seeing. So I can remember her. From the side she looks proud. From the front she just looks skinny.

'Grow a beard.'

She stops. Crows cough and clatter by the foot of B Block. She throws a stone. 'Don't be stupid. I know you're not.'

'What about you? What do you want?'

A car horn. It is her father, waiting for her. The sun is ahead of us. A little boy on a tricycle comes out of the light. His shoulders rock and the wheels creak, creak.

Hanna stops. Red hair and blue eyes. No one has hair like hers. It is the colour of squirrel fur. Beautiful. 'I've got to go.'

'I want to be like snow.'

'Why?'

'The more you press it, the harder it becomes. In the end it's ice.'

I give her her geography books. She takes them without saying thanks. She looks at me again with her thin eyes.

'I want to go somewhere where no one knows I am Jewish. Then I can just be me. Don't get like ice, Ariel.'

She turns away without saying goodbye. In three days I will never see her again. I shout goodbye after her but the car's already going.

'I told you. Look at it. It goes mad.'

In my mouth the spit tastes sweet and rich as blood. I hawk into the silo dust. I hurt from running hard.

He is right; Piotr is usually right. He takes off his gloves, which are dark where the squirrel bit him, and he sits down between Monika and me. It is spring and cold in the silo. The blood hardens fast.

The squirrel goes round and round without falling; there is no up and down in its head. Its red fingers flutter in the chicken wire and Maria tries to stroke them, but she is only four and slow with it.

'Leave it alone.'

'I want to stroke it.'

'No –' Monika pulls her sister away. 'Stupid *Ohyn*.'

Maria starts to cry. Not making any noise, just crying down her cheeks. The squirrel chatters and the cage shakes; it is just sheet chicken-wire pulled up into a ball, messy at the top where I bunched it together. Maria stops crying to watch. Now the squirrel jumps hard to one side. The cage tips over and begins to roll. It goes towards Monika and she screams and kicks at it.

'No, oh no! Get it away from me!'

No one wants to touch the cage because we know the squirrel will bite. It has gone mad, as Piotr said it would. We would bite, if it was us.

Her hands are quite red from work, and the ambers red in them or gold or black, like lumps of tar on the new town roads.

I watch her face. She holds an amber up to the light. The blacks of her eyes go small; they are smaller than a millimetre. She smiles and frowns at the same time.

'Where's that one from?' It's the red amber, from Persia. It's too big for millimetres, it is in centimetres. The light moves slowly inside it.

'You know where.'

'Tell me,' I whine at her. We're at home, no one can hear.

She picks it up, turns it in her hands.

'This is from Persia. Your grandfather bought it from the Gypsies. They came to Kielce every spring and harvest. Their king was richer than almost anyone then, but we were not so poor either. Do you know what your grandfather did, Ariel?'

'He bought amber from Persia.'

She laughs. 'Do you know what his work was?'

'A miller.'

'I never saw him with flour on his skin, not once outside the mill. He was a clean man. He liked everything in its place. You have that from him. And the size of you, and your name. I know it's not much.'

She puts the Persian amber down and I take it. It is smoother than my skin. Smoother than my mother's skin.

'Was he rich?'

'I wouldn't say so. We weren't allowed to own the mill, so he rented it. It belonged to a German called Wagner. He was the only German in town and quite friendly. We weren't rich. Comfortable. My father rented the mill for forty years –'

I look up. She is frowning down at the ambers. 'There were more before the war. He had to sell them.'

'What for?' I keep my voice quiet, like hers. Like church.

'For me. I was so hungry then. For potatoes.'

I look down at the amber and think of potatoes. All the beautiful colours of honey and green water, changed into grey. 'Lots of potatoes.' It is half question and half not. She shakes her head. Her eyes don't move to me.

'No, no. One for each amber. One potato, one egg. The taste of one egg!' Her eyes close. 'Pushing his hands through the wire, my father. Everybody's hands and all their jewellery, the gold worth less than potatoes. And the people outside, who were our old neighbours. Wagner and the rest, taking all they could. I still remember everything. If I am not careful, I remember it all. It is so much better, to just forget –'

She shakes her head. It means she won't talk any more. Already it is more than ever. I don't understand, but I remember for later.

'Why wasn't it his mill, if he was the miller?'

She takes the amber out of my hands. 'It doesn't matter why. It's time for your homework. What do you have?'

'Human Philosophy.'

We go to do the Human Philosophy. It's boring for me and boring for her. Then Dad is home, smiling, with two big handfuls of broken biscuits and poppy-seed cake, and we kiss and laugh with him. First things first.


It was Piotr's idea but I caught it. The Wittlin farm is three fields, three pigs, the duck Archangel and the chickens for eggs and carp in the pond for Christmas, fat as pigs. The barns and the silo, white paint and red rust.

We were in the woods by the top field, where the pines are old and fat at the roots like spring onions. The red squirrel sat quite still. Not looking at us but away to one side, as if it was listening to music.

'Catch it!' hissed Maria.

I leaned forward into my run and pushed hard with my thighs and feet, arms and shoulders, curling my feet into the pine earth. Then I was on to it and it came alive, biting at the sleeves of my winter coat. Piotr said take it to the silo and we did.

In the cage the squirrel stops upside-down, holding the bars. It is a beautiful thing, but it scares us too. A rich little man in a red fur. A speculator, loan shark, Party member. It has hands, face, heart and eyes, just like me.

'What do we do now?' says Monika, and I say, 'We can do anything we want. We are alone.'


'Hey, is that your dad's car?'

'Yes.'

'That's brilliant, that is. A Polonez. When did he get it?'

'Casimir! Is that your car?'

'Yes, it is. He got it yesterday from Katowice.'

'Hey, mister! Can we touch it?'

'Mister Kazimierski, sir? How much was it?'

'No. Four hundred. Oy! Hands off, you.'

The price comes out with Dad's smoke. He has an American cigarette, a Marlboro. The smoke is like a speech balloon in a cartoon, silvery-white.

'Four hundred thousand zloty? Bloody hell. Did you hear, Boleslaw? Four hundred.'

'Thousand? Bloody hell. What colour is it, sir?'

'You ponce, are you blind? It's blue.'

'Hey – watch your language. And it's not blue. It's navy.'

They all crowd round outside the school gates, kids and teachers too at the back, Mr Kruczkowski, the Human Philosophy master, and Mr Grudzinski, who does Arithmetic and PE. Dad doesn't smile, but I know he wants to. It's good that he doesn't. Being too happy is like being the smartest in class. It's better to keep quiet about it.

Ours is the biggest car on the street. It's got a boot and four doors. This morning it took eleven tries to start; it would have been quicker to walk to school but we drove anyway. I'm the second one in school to have a Polonez but it is the first to be navy.


We go on a car trip to see my Uncle Jan. He is a guard at the Russian border. Mother says he met me when I was baptized.

'Be polite to him, love. He can get very angry, your uncle. It is just his temper. Are you ready?'

'Yes.'

'Let's go then!'

She is as excited as me. The car starts first time. It's a March Saturday, and the sunshine comes down between the houses and at street corners, through trees and leant long down hill-sides.

We have Marlboro for my uncle. Dad brings an emergency oil can so if we run out of benzene, we can stop at garages and fill the can for free. He does it even when we already have a full tank. Mum says it's dishonest. Dad says it's the law and he didn't make it. Their voices get louder, softer. Wind comes hushing in the window. Mum sings, not out loud, just humming.

For a time I sleep in the back seat, where the plastic is warm in the sun. Then I wake up and look out of the window. The coalfields have gone and instead of them I see fields of flax, twisted walnut trees, apple orchards in long bony rows with their whitewashed trunks.

'When do we get there?'

'Soon. Go to sleep, love.'

I'm not tired now. I sit up. 'What is it called, the place he lives?'

Mum turns round in her seat. I wait for her to tell me. She turns back again. She talks without looking at me. 'Where are your gloves?'

'Here.' I hold them up drooping from my coat. They are on elastic through the arms. She isn't looking anyway.

'Just sit still. We'll be there soon.'

It sounds like what she said makes no sense, but it does. It means she forgot where we were going too. It happens more and more often, her forgetting. Dad makes a joke of it. He says one day she'll go shopping and forget where she lives. It's not much of a joke.

One time, I was waiting for her in Pieronek's shoe shop and she left without me. I was in the back with the mirrors with pictures of French women, measuring my feet on the foot-measuring stool. When Mr Pieronek saw I was still there he called my flat but no one was home. Then he locked up the shop and took me back on the tram. My mum went back to the shop later and there was a note, so it worked out fine.

When Mum forgets, it's different from the way I do. It's something to be scared of, you can feel it. I don't ask Mum about it because if I do, she'll tell me and then it will be true. My mother's eyes are blue and the brows are thick and the nose is small and hooked. I think she is probably beautiful but I don't know. She is just my mother.

Mother and Father. I look at their heads in the front seats. Their hair is the same colour, black and bright. They grew up together in Kielce. Kielce is at the heart of Poland. Where did I learn this? In school I learn that Silesian anthracite is the richest coal source in the world. My parents' hair is the colour of anthracite. My hair is a different kind of black, more like road-tar. From behind, my parents look like the same person.

Uncle Jan is different. The veins in his face are the road-map across Poland, from Gliwice in the west to Terespol in the east. His hair is white like a grandfather, although he is not even a father, not even married. He is my father's brother and in the Militia Border Guards. His uniform is green and itchy and he has to carry a satchel with a book of the names of all travellers.

He won't show me his gun and he shakes my hand without smiling. He smells hot and sour, like zúr soup. Not like my dad, who smells of his imported aftershaves, sometimes like firs and sometimes salt.

'Casimir? You're getting big. God knows you don't get it from my family. When are you going to start helping Michal with his work, eh? It's a long haul he does now, to Astrakhan. Hard work. Do you know where that is, eh? Astrakhan?'

'No, sir. In Russia.' I stay polite with him, for now.

'In Russia. Go off and play.'

The smell of him is ugly and dangerous. Now he brings out winiak brandy in a brown bottle and I go away while the two of them drink. Mother is standing at the window but she doesn't see me go past. Outside it is not cold at all; I could do without the gloves.

Terespol is two towns with the border through it. In Russia it's called Brest and it looks bigger. It's not dark yet but there are no kids around, only border guards. I play by myself, as far as I can go. There are oak trees here with rook nests in them, big balls of twigs like mistletoe.

I come to a pair of wide-open doors. I look inside and there is flour everywhere, on the machines and shelves. It is a flour mill, like my mother's father's. His mill, which was not his mill. I get some of the flour and put it in my mouth but it doesn't taste of much. I clap my hands to get rid of it.

Outside I can see the railways, lines going away silvery, crossing and separating. There are queues of cars at the border. One lot waiting to go into Russia, one lot queuing to come out. Some of them will wait for days to go through, but when Dad goes he doesn't have to wait long. Uncle Jan gets him through. They work together on the speculations.

I see glasshouses long as trains with giant doors. Sunlight in Russia but not here yet, it moves across the flat fields towards me. On the far side of the glasshouses is where Russia begins. It looks ordinary. There are chimneys steaming in the light. Houses with roofs built heavy for snow. The land white with snow and black with thaw.

'America is the land of milk and honey, but Russia is the land of champagne and caviare.' Dad says that. He tried to give me golden caviare one time. It smelt like cod liver. He sold it to the Finns for dollars. They're welcome to it. I like tinned sardines better.

It starts to rain. I stand by the flour mill, watching the rain in Poland and the rain in Russia. The asphalt smells of sourdough. It makes me hungry. I go back to Uncle Jan's house to see what I can find.


The woods are my special place. I never get lost or forget my way, like my mother.

It makes me angry that she forgets. I know she does it on purpose, because she told me. Forgetting is what she does with secrets. That's what she told me. I think about her at night, under the ceiling cracks. There are new cracks, one like East Germany, one like Great Britain.

The woods start after the allotments with their woodsheds and fruit trees. The allotments start after the factories with their red-topped chimneys. Sometimes there is woodsmoke through the trees and sun through the smoke and what happens is, the trees and the shadows of trees are both bars of dark cutting through the light, you can't tell which is which. I like it.

Today there is food in the kitchen, dried peas soaking in water for the soup and potato pancakes with cheese and eggs from our friends the Wittlins. I am alone. I take one pancake wrapped in newspaper. I take an egg too. I leave a note, so it isn't stealing.

I go westwards into the woods, away from the big towns of Katowice. First I pass the Wittlin farm, round the bottom field. Then I come to a rubbish dump, its bitter smoke catching in the trees. There are fewer firs here in the deep wood; the trees are naked inside and thick at the tops, stands of pine and larch and birch. The bare pine earth rolls up and down where the Germans hid tanks in the war. I see squirrels and I find boar shit. In the deep woods there are bison, they are red and they eat bison grass. Grandad told me that before he died. I don't know if it's true, because sometimes he lied.

Now I go south, then west, then north-west. Walking a circle is more interesting than a there-and-back. It's past noon now and raining. I'm looking for somewhere dry to eat and just when I turn, the ground falls through.

There is no time to scream. The darkness comes down around me and I hit the ground blind and go over on one side. My legs hurt and I cry out, not moving. There is cold black water coming through my coat. The underground place smells sweet and oily. It's the smell of coal, the smell of my town.

I open my eyes. There is light from the hole; it isn't so far up. I sit up and look at my hands and they are black, steeped in coal dust.

I stand up, the water echoing off me in slow drips. I breathe softly, listening. The shaft sounds big. First I look up and there are big tree-roots round the sky. I can climb out; it doesn't look so hard. Then I look around.

In school Mrs Nalkowska told us about the old mines. Some of them are a hundred years old, or hundreds. They were the most dangerous things, more than gun shelters or strangers. But here I am. It's too late to stay away.

The coal shaft goes away westwards and downwards. When

I was small, my friend Karol's brother went into an old mine and found a German shell and died. Still, now I know where I am my legs don't hurt so much. I climb out to make sure I can. I get a birch stick and then I climb in again.

My feet slap against the mine bottom. I tap ahead with the white stick, like the blind. The shaft smells of coal and earth and the trees above my head. I have a good look round for bullets but there's nothing. The shaft is getting bigger and I stop, listening to it.

I look down. There is no reflection off the black water. I tap ahead with the white stick and the ground has gone. The darkness is flat black, without sound. I can't tell how far ahead it goes or how far down. Up above, a blackbird goes singing away in fear.

My breathing starts to go fast and I wait, making it slow again. Then I take a step back, more steps. When I'm sure of the ground, I kneel down, feeling for a piece of loose coal or stone. When I find one I throw it forwards, into the downshaft.

The darkness makes no sound.

I go back to the mine entrance. My eyes are used to the underground now; I can see the walls, shining rough blue-black. I get another loose stone and scratch my name zigzag across the walls, KAZIMIERZ. Now it is mine, a secret place in the deep woods.

I climb back out. The rain has stopped. I eat my pancake and my egg. It all tastes good but it makes me thirsty. I go back home the way I came.


Her hair is tied back in tight red lines, like the copper wire in machines. Her shoulders are goat-thin even though she is tall for a girl. Her hips too. Her father and mother both work in the Office for the Control of Press, Publications and Public Spectacles. Dad says they are high up. He calls them leftover Yids. I also heard Mrs Nalkowska talk about them in the vodka and meat shop. She said it's not their fault the Jews killed Jesus, after all. They had a Fiat before anyone in school but Hanna didn't tell us.

It's not the colour of copper exactly. Sometimes there are goods trains which take old iron cable from the factories. Twisted and tough and rusted. This is the colour of Hanna's hair.

When I was small we were friends and sometimes we still are. When we are not I still dream of Hanna. In the dreams I made love to her. We are underground in the deep woods and naked and I lie flat on top of her in the cold black water. Lips on lips, belly on belly, legs on legs, down to the simple feet.

After three days the squirrel stops moving and watches us. Waiting with its head on one side, the way it did in the forest to begin with.

We take it to the abandoned mine and throw it in. This time you can hear the bottom. The cage clatters once. Then there is silence again and then it splashes. The Black Trout Shaft is called that because sometimes fish swim into the flooded chambers and the miners catch them and eat them. The cooked flesh is black and sweet. Maybe the trout will eat the squirrel, down underground. Maybe the cage came open when it clattered and the squirrel got out in time.

When I was small I thought there was nothing else in the dark except myself, so I knew everything and I loved it. Now there are questions and dangers. The squirrel drowned white in its cage. I don't know the darkness any more. It's my own fault. Piotr takes his father's torch, so we can see where we're going.

In Hanna's house there are white patches where the stove and pictures were. They are the only Jews I know in town, the only ones I have talked to. Hanna says there are more in Warsaw, but not so many. Not since the war.

There was a hole in the door where they kept Jewish things, and candles like trees on the mantelpiece. Her guest room was always dark and smelling of oil and turpentine, but now it's plain, the net curtains blowing outwards, white and ordinary. Her mother sits in the car with their cat in her arms and the bread bin on one side of her and a green glass lamp on the other. I wave at her as we go past and she waves back.

'Where are we going?'

'The woods.'

'How far?'

'They'll wait for you.'

She follows me. A #5 tram goes past us into town and the wire fittings ring together like sleigh bells, long after the carriage has gone.

We pass the last tram lines, then the last houses. There are yellow cranes dropping four-fingered hands, lifting trees. Thin chimneys and fat chimneys. The thin chimneys are red brick with red and white stripes at the top to stop aeroplanes going into them. The fat chimneys have no stripes. If the aeroplanes can't see the fat chimneys coming they must be blind.

Factories, allotments, woods. Hanna walks ahead, then beside me. There have been deer here; you can see where they scratch their backs on the pine trees.

Our hands are close; the knuckles knock together and the fingers catch. No one can see us here, where the light stops in the wings of firs. We can do whatever we want.

It's a long way to the mine but she doesn't talk. When we get there I help her down, then along in the dark.

She laughs. In the dark it is a wild sound. 'What a place. Did you find it yourself? I want to see it. Do you have a light?'

'Yes.'

Now we're at the mouth of the down-shaft. I got matches from the kitchen and tore rough paper from the box. She looks around in their flare. The shaft is round at the end, like the inside of the rabbit's skull in the glass cabinets in room C2 at school. The down-shaft drops away in front of us. Its darkness begins again, ten or fifteen metres down. Hanna doesn't make a sound. She puts out a hand towards the drop, palm out. Steps back into me.

The match goes out. I find her face with my hands, then her mouth with my mouth. I feel her fingers link at the back of my head, where the bone is thinner. Her lips are soft against her hard teeth and I can taste her breath.

'Light another match. I want to see.'

I strike two at the same time. There are two more matches

left. Hanna looks around for a stone to throw. I go back for some birch twigs because they'll show up in the dark.

We throw in the pebbles and twigs. Sometimes the pebbles click. The twigs make no sound at all. Hanna comes up close to me again. She puts something into my hand.

'I got you this, look. Light another.'

In the match-light I see it's a little amber, still warm from her jeans pocket. The thin yellow of honey strung down from a spoon. The edges are not smooth, but carved. There is a face in it. Grinning, full of teeth.

'I got it in Warsaw, when we went to see my new house. It's a lion, you see? For your name, Ariel. It means "Lion" in Hebrew. Do you like it? Who chose it for you, your name? Was it your mother?'

I have time to look at her before the match goes out. Then there is a sound from outside, a pheasant. It chatters like machine-guns. Then it stops.

'When you asked me what I wanted to be when I grew up and I asked you, you said you wanted to go somewhere where no one knew you were Jewish.'

'Yes.'

'Then why tell me this?'

'I don't –'

'Now someone knows. I know.'

'I thought you knew already. Didn't your mother –' She's feeling for my hand, but I step away from her. The down-shaft is close, somewhere beside me. I make myself stop.

'Ariel?'

The amber is still warm from her. Her body must be warmer than mine. I throw the carving out over the down-shaft. It clicks once, twice. Now it's gone where no one will know.

'Ariel?'

Unless the trout eat it. Then the miners will catch the trout. When they cut it open the lion will be there, its yellowed teeth on the cooked black flesh.

'Ariel!'

'Don't call me that.'

'Light the last one.'

'Why?'

'I want to see. Because I want to see your face. Please?'

I do it. Her own face is thin and white. She runs up too fast and I reach out to stop her falling. I hold her for a minute or two. It's true; her body is warmer than mine. It must be that her heart is stronger. Then I let her go.

'Let's go back.'

We get out. Her hands and face are smudged but I brought newspaper to wipe them clean and she does that. We don't say anything now. Underground in the secret place we could say anything, but not here.

She walks ahead of me. Fast, so I have to keep up. We come into sight of the town, yellowed coal smoke rising from all the house chimneys. At the beginning of the tram lines she begins to run. I call her name three times but she doesn't turn round. I called for her three times.

# 7

# Undertakings

'What's up, sir?' Weaver shouts to be heard over the roar of machinery. 'Oy, Cass, what's the problem?'

Casimir glances around. The movement makes him look surprised, lining his forehead, making him old. 'With what?'

'With everyone. The geezer that left.'

'Adams.'

'Him. And you.'

'Me? Nothing is a problem with me.'

Above them the dark ceiling moves and roars. Great tank-tracks of escalator machinery, an armour of steps flattening as they turn.

'Yeah? Well then, I reckon you should all talk more, all the old workers. Get out a bit. If you don't mind me saying. 'Cos some days you're all so quiet down here, it feels like Lenin's Tomb. You know what I mean?'

He smiles. 'Yes, I know what you mean. Do you want to leave?'

'No.' There is a question in the trainee's tone. It is gone when he speaks again. 'No. A job's a job, even if it's underground. I just wish you'd all talk a bit more.'

'I'm sorry. I'm glad you will stay.'

They are in the escalator-machinery chamber, waiting for closing time. To the south, the ceiling slopes upwards over two engines, all steel and axle grease. The engines are surprisingly large, barrelled sides curving above the heads of the two workers. At the southern end of the chamber there is room for two doors; to the north, the glittering movement of escalators almost reaches the floor. There is the fat smell of grease. The sour odour of metal and rust.

He is thinking of Alice. For the time being, nothing is wrong. It is twenty minutes until closing time. Ten minutes along the lines to South Kentish Town. He has left the glass matchbox in Lower Marsh and now he wishes he had it with him. A souvenir of the abandoned station, he thinks; something to be remembered, by which to remember something. He remembers her skin, fine and freckled in late summer, and feels the fierce excitement of attraction. It is not unpleasant or unexpected. Not a problem. In this sense he is not lying to Weaver.

Caterpillar belts and gear chains grind together overhead. When he looks up Casimir can see graffiti on the leathery hand-grips, electric-blue spray paint scrolling out on the escalators' underside. He is too far down to read the ciphers, to see if Alice's name is there. He thinks about running to the chamber's shallow end to look again.

The smell of the escalators reminds him of Polish churches, their black metal and turpentine. A Madonna outside the nunnery in Katowice with a tubular neon halo. Circular, like an insectocutor. The religion of an industrial town.

'Are we finished, sir? Closing time soon.'

'Yes. Almost finished.'

They work for a few minutes more in easy silence, checking for obstructions until each belt of steps has circulated. At the chamber's higher end Casimir stands upright, stretching his arms and shoulders. Weaver stops by the doors, wiping axle grease off his hands, reading the signs: ENTRANCE C, ENTRANCE D.

'That's good, that is. "Entrance-d". Do you reckon they thought of that when they did it? What's down there?'

'You can see. We can go to the platforms that way.'

Casimir unlocks the door and leads the way down one flight of stairs, out into a larger hall. It looms around them, damp and smelling of ozone. Like a sea-cave, thinks Casimir. The walls are cracked with subsidence.

'What do you call this?'

'The substation.'

'That'll be because it's under the station then. It's a bloody maze down here, isn't it, sir? All hidden away. Gothic. Like in that film with the cannibals. You know what I mean?'

'No.'

'Doesn't matter. I mean you could get lost for days down here. Does it happen, people getting lost?'

'I don't know. It could happen. The Underground is old. Older than the states of Germany or Italy. Bigger than London. The deepest subway ever made.'

'Is that right? Is there anything further down than this?'

'Yes. In the war they built deep levels. Shelters. They were never used. The bombs became rockets, and the rockets were too fast to shelter from.'

'Have you been down there?'

'Not often.'

Casimir imagines the deep shelters under him; their massive, locked silences. Around the two workers, panels of red lights flicker on domed ranks of back-up generators.

'There isn't anything living down here, is there?'

Weaver wanders past him, into the dark, looking around. Casimir sees that he hasn't shaved. Stubble emphasizes the teenager's hollow cheeks and the nervous eyes. Fox-like.

'Mice.' He starts to walk, stepping around hooped ends of orange cable, the broken bowls of ceramic insulators. 'Rats from the sewers; they are only small and brown. Much comes in from the sewers.' Five more steps. A pile of emergency torches, a stack of decaying magazines with their sour smell of old perfume samples. 'Once I saw a tunnel wall covered with white crabs. There are plants, mosses, where there is any light. And in the deep shelters there are moles.'

'Bollocks!'

'Bollocks, yes.'

'Oh, right. Nice one. Hold up.'

Casimir realizes he has been walking fast. Trying to get through the dark. Just ahead, steps lead up to a plain grey-metal door. Limestone salts glitter on the raised concrete. Casimir makes himself stop and wait.

'Cheers. What's all that noise?'

He listens. Off to one side of the steps are wooden racks of fuses, bright and intricate as the trays of a beehive. Casimir hears the clatter and spit of electricity coming loose. He turns his head and shoulder, allowing light past his bulk. Water runs down the corner walls in slow, flat sheets. He unbelts his radio, clicks it on.

'Leynes?'

'Cass? You're late. What's up? You struck gold or something?'

'There is water in the substation again. By the fuse boxes.'

'Aha. That'll be why the bog lights are buggered. The monitors are down too. I'll call the Water Board to check the mains, OK? Out.' The radio line goes dead. Casimir turns and goes up the steps, walking between pools of groundwater.

'Sir? Did you get to talk to that policewoman?'

He digs in his overall pockets for keys, looks round. 'Stay out of the water. Inspector Phelps, yes.'

'All right, wasn't she? Bit built, though. Built for the beat. I wouldn't want to walk into her on a dark night.' Weaver is kneading the small of his back, massaging the spine. He screws his face tight, a quick expression of pain. 'Do they reckon she was pushed, then? That woman who fell.'

'They don't know.' He unlocks the heavy door, steps through. 'No one does.'

The door clicks shut behind them. They have come out into the warren of side-passages by the emergency stairwell. The sounds of the Underground change abruptly, from the humanless hum of generators to the commotion of the midnight trains: footsteps, voices. The rumble of train doors closing, the rising whine of acceleration.

'That's weird, down there.' Weaver walks over to the far wall, looks left and right to the platforms, then leans back on the cracked blue tiles. 'Being behind the scenes. I've got a friend, he's Aladdin at EuroDisney every summer, good money but a bit hot. He said it was weird behind the scenes there too. All the characters sitting around with their heads off, drinking tea. Last year he got off with Goofy. She was from Poland. Isn't that where you're from, sir?'

'Yes.' Casimir looks down the tunnel, towards one of the West End- and City-bound platforms. On the corner is a convex mirror and he remembers the dog woman. Now there is only the sound of the crowd, coming closer. 'Stand up. There are people coming.'

Weaver elbows himself upright. An old man with a folding bicycle hurries by, flat cap pushed back on his head. Most of the passengers go slowly, though, making for home at the end of their days and evenings. No one looks at the uniformed workers as they pass by. Weaver grins across at Casimir, rolls his eyes.

The crowd peters out to three girls in purple puffa jackets, the first girl pulling off gloves with her teeth as she walks and talks.

'It's all babies with her now, it's boring as fuck. I don't care if she's my sister, I just feel like leaning over and turning the volume down.' They swagger towards the stairs, laughter carrying back.

Weaver follows them with his eyes. 'They make me feel old. I know I'm not, but still. How old are you, Cass?'

He looks at his watch as he answers. 'I am twenty-eight.'

It is ten minutes until the last train, out north to the depots and yards. Casimir imagines he can feel it approaching through the tunnels and passages, a fractional pressure of air against his face. But then there is wind all the time down here. The air rushes and falters, always in motion. Sometimes if he closes his eyes, the Underground feels like open land. The coalfields of Silesia, anthracite dust blown against his hair and skin. Blue-black, the colour of his parents' hair.

'Is that all? Jesus. Sorry. What time is it?'

He smiles at the other man, amused despite himself. 'Past midnight. We have to check the platforms now, to see they are clear of people and belongings before we close. If you could check Three and Four, I will do the other two. Wait for the last train on Three.'

'No sweat. I'll see you back at the control room, will I?' Weaver is already walking away, looking over his shoulder as he goes.

Casimir watches him reach the Barnet platform, then turns away. In the fish-eye mirror Platform Two looks deserted already, its motionless strip of bright track and black bitumen curving to a vanishing point in the pocked metal surface.

He walks out on to the platform, to be sure. Posters line the opposite wall, massive rectangles of gaudy reds and golds advertising suspenderless stockings and Japanese beer. Small flyers have been stuck across the Japanese beer and Casimir recognizes them from days ago: HAVE YOU SEEN THIS CHILD?

He wonders how the posterer got across the live tracks, shakes his head to clear the crazed image.

The far end of the hall looks hazy and for a moment Casimir thinks it is his eyes before he smells the peppery odour of smog, dust pooled from the streets above. He walks the platform's length, checking the catch pit beside him, remembering other closing times. Umbrellas and cashmere coats left on benches, underwear and used condoms on the track. A broken branch of blossom one spring, laid neatly on the platform's edge. He hadn't recognized what kind. Black bark, and the buds plush and almost blue, the colour of cigarette smoke. Startlingly beautiful.

There are no people sleeping on the benches, no belongings left behind or abandoned. All around is the sound of the station closing down, echoes of movement draining away. A good sound, Casimir thinks. He tries to remember who else will be line-walking tonight. How long he will have to get to Alice, if she is there. If she is waiting.

He turns back, takes the stairs up to Platform One, and comes out of the side-passage beside the southern tunnel mouth. He looks up at the great keystone of its archway. A pair of closed-circuit monitors is bolted to the platform ceiling, placed for train drivers to check their rear view as they leave. Casimir stops under them, looking along the empty hall and then up. The screens are dead, a flat grey-green.

The air here is also hazy, the far tunnel mouth shadowed with dust. Machinery lines the near wall: wall telephones, chilled chocolate dispensers. Casimir screws up his eyes and nose at the harsh smell, trying to see clearly. A crimson plastic bag fishtails in an air current, floats out across the catch pits.

There is something at the platform's main entrance, a hundred feet away. Casimir looks up at the monitors then down, frowning at the lack of a closer image. Something protrudes from the entrance arch, a shining vertical bar and the edge of a small, black wheel. From where he stands, Casimir thinks it looks like the front end of a shopping trolley.

He walks up the platform towards it, the slow steps of his long stride echoing in the bright, empty place. Now he can see that the front of the object is no more than four feet high with a horizontal bar at the top, padded black. An armrest. Casimir breaks into a run.

At the entrance he stops. The wheelchair sits abandoned in the side-passage, skewed slightly to one side. Casimir reaches out to touch the armrest but the brakes have not been set and the apparatus jitters away from him, down the empty corridor. He takes two steps towards it, to halt its movement, then stops. Turns round and begins to move, slowly at first then running, back on to the platform. He sprints north, towards the far tunnel mouth, its circle of dark encompassed by the end wall of the platform hall.

He is still some distance away when he sees the body. It has slumped down, half-hidden by the walls of the catch pit. Casimir backs away, not crying out. After three steps he is able to make himself stop.

It is a woman, slight and blonde. She has been wearing a transparent plastic watch, cheap and gimmicky. Through it Casimir can see blood. The watch-works are still moving, tiny and regular, over the blood. For a moment he can't understand how the watch is still moving, now the woman is dead. The detail pulls at his vision, nagging at him.

The smell of burning and electricity is sour in the air. Under the woman a crumpled mass of litter is charred black and glowing, ready to catch. As Casimir scrabbles at his radio a strand of blonde hair lights, burns and shrivels back towards the turned head.

He covers his mouth with one hand, breathing shallowly. There is a lot of blood, more than he would expect. It is still bright red, oxygenated, staining the piles of trash, the skin and clothes. The radio has become stubborn, banging against his clumsy fingers.

He can't take his eyes off the catch pit. The suicide pit. The watch-face, the tiny wavering mechanism. On the woman's arms veins have broken, a hatchwork of violet exposed in the white skin.

Casimir remembers that the wheelchair is behind him and he looks round quickly, then back at the body. He sees how its nails are painted reddish brown. Sepia. There is blood on the hands too, but that isn't sepia. The nail varnish is cracked – no;

the nails themselves are cracked, like the skin. Casimir's mind races and stumbles. White-blonde hair is jumbled over and through the stained catch-pit litter.

He unclips the radio from his belt. It almost falls on to the track but he catches it, hands held out together.

He can feel the terror rising in him and he makes himself close his eyes and wait, shaking. Clicks the transmitter on.

'Leynes.' His voice is too soft. He tries again. 'Leynes. Aebanyim.' He cannot raise his voice beside the body. The names whisper around him.

'Cass? Cass, is that you?'

He opens his eyes as a shiver runs through him, rocking him forward towards the platform's edge. Abruptly he realizes how close he is to falling himself. He stands slowly, finding his balance. 'Leynes. Turn off the tracks.'

'You what? Cass, where – Is that you on One?'

He sees that behind the watch-face the blood is still moving and gathering. As if the blood, like the watch, has somehow survived. 'Someone is dead. In the catch pit.'

'Oh no, Christ. Jesus Christ. Oh, Jesus.' The supervisor's voice has become a whine, almost blaming. Like a child, Casimir thinks. He closes his eyes again.

'Leynes. Please turn the tracks off.'

A large man standing alone. The wheelchair, skewed and empty. His voice whispering on the silent platform.

'Please. Turn off the tracks.'


'Mister Kazimierski?'

He blinks. Someone is bent over him, silhouetted against bare bulb-light. There is a hand near his face, too close. The first two fingers and thumb are extended in a curious gesture. Like a priest, he thinks.

'How are you feeling?'

He remembers the sound of fingers snapping. The figure draws back, into the light. It is the policewoman, Phelps. He tries to remember what she is doing here, then realizes he doesn't know where here is. He focuses beyond the inspector, taking in the control room. Leynes and Sievwright are there, other people he doesn't recognize. Voices, low and urgent. There are the smells of sweet tea and work-clothes sweat. He breathes deeply, once, twice. The odours become overpowering, like the smell of burning. Of rank fish and caviare in a Russian market, his father's footsteps ahead of him.

He closes his eyes again. 'No. My name is Ariel Casimir.'

'Good for you. Up you come –'

Blinks. The world has altered again. Ahead of him is a street at night, its junctions dark and deserted. The chuff of windscreen wipers. Acceleration tugs him back into the warmth of a passenger seat. It is raining hard, shimmering on the road ahead. Car alarms whicker, disturbed by the downpour.

Fast. Everything is moving past him before he can react. Then he breathes deeply and time slows down.

He turns his head. Phelps is driving. Streetlight passes across her calm face.

'Where are we going?'

His voice is quiet, an accompanying calm. The police officer glances at him, looks back at the road.

'The station. Mine, not yours.'

'Am I under arrest?'

'No.'

Her intonation is level, inconclusive. The police radio stutters news of other accidents, other deaths. She clicks it off. 'I just want to ask you some questions.'

He looks out of the side-window, into the rain. 'What was her name?'

'Asher. Marion Asher.'

They pass between low walls, a view downwards to flat, hazed water. Casimir recognizes the Grand Union Canal and then their route, heading north on the Kentish Town Road.

Phelps's voice is dry and level, used to its undertone. 'She suffered from multiple sclerosis. Recently it was getting worse. She was twenty-four.'

The traffic lights are red by Castle Road. They wait without talking. Outside the rain begins to ease. Neon winks over shop entrances. Casimir sits back, eyes running across the bright names: AL ARAF SAUNAS, CASH CONVERTERS, VENUS OFF-LICENCE NO. 5.

'Sad. She had a Filofax, which helps us. Role Models Islington comes up regularly – it's a fashion agency. We can't get hold of anyone there tonight, but from the diary entries it sounds as if she modelled one day a week. Catalogue clothes. A year ago she was working double that. Remarkable, don't you think? To go on modelling. Beautiful girl.'

Beautiful. He thinks of her hair, thrown out by the impact. Burning white strands. 'I need to see a picture of her.'

The lights change to amber. Phelps turns in her seat, not releasing the handbrake. 'Why?'

He shakes his head. Green-lit rain ribbons the glass beside him. A young man comes out of Al Araf Saunas. Shakes open an umbrella under the doorway's black plastic awning. 'How long were the cameras dead?'

Headlights shine in from the car behind, stark and colourless. Phelps releases the handbrake and accelerates.

'Too long. Hours. How often does that happen?'

He raises one hand, the gesture meant to explain something of the Underground's age and decrepitude. Lets the hand drop back. 'Often. What happened? After I found her.'

'You were in shock. I'd be surprised if you remembered nothing.'

'What time did she die?'

'Not sure yet. The tracks didn't kill her, though. There were stab wounds. In her back. The shock stunned her, but she bled to death. I think the knife was just to make sure, don't you think?'

'Yes.' His own voice sounds brittle.

Phelps clicks on the left indicator, voice rising as she turns the wheel. 'You sound angry with yourself, Mister Casimir. Why is that?'

He allows his eyes to close again. The sense of disorientation grows and fades. 'I would like to have been stronger.'

'Really. Welcome to the human race.' She pulls up, switches off. 'Can you get out by yourself?'

They cross the pavement and go on, under the blue light of a Metropolitan Police lamp. Casimir has never been inside a police station. He imagines the institutional chipped-paint walls, cracked plastic chairs, the smell of antiseptic and linoleum. Then they are inside and it is too late.

A drinks machine hums against the far wall. The cropped office carpet smells of old tea. Casimir is surprised; the room carries no sense of threat, or authority. It feels more like a bank waiting room than a place of law. Posters are arranged on two large pinboards: MISSING PERSON: HAVE YOU SEEN THIS MAN?, TERRORISM: SUBSTANTIAL REWARDS, KNOW YOUR COLORADO BEETLE. Only the lighting suggests any potential for strength or violence, the neon dimmed fractionally behind metal grilles. A desk officer watches them through cash-till glass.

'Hello, missus. Who's this?'

'Inspector missus to you.'

'Inspector missus, ma'am.'

'He's from Camden Tube. Any problems?'

'The Noise Pollution unit clocked off three hours early. We've had eleven complaints . . . Mrs Trueblood of Lady Somerset Road is not happy. That's about the worst of it. Quiet night.'

'Here. Photocopy this lot, will you? I'll be back for it in a minute.' Phelps passes a green card folder through to the policeman, then turns back to Casimir. 'Right. Are you tired? Coffee any help, no? Good.'

She is already walking away. Her heels echo along the unlit corridors.

Casimir follows the policewoman slowly, trying to gauge his own state of mind. His head feels very clear, as if he has recently woken from a long night of sleep. Only the memory of Asher disturbs him. His thoughts slide away from the event, forgetful even when he tries to remember. He thinks of Alice at the abandoned station and wonders if she is waiting for him. He wants her to be waiting.

'Here. Sorry about the walls.'

Phelps opens a door, clicks on a light. The interview room has been painted pastel-pink, the catalogue colour wildly out of place in the institutional building.

There are chairs, a TV. Casimir sits down. 'She must have been able to stand, a little.'

'Why must?'

'It is regulations. Passengers must be able to stand on the escalators. So if there is an accident, a fire –'

'Leynes says you're not supposed to help, is that right?' She half-turns in the doorway, light cutting across her face as she studies him.

'Yes.' He thinks how hard it would be, at his station in a wheelchair. The fear of being trapped underground. 'Did she have no one with her?'

'No one. Leynes remembers seeing her before. He says she made a point of asking the staff for help every time. A one-woman access campaign. Take a seat. I'll be with you in a minute.'

He waits. The rain has eased, he can hardly hear it. Sirens go past outside, heading south. A wall clock clicks towards four a.m.

'I want you to go over the Saville tapes with me, tell me what you see, all right?' Phelps comes back in with folders and a video, its casing marked with the London Transport insignia. Red ring, blue bar.

'Why are you asking me now?'

Phelps passes him the folders, kneels down by the television. 'Why do you think?' The video display lights up. 'Two people are dead.' She unpacks a cassette, pushes it into its slot. An image of a deserted Underground platform appears on the screen, marked with white digits: PLAT 4 CAM TN. 03/09/96. 13:10:26. Eight days ago. The seconds accumulate as he watches.

The recorded picture is linked up to one of the end-wall cameras, so that the whole platform is covered. The far tunnel mouth is tiny with distance. The nearest advertising poster looms up, a giant image of a woman's throat and teeth.

'We're a few hours early.' She looks back over her shoulder. He is struck again by the contrast of her face and eyes. The hard lines of her forehead, the gentleness of her gaze. 'I'll fast-forward, shall I?'

He nods, wondering which is real and which instilled. Looks back at the screen. A Tube train careers towards the camera and stops dead. Crowds flood out of the carriages and disperse. Speeded up, the platform movements make Casimir think of time-delayed nature films – flowers bustling towards light, the circular flight paths of stars. On screen the Underground crowds are reduced to a pattern, simple as breathing.

The image clicks back to normal speed. Two children stand on tiptoes by a chocolate-vending machine, tugging at the wall brackets. Another walks round and round a laughing couple, tying them up with elasticated gloves. The screen readout shows 16:54.

Phelps sits down in the chair next to him. 'Are you ready?'

He nods again, not taking his eyes off the screen. The rush-hour crowd is building up, pushing itself closer to the platform's edge – an ordinary, everyday kind of danger. Casimir remembers the photograph of Saville, days ago in the control room. Now a tall man in anonymous City pinstripe steps closer to the platform's edge and becomes familiar, part of a set background. Casimir searches the mass of people behind him. It is an odd sensation, he thinks, to watch the photograph falling into place. Knowing the future.

A young woman is moving through the crowd. Her hair drapes against shirts and jackets as she turns her shoulders to get past. Faces turn to follow her. From the camera's-eye view they are expressionless with distance.

Casimir leans forward, intent on the recording. For a moment he thinks the woman is Alice, but the similarity is superficial; this woman's movements and attitude are different. More elegant, less quirky.

Rebecca Saville looks down at her wristwatch, then puts her head back, stretching the shoulder muscles. Her neck is startlingly thin, as it was in the photo-booth picture. Figures move in the crush behind her, almost indistinguishable, like forms under water. There is a monotone flash of clothing as someone steps through a gap, back into shadow. A black woman reaches up to adjust her headphones, nodding to their rhythm. Casimir stares, trying to take in everything.

It happens in the space of seconds. Rebecca Saville twists at the white platform edge, toppling forward. The crowd moves back from her as she falls, like water from the impact of a stone. There is a flash of electricity as Saville's arm grazes the negative live rail. Concussively bright.

Motion ripples back through the crowd, as if it is they who have been pushed away. The pinstripe man turns, shoving. The black woman half-kneels, both hands going out. Black skin, pale blouse sleeves.

'It was not her hand. In the photograph.'

'Watch again.'

The tape whirrs. Saville flails back up on to the platform, ungainly and unchangeable. Phelps clicks the remote. Saville stands at the front of the crowd with her head back, eyes closed, stretching her thin shoulders. Inexorably, the sequence begins again.

The woman falls. Every part of Saville is in motion, her face, arms and body turning as she goes down. Behind her the hand is drawn back into the crowd, its outline already lost in shadow.

'What do you see?'

'Nothing. Just the hand.'

He searches the packed faces of the crowd, looking for intent. But the passengers are a grainy blur of movement. The only expression visible is in their motion. The panic of bystanders, fighting clear of violence.

After a moment Casimir looks at Phelps. She is waiting, studying his face. 'I'd have seen you in this crowd. If it was you. But it isn't.' She is thoughtful, her voice quieter.

'I'm sorry. I thought I could help.'

Casimir begins to stand up but the policewoman doesn't move. 'Not yet.'

He sits down again. In his mind he can still see Rebecca Saville, so like Alice from a distance. The body in the catch pit, its hair paler than yellow.

'The photograph of Marion Asher. Do you have it?'

'In a minute. Tell me about the Tube first. What's it like, working down there?'

He sits back, requiring himself to be patient. 'Like anywhere. No.' He is thinking, so that when he talks his English will be clear, precise as his thinking. 'The Underground starts out perfect. At first it isn't like the city above it because it is conceived all at once. Everything must be created, heat and the passage of air. For the engineers and architects it begins as a perfect technical form. Then years go by – decades. Cross-tunnels are found to be unnecessary, so they are bricked up. Deeper tunnels are added by the government, then closed down. Limestone comes through the concrete as if it were muslin. Up above, communities die out. Stations are abandoned.'

He looks up and she nods for him to go on.

'The Underground becomes a reflection of the city above – organic, not perfect. Full of small animals and weak plants. Good hiding places, and places that are dangerous. Some people – Adams – he felt it was becoming more dangerous.'

'Why?'

He shrugs. 'I don't know, but I also feel it. The first Underground trains had no windows. They were padded, to keep people safe. Now there are children who ride flat on top of carriages. They call it Tube-surfing. Dangerous, you see? Muggings, killings. People end up on the Underground who are –'

*Force of gravity, Burton. All the dirt ends up down here.* The voice comes at him out of nowhere. He shakes it away.

'– needing to shelter. Sometimes weak people, sometimes not. It is not only victims who need to hide. You see?'

'I don't know. It sounds like you care about it. Still, you haven't answered my question. What's it like, for you?'

He shrugs. 'It is safe.' Hesitates. 'Most of the time, it feels safe.'

The policewoman sits back from him, as if she is still waiting for something. When Casimir doesn't go on, she reaches down for the files. Opens the newest, leafs through for a sheet of paper. 'Thank you. Here. You asked for this.'

He takes the paper. It is a photocopied snapshot, shades reduced to stark black and white. Two girls sitting on a low wall under broad trees. Looking down as they laugh. Sunlight coming through their hair.

'From her Filofax. The one on the left's Asher.'

He turns the page in his hands, as if he could see more of the photograph in that way. Marion Asher leans forward slightly as she laughs, supporting herself on the flats of her hands. Her hair is much lighter than the other girl's, the photocopy reducing it to page-white. Light is reflected up on to her face. Casimir is struck by the long cut of her cheekbones. The nose curved outwards towards the bridge, not quite aquiline. A small, neat hook.

'Remind you of anyone?'

He looks up fast. Phelps is turned away from him, clicking the video back into its case. 'Like Saville. Don't you think? A little, anyway. Enough for it to matter.'

'Of course.'

Casimir looks down again. Collecting his thoughts. The urge to run is stronger now, to get to the abandoned station and ask Alice – what? At least to see her, to see she is safe. The picture lies on his open hands, almost weightless. He is aware of the policewoman moving around him, clearing things away. When he looks up Phelps is standing in front of him, the folders in her hands.

'That was what you wanted, wasn't it?'

'What ?'

'To see what she looked like.'

'Yes. Thank you.' He stands and stretches, an automatic movement. Rolling the shoulders back, feeling the circulation quicken. He screws his eyes closed for a second and Asher's image flares and fades. He glances up at the wall clock; it is long past five. And there is someone else he has to see. He thinks it is not too late. 'I'm sorry I was no help.'

'You tried. It's more unusual than you might think. You must be tired. I'll get one of the officers to drive you home.' She is already turning towards the door.

'No. I would like to walk.'

'To Lower Marsh?' She opens the door, looking back at him.

'No.' She remembers his address so quickly. He wonders how long she has considered him as a suspect, and if the consideration is over now. 'Just to walk.'

Phelps raises her eyebrows, shrugs. 'Whatever gets you through the night. Just remember you've been through a traumatic experience. I wouldn't advise walking along the canals, or down to any King's Cross nightspots. Not tonight.'

'Thank you for the advice.'

Together they walk back, past the desk officer to the station doors. Outside, Casimir can see the sky beginning to lighten. Over the rooftops, the dark is faintly hazed with blue, like dust.

'I may need to talk to you again. And call me, if you think of anything.'

'Of course,' he says. He lies. He has never liked authority and he doesn't need its help now. Casimir opens the doors, steps out. The air is cool, still smelling of rain. It makes him feel alert. And he likes to be alert.

Phelps waits in the doorway behind him. 'Thanks again. Remember you're in London. It can be dangerous here, even if you're big and strong. Especially then, Mister Casimir.'

'Yes. Thank you.' He walks down the steps without looking back.

On the Kentish Town Road he turns south, heading back towards his station. The streets are still almost deserted. When cars pass Casimir can hear them coming from far off, tyres hissing against the wet asphalt.

It feels colder now he is outside and alone, and he presses his hands down inside the pockets of his uniform jacket. Somewhere behind him a burglar alarm begins to ring, the sound going on and on over the Victorian terraced streets and railway arches.

The Castle Road junction is empty, traffic lights clicking through their sequences, red and green reflected across the wet ground. Casimir crosses over and stops, breathing slowly, feeling the gentle adrenalin of walking go through him. Outside a row of shops he stops.

He looks up at the shop signs: 'Cash Converters' on a white Perspex lightbox, 'Al Araf Saunas' in pale green neon, the tubular letters looped together like graffiti. Both shops are housed in the same two-storey building. From where he stands Casimir can see the whole façade. Rain against plate-glass shop fronts. Oxblood tiles, gabled and patterned with old lettering. The second-floor windows are flat and arched, like tunnel mouths.

The design is familiar to Casimir as the warren of his own station. Above the arch windows, foot-high letters are moulded into the ceramic tiles. Even in the streetlight they are faint, the colour weathered away. Casimir moves his head so that the illumination catches the raised characters. Narrows his eyes against the rain as he reads: SOUTH KENTISH TOWN STATION. Lower down, UNDERGROUND.

He drops his head and looks around, but the street is

empty. Casimir is breathing faster, already nervous at what he is about to do. Exhilarated to have got something right; the concrete fact of the abandoned station, here in front of him. At the side of the building an alley leads off towards high blocks of post-war flats. Casimir ducks down past the Al Araf Saunas plastic awning, following the old station wall back out of the streetlight.

The side of the building is untiled, bare brick covered slap-dash with mortar. There are no doors or windows, only wild screeds of graffiti in bright silver spray paint, towering over Casimir's head: SEX IS GOOD, TIME FLIES BUT AEROPLANES CRASH.

The back of the building is surrounded by a rambling fence of corrugated iron. A small door has been blowtorched into the fence and padlocked shut, and Casimir puts his face up to the wet iron edge, looking through the gaps. Beyond are a few yards of wasteground, old carpets and empty boxes half-lit by the lampposts on Castle Road.

Casimir reaches down for the padlock. The bar is clamped down over the latch. He pulls hard. Harder. The bar chafes open, stubborn but unrusted. He wonders how many times someone has come here, at night, unnoticed. Whether it is always Alice, or Alice alone. Carefully, he lifts the door open and goes through.

The yard is uneven, with piles of rug ends and carpet stair-lengths. The ground is covered with their waterlogged patterns: mottled purple flowers, yellowed kilim abstracts, a deep greenish design of branches and birds. The back of the station is windowless, cracks opening in its damp brickwork. A peeling wooden door has been propped open with a sagging roll of blue linoleum. The doorway itself is blocked off with a jumble of barbed wire and red-white striped emergency tape.

He squats down. The carpets are heavy and very cold in his hands, slippery with an accumulation of grease and dirt. Casimir shoulders them away layer by layer, working down until he finds a piece small enough to make use of. He wraps it around both hands like a muffler and goes up to the doorway.

The barbed wire scratches against his forearms as he gets a grip. When he pulls it comes out easily, bouncing and skitter-ing against the walls of the doorway. The warning tape flutters its writing into his face: LONDON TRANSPORT PROPERTY. KEEP OUT. Beyond the obstruction is a straight unlit staircase, leading down.

The mass of metal is surprisingly heavy. He turns at the waist and drops in on to the carpets. Their fabric oozes groundwater. In the streetlight Casimir can make out one flight of descending steps. More faintly, light from behind him illuminates a square white patch of floor further down. It is hard to tell how far down the stairwell goes.

He thinks of Phelps. Her voice measured, like hard footsteps. Something about strength and danger. It reminds him of childhood, the time he went through spring ice on the canal. The sour taste of ice and the feel of it against his face, coming up under a frozen surface. Something behind him in the dark green water, beautiful and monstrous.

He pushes the thoughts away. For now there is only Alice, the killings, and the dark stairwell in the abandoned station yard. Casimir looks back at the lampposts behind him, blinking in their glare, grateful for the after-images of light. Then he goes through the doorway. Edges forward, feeling the ground with his feet.

At the third step he stumbles and again at the ninth. He makes himself stop at the first landing, waiting impatiently until his eyes adjust. The staircase is not truly dark, but his pupils are still narrowed to the strength of surface light. Mica flecks glitter in the stone under his feet. Illumination comes down from the street above but also dimly from below, filtering up the shaft of a spiral staircase. A huge worm-like ventilator extends from the vertical well, segments curving upwards to its silver turbine mouth.

Sound carries up from the tunnels underground, faint as the light. There is a rumbling gust of air as a train passes, north or southwards. An irregular musical banging, metal against metal. Casimir stands entirely still, listening. He can make out voices, high and childlike. Like something out of *Alice in Wonderland*, but more real. Down to earth.

'Kevin would strip your hide, man.'

'Yeah. But I'd slap him though. I'd kick him with six legs though.'

'He'd strip your hide.'

'Yeah.'

The core of the spiral stairs is iron mesh, furred with dirt. Casimir can see lift cables and pulleys inside, moving in the air from the doorway above. He puts his face up close to the wire, then pulls back. There is a door in the mesh and next to it a palm-sized red button on a flat metal panel.

He presses the button. There is a jerk of machinery from above his head and voices below cut off abruptly. Casimir steps back as engine machinery clatters into life, shockingly close to his face.

The lift cables loop and wind. A red cage-work lift rocks up into place and Casimir pulls at the door. It has been wired shut, but his movement breaks the wire cleanly. A bundle of tunnel workers' clothes is slumped in the far corner. On top of the bundle someone has propped a London Transport sign: THIS LIFT IS NOT IN USE. PLEASE WALK DOWN.

He swears softly and turns away, going on down the spiral staircase. Carefully, staying close to the outer wall, where the steps are at their widest. At the bottom a metal door leans open in the staircase's core and a pair of archways lead off through the stairwell's curved walls. Casimir reaches out and carefully opens the heavy door. From experience he knows that this must be the entrance to South Kentish Town's substation. But he can see nothing, not even the steps that will lead on down. He can hear the soft lapping of floodwater, and against his face the darkness is solid and cool. He steps backwards towards the nearest archway and through it, breathing fast. Turns round.

He is in an Underground cross-tunnel, a long low hall, lit by a row of light bulbs hanging from the roof. There is the church crypt smell of damp and sweet dust that he remembers from the abandoned platform. The harsher smell of urine fermenting in closed-off rooms. There is writing all over the ceiling in neat black charcoal, and Casimir cranes his head back to read the nearest message: '*Royal Lincoln bound for Malaya 1955. RSM Brown is a fat ugly barrel-gutsed bastard.*'

He looks down again. At one end the tunnel stops dead at two public lift doors, their square apertures bricked up with breeze-blocks and sloppy mortar. At the other, the corridor turns away out of sight. Casimir walks down towards the corner, quiet and alert. Here the cream-and-oxblood-patterned walls shine with damp, wet as bathroom tiles. There are wooden storeroom doors along the walls, but when he tries them they are all locked up.

There is the sound of running water, and Casimir stops again to listen. The voices have gone quiet but the metallic hammering is still audible. Casimir bends forward, frowning, trying to make out where the sounds are coming from. But it's hard to tell; the tunnels and chambers trap the sound, echo it, turning it back on itself.

Ahead of him is another flights of steps. There are no lights here, but stuck to the walls are long strips of luminous tape. They cast a faint, greenish radiance around Casimir as he walks down. A narrow arched cross-tunnel leads off left and right. In the wall ahead are two enamelled Underground maps, South Kentish Town circled in red and black like a bull's-eye. Between the maps is a high, thin wooden door. Light shows under it. Without letting himself stop to think, Casimir turns the handle. Steps in.

'Did you put it back?'

He blinks and stares, trying to take in everything at once. The room is long as a train carriage. Near the end where Casimir stands are a tall wooden lampshade and a bar heater, wires trailing away. The Underground air is uncomfortably humid. There is someone humped asleep under a pile of blankets, grey rat's-tails spilling out across the floor. A man sitting against the near wall, broad head shining with sweat, staring back at Casimir.

'I said, did you put it back?'

'What?'

The man turns his face away, expelling smoky breath through clenched teeth. There is a cigarette in his hand, burning down into a horn of ash.

'He means the barbed wire. In the yard.'

Casimir turns around. Alice has come in behind him. She is

standing so close they almost touch. Her hair is tied back, and Casimir can see the collarbone under her skin. Like wings, he thinks. She reaches out and takes his hand. Turning it, feeling for the pulse with her forefingers.

'Your pressure's really low. I like your watch. Who's the head?'

He looks down. A tiny profile is embossed on the white face. 'Lenin. The watch is from Russia.'

'I like it. Two faces. I've got one too.' She holds it up fast and close. He doesn't jerk back. 'It's only digital. I set the alarm for 2.12 p.m. Not because I have to be anywhere. It's just to see what I'm doing each day, at 2.12. It's never the same, unless I'm sleeping. I'm glad you came back.'

'Why?'

She smiles. 'I'm just glad. Why do you think?'

The hammering starts up beyond the door at the far end of the long room. From here it sounds like an anvil being worked. When Casimir looks back at the Underground girl, she is still half-smiling, waiting for him to talk.

He reaches out with his free hand, takes her hair, as if he is weighing its smooth mass. Lets it fall. 'A woman died at my station. Did you know?'

'Yes.'

'Another died last night.'

Behind Casimir the man begins to cough; a hacking rhythm, three times.

'I want to know why.'

She watches him, sharp and feral. Gauging him with her quick eyes. She is so quiet he wonders if she is holding her breath. Then she is reaching out, putting her hands on his shoulders. He can smell food on her breath, warm and salty.

'If we kissed, I'd have to stand on tiptoes.' She leans on him, pushes herself away. 'I've got to go. OK? I'll be back soon. Wait for me.'

'Where are you going?'

She doesn't answer. He goes to the door in time to see her run down the cross-tunnel, out of the staircase's green lumi-nescence.

He turns back. The man in still watching him. He is big,

shaven-headed like a wrestler. When he speaks again his voice is thick with phlegm.

'You're a worker, ain't you?'

Casimir walks over and sits down. From here he can watch the greenish darkness of the doorway as he waits.

'Yes, I work. On the Underground.'

'A worker. Bloody hell. Congratulations.'

The man smells of Elastoplast. His thick neck is wound round and round with skin-pink lengths of it.

'Where did she go?'

'Alice? Got to see a man about a god. No, that's not right, is it? Spit meth, she's gone for. Are you comfy? There's blankets, if you want. Alice got them in a launderette.'

'What is spit meth?'

He leans towards Casimir, whispering and grinning. His nose is flattened out against broad cheekbones. 'She's good at getting things, she was in the papers for it. Blip Girl, the one-woman juvenile crime wave. That's what they said. Spit meth? Some of the people on methadone want the stronger stuff and some of the people get a taste for methadone, so the people with methadone puke it back up and sell it. That's spit meth. Everyone gets their poison. What's yours?'

'I don't know.' He checks his watch, then looks back up at the doorway. It's long past dawn. He feels wide awake. 'Not spit meth.'

'You didn't take the lift down then?'

'No. Why?'

'It's out of order. There was a worker like you, got stuck in there for three days. Well out of order.'

'I heard the story.'

'It's true. Have you got anything to eat?'

'No.'

'Fuck and buggery. There's nothing here either. Last thing I had was from that bloody Chan's Kitchen, some Chinese crap, crispy arthritic duck. That's a joke. Laugh like a drain, why don't you? I used to live in a park, but that was crap too. It was crap spelled backwards, that's why it was so shit.' Something else juts into the man's brain and he looks back at Casimir. 'Are you wearing working underwear? Do you understand underground underwear, Mister Worker?'

'My name is Casimir.'

'Nice name. I'm Bill. That's my wife, Hilary.' He shakes Casimir's hand and begins to talk rapidly, still holding on to Casimir's fingertips. 'Bill Aeaeae. That's a nice name too. Like Circe, that was her other name you see. Names are important, aren't they? Miss Circe Aeaeae – Miz of course, Miz nowadays, Circe was some time ago now. It's all a matter of time. A stopped clock never boils – no, that's not right, is it? Even a stopped clock tells the right time twice a day. That's it. That's me, you see; a stopped clock. Not like you, poor you, always running, Mister Worker with your shiny watch. Always watch-watching, always running fast. You see? A fast clock never tells the right time at all. Better off stopping than window-shopping. You should come down here more often, sweetheart. Take a break, take a knick-knack. Like this.'

He pulls out a hip-flask bottle from his parka. It is half-full of a gritty, brownish liquid. 'Do you want it?'

'What is it?'

'Spit meth. I told you. You can have it.'

He shakes his head. Sits back from the man's leering face. 'Is Alice her real name?'

'Alice? Why not? It's very nice.'

Casimir stands up, walks to the open door. Outside there is no sound except the hushed movement of air. Another train is coming, still far off.

Bill yells after him as he walks aways down the cross-passage, 'Are you going? Not out there? Ooh, how low can you go?'

There is yellowed light ahead. Casimir turns a corner and finds himself at the end of the cross-tunnel, a bare light bulb hanging down from the arched, tiled ceiling. Three steps lead down to the southbound platform, and Casimir ducks under the bulb and walks out and stops in the centre of the ruined space. The echoes of his footsteps fade around him.

The darkness is more substantial here. Casimir's breathing comes quicker. He forces it slow. Across the tracks, the hall's curved panels have been removed. An intestinal mass of pipes, cables and iron ridges has been exposed, their shiny lengths and knots running off towards the distant tunnel mouths. From the south come the sounds of trains, the whine-down of deceleration carried along the miles from other lines or stations.

'It's like that film. When they go into the mother ship and the walls get alien.'

He turns round. Alice is further up the platform, sitting on an old ironwork bench. Her hands lie on her knees. Like a pianist waiting to play, he thinks. The tunnel wind is picking up, and it tugs against her open coat and hair.

He walks over, sits down beside her. 'I don't see many films.'

'You wouldn't like it.' She turns to him, pushing back her hair. 'No films, no clubs. What do you do at nights, Casimir?'

'I work. When I am free, I go walking. I learn English.'

'Do you like England, then?'

He shrugs. 'When I came my life was very bad. Now it is not so bad. I made my own life here. Yes, I like it.'

Alice is smiling, lips pulled back against her gappy teeth. 'I like sitting here, watching the trains. All the people inside them. No one ever looks out of the windows. You can run around and scream at them but they never notice. It's like being invisible. When I was little I always wanted to be. And now I am.'

'Why did you want to be invisible?'

She stops smiling. 'Don't do that. You sound like a social worker. Everyone wants to be invisible sometimes. You do. Don't you?'

The wind is stronger now. He sits thinking, face lowered against it. Shakes his head.

'Liar. Why did you come here tonight? Because of me or because of those women?'

'They looked like you. I thought you might be in trouble –'

'You came because of them.'

'No.' He meets her eyes and holds them. They are too close for the contact to be anything except aggression or desire. 'I came because you are here.' He feels no aggression. He needs to know what she feels.

'Someone is following me.'

'Are they here?' He forces his words to be heard, eyes narrowed against the wind.

She has been watching the northern tunnel mouth but now she looks round at him again, unsmiling. 'No. No one finds me here, unless I want them to.'

'Who is it?'

'I don't know. Just someone. I've never seen him.'

'How do you know it's a man?'

She shrugs and looks away. 'I've heard him breathing. There's a train coming.'

The air pressure is rising to a roar, louder and more violent than at an active station. Behind the bench, a storeroom door begins to rattle in its frame.

The air hammers against them as a train goes through at full speed. Windows flicker past, crowded bodies and profiles lit up and instantly gone.

He looks back round at Alice. 'Their names were Marion Asher and Rebecca Saville. Someone killed them.'

She is still watching him. The roar of the train fades to a thread of sound. He leans towards her. 'It was you, wasn't it?'

'No.' She looks past Casimir. Eyes unfocused, giving away nothing. 'I was sleeping in your station. Then that woman died. I started hearing someone, in the station at night, and then all my stuff got stolen. My blanket and everything. So I came here. I ran along the tunnels and this is where I came out. Do you believe me?'

'Yes.' She is sitting so close they touch. He can't feel her body's warmth or coolness against his own. As if they are too similar, or as if she doesn't exist. Invisible. 'You were sleeping in the old cross-tunnel. By the railway sleepers?'

'Yes.'

'You must have seen him.'

'I don't know. I wasn't sure. There are so many people there. Once I heard him in the cross-tunnel, in the dark. I kept still and he went past me. I came here a couple of days after that.'

Casimir leans his head back. Takes a breath and lets it out, a long sigh. Mostly he feels relief, to be here with Alice, to hear her talk. But there are other feelings too, disturbances. She has always disturbed him.

'You don't need to stay down here. I have a room. You could stay with me.'

She grins and tuts, kissing the back of her teeth with her tongue. 'No one's going to find me. I like it down here. There's plugs for music and lights, room for my friends, and it's warm. It's safe down here, don't you feel that? We don't die if the bomb falls. It's a good place. And I've got you now. You're on my side.'

'How long has he been following you?'

She shrugs. 'I don't know. A long time. It doesn't matter now.'

She leans over him and presses her hand against his chest. Hard, so that Casimir can feel his ribs and sternum against his lungs and heart. He isn't surprised by her strength. She kneels up, close to his face, staring. Her eyes jitter, as if she is trying to see round his own, to get inside him.

Then she kneels back, letting him go. 'You can stay with me, if you like.'

'I can find out who is following you. There are places I can go.'

'Good. Stay anyway. As long as you can.'

She takes his hand as he stands. Her fingers are bony and cold and too small to reach across his palm. He follows her up the half-lit platform, past rusting escalator steps, their vertebrae of chainwork laid out flat. There is another side-tunnel here, another staircase. The darkness makes him blind and he closes his eyes against it, one hand on the worn wooden balustrade and the other around hers. At the top of the stairs is a door and she unlocks it in the dark and pulls him in and kisses him, reaching up against him. Pulls him down.

There is bedding under them as he kneels, a thick pile of unzipped sleeping bags and blankets. Alice sits back from him, silhouetted dark against the dark as she pulls her skirt loose over her head. Her hair catches in the collar and he lifts it out. Lies back as she undresses him. He closes his eyes, feeling her hands and kisses against his chest. Her skin is very smooth, colourless in the dark. The cold lines of sleeping bag zips press against his back. Their lining is smooth as her skin.

She makes almost no sound, nothing except the breath forced out of her by their movement. When he enters her she holds on tight to his arms, gripping the sides of his biceps, eyes open and watching. He lifts her under him, her smaller body moving against his, his hand around the small of her back.

Even when she comes he can't tell whether she is about to embrace him or push him away. Then she shoves him off, reaching down to strip off his condom, throwing it away. Curls up into herself, instantly asleep.

For hours he watches her, naked against the arch of her spine. She mutters and laughs in her sleep. It surprises him that she gives away anything. Once – when he is on the verge of sleep, still raised up on one elbow – she begins to sing in a small, private voice.

White scars run up from the curve of her hip to the hollow, angled blades of her upper back. Casimir counts their seams. There are seventeen, wrinkled and ugly, a patchwork of old violence. He doesn't touch them. He thinks of knives. The movement of watch-works over blood.

He kisses the backs of her thighs. The skin there is hot and still damp and salty, as if she is feverish. Her body has the rank smell of honey. He kisses her lips and temples and the thin back of her skull, at the roots of her wet hair. Her movements move his heart.

He stands up. If he is to try and help Alice, then it is time to go. For a moment he waits, planning his route upwards through the dark.

'Don't look back.'

She speaks without turning over. Casimir curses himself for waking her. Only as he bends and kisses her shoulder does he wonder how long she has been awake.

'I have to go. Sleep well.'

Her mutter is thick and anxious, running over itself. A voice out of dreams. 'Don't look back though.'

'Why?'

'You just mustn't.' She is whispering now, subsiding back into sleep. 'You just mustn't.'

He kisses her again. Then he goes. The streets outside are crowded with people and bright under a clear white sky.

# 8

# The Feeling of Sight and the Feeling of Sliding

I'm tall as my father. I am twelve and he is old.

One time I was with my class in the school bus and I saw my father drunk. He was wearing a check suit. He was leaning on the windowsill of Kapelusze the clothes shop. The window is very big, with stone around it, so Dad looked smaller. Like a kid. His name is Michal.

No one else saw him; they were shouting about Kozuck, the blind champion runner. I turned my back on the window and shouted too. My dad didn't see me either because he was looking down, with his legs apart to steady himself. It was only me who saw what happened there.

This was a while ago. It was easy to tell when Dad was drunk round then, because everything got more. More radio music to dance to. More happy, more angry. Nowadays it's even easier. The only hard thing nowadays is finding him when he is sober.

My mother forgot the morning of my birthday. It was only for a few seconds. I went in and she was reading at the glass table. I waited for her to say something and she didn't know why, I saw it in her eyes. Then she remembered and she kissed me and we went to open the presents.

My life is ordinary. Not good, not bad. Sometimes it feels as if it's getting worse. I dream of it as a feeling of sliding. My life sliding down a steep, dark hill, going under the ground. I can't stop the slide, it is out of my control. It is my worst dream, but just a dream. I do not think my life is so different from anyone else's.

I got zúr soup the way I like it best, with horseradish and two eggs and a whole garlic sausage in, and I got marble cake and blue track-suit bottoms and blue trainers with white stripes. The trainers are imports, Made in the UK.

I go running down through the Old Town. Smoke goes up from the apartment chimneys straight and brown as dead grass. When I get back I clean the dust off the trainers and put them neat together in my cupboard. There's the smell of mushroom and cabbage dumplings frying for supper. Starlings outside, arguing for somewhere to sleep. The sound of my parents' voices through the wall, high and low.

'More than we can afford. Could've shown it a bit more.'

'. . . quiet. He liked them.'

'Never used to be.'

'Growing up quiet. You know him. Still waters run deep.'

My dad's voice, louder. The screech of his chair going back. 'Still waters run deep! "Deep water's dangerous" – how's that? What's so good about deep water, eh? He'd be better for some work. I could use help anyway.'

'No.' Her voice is small and frightened and strong.

'I could use him. How long's that going to be?'

'It's almost ready now. Almost done.'

I go on through. From the corridor I can smell the horseradish in the soup. The wooden floor tiles are loose under my bare feet.


On my dad's last birthday the TV weathermen said the moon would disappear. My father got everyone on the roof of Block C, but Piotrowski the caretaker made him pay dollars. We sat on the roof and drank Lech beer. It was evening and so cloudy, the sky looked like the inside of a bucket. The girls played the Shoe Game: lining their sandals and heels and house slippers up, and whoever's shoes reached the edge of the roof, that girl would get married next. Then the rain came down so suddenly, it was like the bucket had been turned over on us. Dad shouted that if that was an eclipse, God could stick it where the sun doesn't shine. After he shouted that, Piotrowski never spoke to us again. His skin is red under one eye, as if someone spilled hot wine on his face.

Between the Strug Blocks the little kids and old men are playing. The old men play Pan at a pink plastic table, holding the cards down with their shirtsleeves. The little kids are choosing who will jump off the Block D entrance steps. They sing the choosing song.

'Ana Dua Likka Fakka Torba Borba Ussmussmaka . . .'

When I was little I sang it often, but it's a long time since I heard it. When you are little the years go slower because they are a bigger part of your life. Time goes quicker for me now. I'm bigger; the years are smaller.

Piotr says I'm wrong. He says it's our galaxy going towards a black hole and the closer it gets, the faster we go. I think he's right too. Ideas aren't like real things. Sometimes they can be two things at once. That's what I think.

'It's you, Maria! You!'

She is bony and very small. She climbs up on to the steps' concrete edge and jumps. Her skirt flies up into her face and all the kids laugh. She comes down on her feet, slap in the dust; it doesn't look too bad. Then she falls over and balls up and begins to cry.

'Eee hee. Uuu huu. Uuu.'

I look away from them all, across the town. The sun catches in the waterways, over towards the docks. I'm facing London Piccadilly England. My mother chooses to forget and my father holds me so hard it hurts, but I can go west. When I'm big I'll do that. In the West no one will know me. In the West I can be whatever I want.


I say winiak is the colour of my mother's Baltic amber. Piotr says it's the colour of piss in summer. I say we're both right. We sit looking at the bottle with our backs against the wall of the Laboratory of Oncology. It's sleepy here with the thaw sun on us; no one comes and there are no windows for them to see us by. I pass the bottle to Piotr and he holds it up. The sun comes shining through it.

Piotr unscrews the cap and takes a swig. His eyes go all bulgy. He looks like a shot rabbit at harvest. The rabbits come out of the high rye and roll when they're hit, and the pheasants run up the air like stairs and the skylarks twirl upwards like paper ash from a fire.

'Hoooah! I need some water.'

He doesn't get up, just leans back again and closes his eyes. He doesn't pass the bottle to me either. I take it myself. He didn't drink much, but then Piotr is small. Me, I am not so small.

The screw-top scrapes against the glass. It's an old vodka bottle, there are Russian words stamped into the neck. I raise the bottle and toast Piotr and Poland and my mother. When Dad drinks he toasts Stalin. He dedicates the winiak, the coffee cups, saucepans, the blue-green curtains and the four boxes of shaving foam aerosols stacked in the hall: *To the name of Jozef Stalin! Na zdrowie, Na zdrowie!* Throwing his arms about. It's one of his jokes. He doesn't care if no one laughs. He laughs himself.

When Mother drinks she toasts no one. Drinking is another of her secrets. I take a good long swig.

'Hoooah! Christ. It's fine, isn't it?'

The sun is also fine. It feels like my guts are on fire with the season. Seagulls go over towards the canal, calling and laughing. 'Here. You want some more?'


'Her body tanned and wet down by the reservoir.'

We walk along by the canal in the hot sun, looking for pike. It's me and big Wladislaw and Piotr and Karol. Wladislaw sings.

'River was dry. Down to the river. Ay. Ayayay. That's the best song. He's the king. Isn't he, Piotr?'

'Sure.'

'You don't even know who he is. Do you have a music centre, Piotr?'

'Yes.'

'*Borja!* Farm boy. You're such a liar.'

'I do, though. My grandfather Roman does. Because Roman loves to listen to Iron Maiden.'

Our laughter goes bouncing away along the towpath wall, towards the docks and factories. Scrawled on the brickwork are gibbet pictures in red chalk and white paint. In each noose is the letter of an enemy: L for Legia Warsaw, J for the Jews. Piotr kicks up against the wall. For two steps he's running sideways. It's February. You can still feel the cold on your face.

We took the winiak from Piotr's dad, who gets it free from Mr Krajewski, who lives on the fourteenth floor of Block A and married a German before the war and now he sells rotgut to half the town.

Everybody wants to be friends with Sir Farmer Wittlin. Even now when there is nothing in the shops except glass shelves, he has food. This last Easter, Piotr had pig's knuckles and duck's liver. There is still one pig left. It's Lech, who is the fastest and has warts. Piotr tried to save some for me but his mum wouldn't let him. We had mushrooms in soured cream, and the cream was too sour.

I have many secrets now. Hanna Tuwim is one. When I learned how to come I thought of her. At night I stood at the window looking out across town, thinking of her until I came into my hand. No one taught me how to do it, I just knew. I was glad when she went away. It's too late now.

My mother is another. The way she sings in her foreign language sometimes when she works. Quietly, not to be heard, only to make sound. I know she sings in the language of Jews.

'See anything?'

'No. Just a bottle. I thought I did.' Karol slaps his knees clean and stands up and we go on.

Lots of things get frozen into the canal ice. Just here there's green bottle-glass, wooden apple crates, pages of a torn-up book, a pram with no wheels. We are looking for pike. Last thaw Karol came walking back to the Strug Blocks with a piece of ice bigger than himself. A pike was frozen into it. It was striped green and gold and the belly was white. That year there were pictures of dinosaurs in 7c's biology books. The pike was the colour of the dinosaurs. When the ice melted Piotr cut it open and inside were eggs, like green caviare, and seven fish, each one smaller than the one before. So here we are.

'Have you got more than ten records, Casimir?'

'I don't have any records.'

'Who's your favourite band? Is it Iron Maiden, like Piotr's grandad?'

'I don't like music.'

'Everybody likes music.'

'Not everyone.'

'Why not, then?'

We stop to look at the ice. Already it's melting at the edges and around the bridges. All winter the dock boats break it and then it freezes again behind them. Now it's heaped up like broken windows. Some of it's milky and some clear.

'Why don't you like music, Casimir? Is it because of those foreign songs your mum sings? Karol heard them.'

Across the canal is wasteground, then a red building with a big sign for the Association of Cattle Head De-Boners. There are girls across the next bridge, walking together in last year's long grasses. I recognize Monika from the way she walks, her arms folded across her belly. She's wearing a skirt. I wonder how she got tanned so quickly.

'Is your mother foreign, Casimir?'

I look round at Wladislaw. I wait for him to say anything more but he doesn't. He sees I'm waiting and so he gets a stone and throws it whickering across the ice. I look back at the girls.

'What do you see?' says Piotr. Light reflects off the white-washed bridge. His face is all freckles and wrinkles, screwed up against it.

'Them.'

When I was small we played with Monika all the time. Now I don't know her. The girls are separate from us. It's like the dinosaur pictures from last year's book, each different-shaped creature standing in its own group. It's not really like the dinosaurs. I made that up.

Piotr looks across at them with his screwed-up face. 'Which one would you have? If you could.'

'Monika.'

Karol comes up beside us. 'The Tomassi sisters have got a notebook with all Led Zeppelin in it. English and Polish.'

The girls are closer to us now. One of them sees us, her face lit bright and heart-shaped, turning away.

'Wait –' Piotr squats down at the canal bank, arching his head first left, then right. 'There's something under the bridge.'

We all look round where Piotr points. There is something, for sure. It curves like a tyre where the ice has melted, twisted out of the slush.

'One of us could walk to it. Piotr, I dare you.'

'The ice is too thin.'

'Karol? I dare you.'

'No.'

'Casimir, can you see it?'

'Casimir, you see the best.'

Piotr is taking off his glasses, wiping hair out of his face. I look away from him, out into the shadow of the bridge. The object is smoother than a car tyre and not as wide. Green and muscular.

'I'll do it.'

'Casimir, don't. The ice is too thin.'

Wladislaw pushes Piotr back against the towpath wall. 'It's thicker than your fucking glasses. Look at the barrel, will you?'

Near the bridge are all the things people have dropped down on the ice to break it, stones and half-bricks. Close to the bridge is a metal beer tun. It's small for a barrel, but even so. The ice is grey and flat under it.

'Look at that, will you? What's wrong with you all? I dare you.'

'You do it, Wladislaw, if you think you can.'

'Who asked you? Casimir?'

I reach down the canal bank, into the cold water. There is a gap between the side and the ice. I put my hand under the ice, feeling its thickness.

'Casimir? It could have broken and frozen again. If they dropped the barrel and it floated, the broken ice would freeze underneath it –'

'I said I'll do it.'

I stretch one foot out on to the wet ice, then lean on to it. The ice creaks like polystyrene packing. Then the other foot. Now I'm standing on the ice, it only took a few seconds. My shoes are thin and the cold makes my feet hurt.

'Bloody hell, Casimir,' says Karol. Quietly, as if shouting could break the ice under me.

He and Wladislaw are still standing next to me, close as if I was on the ground. Wladislaw smiles and stares. It scares him, which I like to see; I scare him. I can't see Piotr now. I turn around and start to move. The ice creaks at the third step, and the seventh.

'Casimir?'

I look up. Monika is on the bridge. When I wave she starts to laugh.

'Casimir, what are you doing?'

I laugh back. I start to say I don't know when the ice goes through.


At night I count red lights from the rear window, but if it's daytime like now I ride with my face against the side-window. The light catches in its dust and it changes as you drive, rolling against the glass.

We're on Constitution Street, going slow. I see the luxury shops with floured pastries in glass cases. Old women selling plastic bags by the Old Square crossing. One man with his suitcase propped open on a dustbin. There are bottles inside – Head and Shoulders, I know the shape of them. One man in a trench coat and hat with a cigarette. You can tell he's a speculator too, even though you can't see what he sells.

'Small-timers.' My dad kisses his teeth with his tongue, a long drawn-out tut. The steering wheel straightens inside the ring of his hand.

'How soon?' says my mother.

'Tomorrow, late. I could do with help this time.'

'No. You don't know if Jan is on duty.'

'Not yet. I can telephone.'

'Why so quick?'

My dad is going away again. Astrakhan is where he has friends in furs. It's four days' drive but the friends are what counts. They're made from dead lambs stitched together, but the wool is soft and the inside is also soft, like skin. This is the furs I'm talking about. The friends give Dad presents. A Russian Army watch that glows in the dark. The pistol of a cosmonaut. Only the best for the best. That's what they said. Dad told me. We were playing Pan. I almost won that time.

'Michal? Why does it have to be –'

'I don't know. Because it does.'

Outside are more old women with plastic bags. Women with grey cauliflowers and dusty bilberries and branches of yellow broom laid out on newspapers. Two Gypsy men with jars of live fish around their feet, all of them turning the light slow and orange. The old women look at nothing. The Gypsy men look at everything.

'I could use him. He's big enough now.'

'I said no.'

'Big enough. We'll see.'

'Look, Mum. Mum. Mum?'

She looks. 'Goldfish.'

'They're great, aren't they?'

'Yes, they are. Beautiful.'

My mum's hand and mine hold each other; I don't look round but I can feel them. A big ball of knuckles on the plastic seat between us. When it moves the plastic burns my fingers, but only a little. I keep my face to the glass, watching the light change.

The cold rushes up around my knees, cock, chest and head. My hands go into the water last and when they are through I pull them down, wrestling upwards. My eyes have closed themselves and I open them and look.

The ice is full of light. The water is clear green from inside. My mouth starts to open itself and I taste the ice, which is sour, like iron. I close my mouth and kick upwards. The water won't let me up. Instead it turns me round to face the bridge.

The pike is there after all. It leans away from me, a long trunk the colour of the water. Its mouth is open, a white crack in the greenness. The teeth are shining white inside the hooked jaw, the hook of it curving up through the lit ice.

The water is getting darker. I kick again and come up under ice. My face presses against it. Now I can bring my hands up and I hit through the ice, into the air. I think, 'Still waters run deep'. *Cicha weda brzegi rwie.* There are voices screaming my name and one voice breathing. The one voice is mine. I make it go on breathing. I hold on to the ice and wait until something else happens.

My mother keeps notes in her pockets. If you're in a quiet place with her you can hear the rustle of them. I've only seen her read them once. She does it in secret. We don't talk about it.

One day in June I came home from school. I called out but no one answered. I walked in through the empty rooms, which were full of light and me sighing in the warm air, stretching the work out of my arms.

The bathroom door was open and my mother was there. She was standing by the basin with her skirt hitched up. There was blood on her hands and on her legs. She was staring at her palms. I tried to look away but she looked up at me and I couldn't.

She was as scared as me. I know it was her period now but then I didn't. After that she saw Dr Berman. He said she had Alzheimer's Disease and that she should go away. That was his diagnosis. But I know he was wrong. What my mother has is not a disease. It is that she wants to forget so much.

It's getting dark when Dad goes. I push open the window to call goodbye to him but then I wait. He walks to the car, looking both ways across the railway sidings with their blue signal lights and the allotments with their tinfoil scarecrows glittering white.

Our car is navy, not blue. Against the edge of the birch woods navy is the same colour as darkness. If pine trees grew there and not birch you wouldn't see the car at all. It's the right colour for a speculator.

He stops by it, not getting in. It's just spring; the nights are still cold. His face is clear in the dark, like the birches. It turns quickly and I look down the road and there are people coming. Two men in uniform, army or Militia.

The woods are near him, so he could run. I would. But he just stands with his face turned, watching them come up the back road towards him.

At the car they stop. I count time passing by the alarm clock's tick. They couldn't stand for so long without talking. One of the men lights a cigarette, dropping his face towards the match, and I know him. It's Tomek the Militia man, Wladislaw's father. He holds out the match to my dad and lights his cigarette too and then waves it out.

They go on talking, and then Tomek and the other Militia man take off their gloves to shake hands. My dad throws away his cigarette and shakes their hands but he doesn't take off his gloves. Then he gets into the car and the tail lights come on. I lean out of the window, holding on to the Singer's heavy iron frame.

'Dad!' It's too late. 'Dad!'

One of the Militia turns his face up to me as they walk away. My father's car goes east, towards the highway.

I get into bed and think of my father. It's an insult to shake hands with gloves on. My dad insulted the Militia and they did nothing. Outside the lampposts come on. Their light stutters across the ceiling from ten storeys down. Through the wall I hear my mother's bed creak as she lies back.


'You could have died.'

'I was all right.'

We sit on the stairs, Monika and Piotr and me. You can hear the echoes coming up from each floor. Voices and doors and dogs. The clatter of pigeons around the entrance.

'I got out by myself. I was all right.'

'I could see you through the ice.'

My arms are still cold, so that I shiver a bit. Monika is warm beside me. It's good, having her here.

'You were looking up.'

'I told you it was thin. You knew. Why did you do it?'

'I don't know.'

'Was there anything there? Was that why you did it? Was it because of Wladislaw?'

'Maybe.' I stand up. I don't tell them about the pike. It's my secret. I know it must be still there, dark in the dark water. It feels good, the seeing and knowing. 'Do you want to come inside? My mum made zúr soup. There's plenty.'

I remember how it felt. The taste of ice was sour, like metal or snow. There was the terror of coming up under it. Then there was the feeling of breaking through the ice. That was great, though. I just reached up with my hands and broke through to the air. With it came the feeling of sight. It was worth doing just for that.

# 9

# The Low Road

In Casimir's dream there is the Underground and the sound of the squirrel-cage. He is down in the tunnels. The ballast stones are uneven and sharp against his bare feet.

Between the rough gravel are track sleepers, wood flush with the tunnel floor. Smooth and dangerous, smelling of damp and creosote. It is a paradox of his dream: the smoothness of the danger, the pain of what is safe. He takes small steps. He has no torch, no lasting source of light.

He is holding out his left hand so that his watch-face is ahead of him. The luminosity is already fading. He doesn't take his eyes off it as he walks. The tunnel wind beats against his bare skin. Soft and insistent, like moths.

The Underground closes around him. Its dark presses against his face. It is safe as a locked room; it is terrifying as a locked door. He is shivering, his head is shaking with it. As if he is refusing to go further, even as he walks. He tries to think where he is going but in the darkness he knows nothing. It is like having no thoughts at all. He stumbles and cries out as he falls.

The ceramic bowls of the current insulators loom up. The live track is so near his face he can smell the acid wetness of its metal. The insulators are white and featureless. Faces in the crowd of a northern country.

The track hums with power. He backs up from it with his father's watch against his chest. Then he begins to walk again. The ballast stones have cut his legs and the palms of his hands. He is glad of the feel of it. It is something to be sure of.

The noise begins as a wheedling echo in the track. It is the sound of a train coming and he puts out his right hand, feeling for the point where the wall opens out. The train doesn't frighten him. He knows this dream. There is a crossover point here, the tunnel widening around a junction. There is room for him to stand and not be killed. And the train will bring light. Everything is wrong in the dark; but what he can see, he can make right.

The wall beside him gives way to space. He steps sideways, ducking under the loops of cables and the bright coppery lines of the old line-telephone live wires. Beyond is a warren of tunnels, branching away. He turns around, pressed into the space between rails.

The train is much nearer now. Already the sound of it is going wrong. Casimir can hear something metallic, a skitter of movement against wire, the sound of something wild trapped in a narrow cage. A crash on stone and the sound of water. Echoes distorted back up the sightless black shaft.

The train roars past him. Grids of light move across his face. He looks up into the train, face screwed up against the light but grinning, teeth set. The light feels so good.

The train is deserted. The carriages press tunnel air against Casimir's face and chest as they pass, windows empty and bright. He can feel himself beginning to wake and he turns, eyes closing, as if he will walk out into wakefulness.

At the last window is a figure. It is indistinct, gone before he has turned properly to see. But he recognizes Alice. She is not singing any more, just looking out at him. Looking out of her eyes but giving out nothing, no humanity. Her eyes are so familiar to him now. The colour of blood seen through muscle.

He wakes. He is cold with the late afternoon sun on his face. The rims of his eyes still sting with sleep loss. He is sitting on a bench, its ironwork hard against his spine. In front of him is a wide stretch of concrete paving. The pavement is littered with broken bottle-glass and curlicues of plane-tree bark, split from the trunks in the September heat.

He can smell river mud. A girl with red hair and blue sunglasses roller-blades past, slaloming between pedestrians. Beyond them is the Thames. A pleasure boat hoots as it passes the Houses of Parliament, light criss-crossing in its wake.

He shifts upright and immediately he is alert, the sleep leaving him cold. He leans forward, elbows on knees, head in hands. His face is warmer than his fingers.

Across the river, Big Ben strikes four. The giant clockface shines white in the autumn afternoon. Casimir makes himself stand. He has been asleep for nearly four hours and the light hurts his eyes.

He walks across to the embankment railing, passing easily between the slow rush-hour of pedestrians. Leans against the railing, stretching out hands and arms.

This is one of his routines, the embankment bench. Often when he has finished a day shift he comes here before going home, walking down from Waterloo station, past the arched glass of the Channel Tunnel terminus. He sits for a while even in winter or spring, when the cold rain drips off the plane trees and soaks his uniform. Partly he does it because he loves the river, but mostly because it is a routine. Routines are important to him. They make things clear and certain, like light.

Now he tries to remember the last time he came here. It is a week ago already. The day he heard of Rebecca Saville's death.

He blinks, and for a moment there is the overpowering sensation of Alice kissing him. Her breath, its warmth and sound and feel. He keeps his eyes closed until the memory is gone. On his work clothes the dirt is a dark sheen at the folds of the knees and the jacket lining. He feels good, still tired but sharp and hungry. Sleeping underground; he smiles at the idea of it. Like something from a children's story or folk tale. Persephone or the Ohyn.

The railing is warm against his hands and he leans over it, looks down. Low-tide mud stretches out to the water. Casimir can see people sitting down there: an old man in a torn sports shirt and stained check jacket; a woman with a bottle in her hands, light catching its clear glass. The homeless. He looks away.

The days return to him haphazardly, in distinct images. He lets them come. Photographs spread out on a grey-lit counter. A child turning, neck stretching monstrously. The wheelchair, edging away from him. The hand in the crowd, blurred by freeze-frame, reaching out; and then the crowd itself, its faces in shadow. Casimir wants the faces lit up clear. Where he can see them.

He looks upriver to Westminster Bridge, yawning as his

mind clears. The sound of car horns carries down. A double-decker bus sits in the grid-locked traffic, stranded diagonally between lanes. Casimir watches, taking in none of it. He turns away from the river and begins to walk, back along the embankment. The thin crowd moves around him and past him.

The Tube train to Camden is old rolling stock, a rush-hour replacement from the depot yards. Its green sides flare out-wards at their feet, and inside the wooden floor is worn smooth, lit by light bulbs under scalloped glass. Casimir sits in the last carriage. There is less crowd this far down the train, and in Casimir's section there is only a single other passenger, a gaunt man with a purple sports bag gripped on locked knees.

The old carriages pick up speed, rocking into the dark. Casimir thinks of the first trains on the Underground. Loco-motives with breathing holes in the roads above. Sleek indus-trial brass and steel, letting off steam like whales.

The stations pass: Goodge Street, Warren Street. The thin man unzips his bag, takes out a dozen lottery cards and scratches them out with a ten-pence coin. As the train slows towards Camden Town, Casimir sees the man is wearing a name tag on his jumper: *Sam Deane – 'The Human Fountain'*. When he has finished, the man reaches into the bag's bulk again. Takes out another handful of cards.

Casimir gets out with the crowd. He is glad of the crush as it moves him along towards the escalators, up towards the sur-face. He is here on his day off, on his own time, his uniform seamed with dirt. There will be questions to answer if he is seen; where he has been, where he thinks he is going. It is sim-pler not to be seen.

He steps out on to Camden High Street and immediately twists back out of the path of a pavement cyclist.

'Oyoyoy!'

Around the oxblood tiling of the Underground entrance are a few stalls, bunches of henna-coloured incense and oiled hot-plates of thick, pepper-red pizza. Trade spilling over from the big markets on Chalk Farm Road, the Lock and the Stables. Casimir turns north towards them, moving slowly through the shoppers and sellers.

It is not often he comes above ground at Camden. There is rarely any reason to do so. It reminds him of Adams: *I'm just going upstairs.* He was right to stay out of things, Casimir thinks. And I am wrong again. Not really careful, not like Adams. Needy. Needing to know everything. Walking out over wet spring ice.

He walks north-west. The bulk of life up here surprises him. A laughing woman with a tall bucket of green sugar cane, next to a tiered trestle of black-bruised yellow peaches. White posters spiralled around lampposts, zigzagged across building site walls. Samosa salesmen leaning between shop fronts of black leather and white goods. Voices –

'Any wear you like, ladies!'

'Shh! Hash? Hash?'

'Rass, man! You need new clothes, you start looking like a tramp. Hey! Hey, big man!'

Teenagers in bright clothes and office workers in grey, all of them walking too fast in the gutters and road. A fire engine slows, thundering at them with its horn.

The pavement ahead is blocked with a red tartan blanket, an obese skinhead brooding over his merchandise. Mechanical sniper figures snake across the blanket. When they go too far the skinhead prods them back with one steeler boot. Behind him is a fenced square of clothes stalls, electric-blue halter tops and sequinned tie-dye skirts. Casimir steps over the blanket and stops, looking across the stalls.

A small building rises out of the sea of clothes. It is simultaneously anonymously placed and curiously shaped: a conning tower of pinkish brick, ventilation slits near its small, flat roof. The brickwork is covered with giant graffiti, SUB 73 on a scrawled background of silver, purple and crimson. To Casimir it looks as if the colour of the market is creeping up the walls, a bright lichen.

He turns right at the edge of the clothes market. The smell of street foods is stronger here, air sweet and fat with the fumes of chilli and lime leaves, cumin frying in ghee, almonds browning in hot caramel. Casimir tries to remember how long it is since he has eaten, his stomach turning over with hunger.

The flank of the building protrudes to the market's edge. A metal door is set into its side. Next to the door is an intercom, an inconspicuous plaque over the verdigrised metal: DEEP SHELTER ARCHIVES INC. NEWSPAPERS & RECEIPTS. Casimir presses the buzzer and steps close to the intercom, turning his face sideways to the smell of urine.

'Yes?'

Casimir smiles, eyes resting on the brickwork. '*Jak sie'n chuyesh*, Wanda? Are you well?'

A pause. '*Jako tako*, so-so. Who is this?' The voice is female, and Polish. The heavy accent of someone too old to ever lose it.

'Casimir. From the Underground.'

'Ah? Ah. Yes, I remember you, Kazimierz Kazimierski. Wait.'

There is a rattle of metal and Casimir looks round. A diminutive man in white jeans is pulling a shop grille down. The showroom lights are still on, gleaming through rows of lava lamps. Globules and teardrops of orange and organ-pink.

When he turns back, Wanda is standing in the open doorway. Her broadness is emphasized by thick bifocal glasses, a great head of steely white curls and an oversized jumper patterned with trees, sheep and a small cottage. She is holding a large paperback in one hand, a Danielle Steele in Polish translation.

'Hello. I close soon. Is it the ventilation?'

'No. I need – there is some information I am looking for.'

She frowns. The bifocals press up against her lined forehead. 'You are not here on Underground business?' Casimir shakes his head. 'You have authorization to see the records?'

'No.' The old woman waits, looking Casimir over. 'It is important. Please.'

After a moment Wanda stands back, holding the door open with her wide, pale hands. 'Quickly. I am in a hurry tonight. I go to the club. You want to come?'

'No. Thank you.' Casimir knows she means the Polish Hearth Club, in Kensington. A place filled by older Poles, wartime refugees, critical of the new waves of immigrants from home. It is not a place in which Casimir feels comfortable. The eyes of the old people on him. Expecting little, assuming too much.

'I will not take long.'

'No, you won't. What information is this which is so important?'

'A newspaper story.'

She stops moving and turns awkwardly towards him. They have come through into a poky office room. An Elvis Presley picture calendar half-covers a bricked-up window. Both side-walls are hidden behind filing cabinets the colour of gunmetal. At the back of the office is a small red cage-work lift.

Wanda begins to cough, staring at Casimir. It is only from her eyes that he realizes she is laughing. 'This is Newspaper Storage. We have every story here.'

'A death on the Underground. Someone was caught for it – 12 June 1987.'

'Ah? That's better. Maybe I can help you.'

The archivist backs away to the lift, hauls open the folding door. It is years since Casimir has been here, checking some common ground between the subterranean properties of London Transport and Deep Shelter Archives – crossroads of ducts and pipes, knottings of cable thick as a torso. The archivist looks unchanged. Even the jumper is familiar. Casimir sees that she still limps, her left leg longer than the right, the shoulders slightly tipped.

'Come on, please. In here.'

Casimir gets into the lift. Immediately it starts to descend, jerking back against the shaft walls. When Wanda speaks again her voice is softer, adjusting to the packed space.

'It is important to you, this death? Maybe you know who died?'

'No.'

It is a long way down. Outside the lift, the concrete shaft; outside the shaft, blue London clay. He is thinking of Alice waking in the abandoned station. The smell of him on her. He wonders how she can recognize morning, without light to touch her eyes.

'Ah. Well, it is nice to have a visitor. To tell the truth, things are not so good here now. No one comes. The libraries, they have all the newspapers inside computers, and warehouses are cheaper for storage, so why come here? This is not to be repeated, you understand.'

Casimir nods. The lift is small, so that he is pressed against the archivist's soft bulk. The smell of her jumper is as strong as that of the market above: lanolin and a bitter, trapped sweat. He watches the black shaft passing outside the diamond lattice of the door.

'This week my son and my daughter-in-law go back home to Warszawa. I will miss them but I am glad. Why do you stay in England? And just to work underground. You will go blind, like a bat – I am going blind, you see? When will you go home?'

Home. He thinks of his father, an old man in misfitting clothes, wasteground around him. He wonders if it will be necessary for the old man to die before he can go back to Poland. He thinks it will be this way. Otherwise there would have to be forgiveness. Casimir cannot imagine any means of forgiveness.

'Eh? You don't talk much. Still waters run deep, that is what the English say. The Polish is better, of course. *Cicha weda brzegi rwie.* "Quiet waters break the river's banks." You should talk more, Kazimierz Kazimierski.'

Wanda narrows her eyes and he sees it is meant as a smile, although her mouth is unsmiling.

The lift slows, two hundred feet down. Wanda pulls the door open and Casimir follows her, out into the deep shelter.

'Now we will find your story.'

They are standing at the edge of a great hall, broader than a Tube tunnel, its massive dimensions sectioned off by miles of shelves and walkways. The curved walls are painted two-tone, black and beige edged off at chest height. The floor of the deep shelter lies across the tunnel's widest point, creating a single arched chamber. Casimir remembers a second level, curving downwards like the belly of a ship.

'1987 . . . 1987 is this way. Come on, please.'

Wanda turns down an aisle between the shelves. As Casimir follows her, he sees that the shelves are packed from floor to ceiling with filing boxes, cardboard caked with dust.

'Tonight is my games night, you see. We play Pan for pierogi! So I get fat, because I am so good. But maybe you are too young for games. Maybe tonight you have a girl to be with.'

Ahead and behind, the black-and-tan walls run off into the far distance. Casimir bends his head, trying to see past Wanda to the chamber's end.

'How far does the deep shelter go?'

'From here to Lvov. No! A kilometre or two. And the same downstairs. Too much room. There is space now, where the shelves end. I never go down there.' She smiles back at him. 'It gives me the willies. The willies. You know what this means?'

'Yes.'

The archivist's teeth are the same pearly grey as the frames of her glasses. They walk on. In the overhead strip light Casimir can see that the walls are marked by slight, spiral ridges. He recognizes the pattern of a drum digger, the Underground's tunnelling machines. But I am deeper here, he thinks. Under the Underground.

'Now we are back in the 1980s. Not far to go now.'

The hall itself feels newer than the train tunnels above. There is no smell of limestone and water here, less sense of a human construction becoming natural. It is because the deep shelter is wartime, Casimir thinks; six decades old. The Underground above is twice its age.

Casimir can see the end of the shelves now. They stop dead a few hundred feet ahead. The strip lighting penetrates some distance further, before fading into darkness. The end of the chamber is out of sight.

In front of him Wanda comes to a halt, out of breath, holding on to the shelves. The boxes are wedged in tight, cutting the light down between rows.

'Here we are!' The old woman's voice is sing-song, artificially bright. She edges one box out, puffing and muttering. There is a string of letters and digits on the box lid: LONDON GDN, 06/87. Wanda dumps it on the floor in front of Casimir.

Dust billows around him and he wipes his face. The boom echoes away as he reaches down, lifts off the lid. Inside are copies of the *Guardian*, wrapped in plastic, pages compressed together.

'There! Now you must look for yourself. If you want more papers, they are all here. I am going upstairs to sit down. In twenty minutes I lock you out or lock you in. Yes?'

'Yes. Thank you, Wanda.'

Casimir is already lifting out newspapers. He doesn't look up at the archivist. Her footsteps echo away as he kneels down, hair falling forward, shadowing his eyes.

Tenth of June. Eleventh, twelfth. Casimir carefully unfolds the newspapers from the plastic wrapper. The newsprint smells fresh but the paper peels apart slowly, like onion skin. The first few pages are full of election news, then sideshow stories: *'Cecil Parkinson Gets Energy'*, *'Portrait of the Artist as a Young Dog'*.

Casimir lays the newspaper out on the aisle floor. The pages hiss as they turn. After some time he stops. As he reads, light is reflected upwards from the white paper, emphasizing the flat blades of the cheeks.

## 'RUSH-HOUR KILLER'
### Suspect Arrested at Scene of Third Death
**by Li Ailema, Crime Correspondent**

Police have confirmed that a man has been arrested in connection with a third death on the London Underground. Thomas Gray, 32, a mental hospital outpatient, was apprehended yesterday morning at Camden Town Underground station. Shortly before the arrest a man was fatally injured after falling on to live rails. Sean Harris, 42, of north London, was announced dead on arrival at the Royal Free Hospital, north-west London.

The death of Harris follows a chain of similar incidents over the past six months which includes the deaths of two other London Underground passengers. A poster campaign on the Underground is said to have led to the arrest, when a member of the public identified Gray on a crowded platform immediately after Harris had fallen. The victim died after injuries sustained in the fall led to a massive heart attack.

Passengers' groups were today calling for an independent government inquiry into why Gray, diagnosed as a paranoid schizophrenic with violent tendencies, was released into the community. Thomas Gray has been shunted between hospitals, hostels and prison since his release from Marginfields Home for the Mentally Disabled, East Sussex, in 1981. Pressure on NHS beds has meant that Gray has been either discharged prematurely or refused admission to suitable facilities since that time.

No police comment has yet been issued as to whether Gray will be charged with the Underground deaths of William Tull and Lawrence Cluny, who died on 10 May and 21 March this year. However, all three victims bear a clear physical resemblance to Gray. If convicted of all three deaths, Mr Gray is likely to be kept permanently in a secure medical institution, although the final period of detention will be decided by doctors and medical staff.

Beside the writing are four photographs. The first three are mugshots of the victims' faces: white-haired, white-skinned men. Their physical differences are emphasized by different lighting and background. Casimir is aware of their similarity without being able to place exactly which features they have in common. Harris is standing outdoors, a high white sky behind him as he grins ludicrously. Snapshots, taken in lunch-breaks or days out. Never meant to be this important, as records of death. They remind him of Saville, unsmiling and badly lit.

The larger photograph shows Gray being pulled along through a crowded hall by police officers. Casimir screws up his eyes, trying to make out details in the blurred newsprint. With a shock he recognizes his station, the surface concourse at Camden Town. Gray is stooped between the policemen, a head taller than either of them, light hair falling across his face. The mouth is visible, thin-lipped and curved downwards. Without being able to see his eyes, it is hard to gauge the expression. It could be anger or satisfaction. He could be crying or smiling.

Again he remembers Adams. The room full of surreal, watered light and the supervisor's voice, angry and haunted.

*He was living down in side-passages. Got away with it for months,
staying down there all night, out of the way of the cameras . . . In a
place the size of London, there's somebody pushing all the time.*

Casimir closes his eyes tight. The archives make nothing
clear, disturbing everything. Thomas Gray has been locked
away for life. There is no sign that this is the man who is following Alice. This is not the man he has been looking for.
'*Kurva!*' He whispers harshly, under his breath. The sound ricochets away along the tunnelled walls. Away past the last
shelves where the dark begins, like deeper water. He is still
thinking of Gray's killings as he folds the newspapers back
into their box. The repetition of a pattern. Gray killing the men
who looked like him. Alice and the dead women, their hair
and skin and eyes.

As he walks back along the hall to the lift Casimir can feel
the dark behind him, deep and cold. Wanda is waiting for him
by the exit, buttoning a woollen coat over her jumper. Casimir
walks her to her car. Kisses her goodbye on both cheeks, her
hands gripping his forearms. Turns back towards the station.

It is not long until evening. To the south the sky is darkening with rain, and over the market streets runs a great skewed
track of cloud the colour of neon. Casimir narrows his eyes to
make out the scale. It looks gigantic, curving out towards the
city's western edge.

Then he is at the oxblood entrance of the Underground. He
bends his head and goes inside.

By the time Casimir arrives at Waterloo the terminus is full of
the sound of rain, a fine hush of water against the glass vaulting.
He walks across to the side exit, out between the shining black
bulks of the taxi rank, down the steps towards Spur Road.

A figure sits against the metal balustrade, one arm held out
sideways, hand resting on the head of a white dog. The stray
looks round at Casimir first, eyes white and pink in the rain.
He remembers it from days ago, before the news of the first
death. He doesn't recognize Alice until he is standing beside
her and she looks up, eyes narrowed against the hazy downpour.

'I love rain. The sound of it. I miss it underground. You do too, don't you?'

She is wearing a black wool hat, and the length of her wet hair is tucked inside the collar of a green duffel coat. Water shines against the flat of her forehead and he sits down, reaches out, wiping it or warming it with his hand.

'Yes. How did you know I live here?'

Alice reaches into the coat. She smiles as she passes him a square black wallet, as if she is giving him a present.

It is his own, cheap plastic impressed with the Under-ground roundel. Casimir turns it in his hands, not frowning. He pockets it without checking inside for the last of his month's wages, the London Transport identity card.

'How long have you been here?'

She shrugs. The dog turns its long head away from Casimir, grinning down at The Cut market.

'You cannot have known I would come this way.'

'If I didn't know, how come I'm sitting here?'

'When did you take it?'

'Last night, when you were asleep.'

They are sitting close, not looking away from each other. Rain runs down the sharp jut of Casimir's nose and around the cavities of his eyes. 'I didn't sleep.'

'Whenever then. You told me I could come here. Stay with you.'

'Stay. Not steal.'

'It's not stealing.'

'I don't see –'

'Which part don't you understand? I gave it back to you, it's not stealing. Did you find out who's after me?'

'No.'

'You said you could.'

'I was wrong.' He stands up. Puts out a hand. 'If you're hungry, I have food.'

She gets up by herself. They walk together, down the steps to Lower Marsh. Behind them the dog stands watching, pant-ing into the sound of the rain.

The shop front is bright and quiet. A few stall-holders sit inside, cradling tea, sheltering their cigarettes away from wet faces. A fat man in sodden black jeans and T-shirt hunches over five polystyrene bowls of mushy peas, shovelling them into his mouth, hair plastered against his forehead. Casimir goes past the shop door to the lodgers' entrance and leads Alice up the uncarpeted staircase to his room. He closes the door behind them. Plugs in the bar heater and feeds the meter. Stands, awkward, as she looks around.

'I will get some food. There will be something left over from last night.'

'I'm not hungry yet.' She walks over to the window, looks out, then draws the net curtains shut. 'How long have you lived here?'

'Eight years.'

She is taking off her hat, the coat, not turning round. When she says nothing else he walks up behind her and she leans back against him and he puts his arms around her waist, breathing in the smell of her wet hair, hardening against the small of her back. They make love there, at the window. Quietly, Alice's cries almost as soft as the sound of the rain. Once her forehead bangs against the glass and when Casimir begins to apologize she laughs, breathless, turning her face to kiss him over her own shoulder.

Afterwards he goes downstairs for food. There are reheated chicken portions on the glass-fronted hotplate, dull and crusted with old oil. He toasts thick slices of white chip-shop bread, butters them with margarine. Warms up glutinous minestrone soup, ladles it into tall polystyrene cups.

When he gets back upstairs the door is unlocked. Alice is sitting on the bed, naked and cross-legged, drying her hair with Casimir's bathroom towel. Her cheeks and breasts are flushed with heat. He feels a sharp sensation of physical desire for her near his heart, almost painful.

'I needed a shower. I wasn't sure which was your towel.'

'You chose the right one.'

'I know. It smells of you.'

'What kind of smell is that?'

'Like fish blood. It goes with the sound of your name. I like it.'

He sits next to her on the narrow bed, carefully putting

down the food between them. Alice eats quickly, head lowered, not speaking. Casimir is too hungry to watch her. When her food is gone she leans against him, side to side, breathing out once with satisfaction.

'It doesn't feel like you've lived here for eight years. It feels as if no one lives here at all. Don't you have any things?'

He drains the last soup, then looks up at the room, trying to see it as she does. 'I like it to be like this. But yes, I have some belongings.'

He puts the cup down on the floor and goes over to the wardrobe. There is a single drawer under the main cupboard and he pulls it open. Inside are his books of street-plans and poetry. His birth certificate, passport, London Transport work permit. An old shirt of soft grey cotton, rolled up and tied with elastic bands. He brings the bundle back to Alice, strips off the bands, unrolls the cloth. Inside is a black-and-greenish lump of material with the texture of plastic. It is large as Casimir's closed, white hands.

'What is it?'

'Amber. From the Baltic. It was my mother's.'

She touches her fingers against it. One side of the amber is smooth and golden-green, the colour of a pike's scales seen through water. The rest of the piece is blackened and gnarled with a hatchwork of cracks. 'It's beautiful. What happened to it?'

'It was burnt.'

'Yeah, I can see that. How come?'

He shrugs. 'A stove. My mother was cooking duck eggs. It was when I was small, before I remember.' Out of nothing, he thinks of curtains. The smell of coal, the smell of snow. He moves his hand near his forehead, as if batting the images away.

'Was she hurt? Your mother.'

'No one was hurt.'

'Don't you miss her?'

'No.' His heart judders at the lie. 'She left us.'

'Yeah? Join the family. How old were you?'

'Twelve. I went on a journey with my father. She waved goodbye to us when we left. She told me to love my father,

[176]

because she loved him. When we came back home, she was gone. No one saw her go and she took nothing.'

'Why did she leave?'

'I don't know.' All at once the words well up in him. He swallows to force them down, but it is too late. 'To put us both behind her. She should have left a long time before. She should never have married my father.'

From outside comes the sound of an ice-cream van, its mechanical music cut off abruptly, repeated, cut off again. The tune sounds familiar, although Casimir has no name for it. Already the sound of it is distant, streets away.

'Why not?' Alice's voice is soft, careful. Casimir leans back against the wall. Beyond the window, the dark rain sky has merged into early evening.

'My father never deserved her. He is a bad man.'

'So why did she marry him?'

He pauses again. 'I think it is that she loved him.'

Alice looks away. Carefully, she begins to cover the amber with its cloth, wrapping it away. 'So where are they now? Your mum and dad.'

'My father is in Poland. We do not speak. My mother I never saw again. I used to think she died at sea, but I don't know. After she left, I couldn't live with my father. I stayed in youth hostels in Praga, downtown Warsaw. Then on the streets. Then in hostels again. I lived there for some time.' He takes the wrapped amber, holds it in his hands. 'And then it was as if I woke up. And I came here.'

'What was wrong with your father?'

'There were things he did. In the war, and after.'

'Everyone did something in the war.'

Alice moves away from him towards her clothes. Casimir had forgotten her quickness and for a moment he thinks he has said too much, that she is leaving. But she is reaching out a cigarette towards the heater. The filament dulls where the tobacco touches it, flares as Alice lights up, sits back.

For a time they don't talk. He listens to the sound of the depot yards from outside, and the hoot of a river boat. Alice is warm against him, a slight pressure on his heartbeat.

'You're very beautiful.' The words sound clumsy in his

mouth, in the English which is still alien to him.

She laughs, a ripple going through her, through him.

'No. I'm the girl on the train, Ariel Casimir. That's all. I'm the girl on the train who you never see again.' Over her shoulder, he watches her smile to herself. 'But here I am. Go on, it's your turn. Ask me something.'

He doesn't stop to think. 'What is your real name?'

'Jacqueline Chappell.'

She sucks at the cigarette. It is quiet in the unlit room. Casimir can hear the crackle and wince of tobacco and ash. She shifts against him, getting comfortable.

'The other names are pretend. I used Alice when I went underground. I've got nine National Insurance cards, nine names. All you do is tell Social Security you're a traveller and your parents are travellers. Then when you've got your National Insurance number, you can get everything. The more you have, the easier it is. But my real name is Jacqueline Chappell. Do you believe me?'

'The man at the abandoned station. He called you Blip Girl.'

She picks a strand of tobacco from her teeth and tongue, then laughs. Casimir realizes he has never heard her laughter before today. It is startling. Clear and musical, like her voice when she sings.

'When I was smaller I used to get caught doing stuff. The police called me Blip Girl because wherever I was, I messed up their crime figures. They couldn't lock me up because I was juvenile. They tried to load me off on foster carers. Now I'm older, I don't get caught any more. Not much anyway.'

'What did they arrest you for?'

She shrugs, shoulders thin against his shirt. He reaches around her, stroking her breasts. The smooth warmth of her skin against the roughness of his knuckles, palms, the backs of his hands.

'Nothing bad. Just stealing. Drugs – no needles. Once there was a man who tried to hurt me, so I hurt him back. That's all.' She folds her arms, trapping him against her. 'Foster homes were the worst. Worse than being homeless. Your hands are so big. Giant, like that statue, the marble one. It'd be good, being like you. You must scare people.'

'How long have you been homeless?'

He feels her breathing change against him. She picks up her polystyrene cup, delicately stubbing out her cigarette in its wet base. 'I can't remember. A long time now. Time goes different when you're on the streets. You get old fast, but then you know that.' She shifts, looking back at him. 'I'm not staying here tonight. I'm going back underground. Do you mind?'

He wants to ask her to stay. He wants her to tell him about the seventeen scars that run from the wings of her shoulder bones to the curve of her hips. Instead he stops himself, shakes his head. 'No.'

'It's safer. I don't like the way he keeps on. He's so – in Camden at nights he was so quiet, it was like he was everywhere. But I do feel safer, underground. Don't you?'

'Yes.'

'Will you come and see me tomorrow?'

'Yes.' She is moving away, picking up clothes, pulling them on. When she is dressed she turns to Casimir. He hasn't moved from the bed. One arm is still loose, where it held her. She comes up and leans over to kiss him, fast and supple, her mouth tasting of food and cigarettes. Then she goes quickly, without saying goodbye.

For some time he sits, thinking. His eyes adjust faster than it becomes dark. Too needy, he thinks. Adams was right after all. I need to know too much; it makes me careless of myself. He remembers the pike under canal ice, white teeth in a green mouth. No one else saw that. Such a beautiful monstrosity.

After an hour the sky is the blue of slate between the half-drawn curtains. Casimir gets up and takes off the work shirt and trousers he has worn for two days and a night, dropping them to the cold linoleum floor.

He gets dressed again mechanically, pulling on a pair of lightweight cotton trousers and a blue shirt bought cheap from the weekday market. His work jacket is hung up against the back of the door and he puts it back on and leaves quietly, pulling the door to behind him. As if someone were still sleeping in the empty room with its thin curtains and half-light.

In the Stamford Street telephone box a female skinhead is arguing about money, leaning forward over the chrome machinery and dial. Casimir waits in the rain, his back to the Bull Ring and its circling traffic. The phone-box door is wedged open with a shopping trolley. In the trolley a small boy is curled up asleep next to an empty fish tank. The woman's voice yells over the sound of cars. She slams the phone down into its cradle and backs out towards Casimir.

'Fucking cunt-fuckers! Go on then, it's your turn. Hope you have better luck with the fucks than I do.'

'Thank you.' Casimir watches the skinhead walk rapidly away towards Southwark, the trolley skewing ahead of her. Then he goes into the box, dials Operator Enquiries and waits, the door easing shut behind him.

'Good evening. Which number do you require?'

'Kentish Town Police Station. London.' He memorizes the number, feeling in his pocket for change, sorting it out on the flat of his hand. Then he hangs up and redials, holding the bust receiver together.

'Kentish Town. How can I help you?' The voice is male, with the same quality of control that Casimir remembers in Phelps's speech. 'Hello?'

It is hard to speak, the words grating in his mouth. Part of him stays detached, disgusted. But he needs the authorities now. Needs their control. 'I need to speak to Phelps.'

'Police Inspector Phelps is in a meeting. Can I help at all?'

'No. I will hold.'

'She may be some time. Can I ask – hang on, she just – just a minute, please.'

The line goes quiet. Casimir looks up at the telephone-box windows. They are crammed with prostitutes' advertising cards: FRESH GIRL, PRIVATE FUNCTIONS, HOLE IN ONE. The line clicks open and he turns away. 'Phelps here. Who is this?'

'Casimir.'

'I'm busy. What do you want?'

'You asked me about homeless people. There is something I didn't tell you.' He closes his eyes. As if the movement could stop him hearing his own voice. 'There is a girl. At nights she sleeps on the Underground. She looks like Rebecca Saville and

Marion Asher. Enough for it to matter. She has been arrested many times as a juvenile, at least once for violence.'

The line goes quiet again. From outside the telephone comes a rattling sound. Casimir opens his eyes in time to see the skinhead with the trolley go running past, back towards the Bull Ring.

'I made a mistake.'

'Yes, you did. How long have you known about this?'

He thinks back, trying to ignore the checked anger in the policewoman's voice. 'A week.'

'A week. What you're saying is, you knew about this before Asher was killed. She must be pretty, your Underground girl, if she looks like Saville and Asher. A week. I hope it was good, because it may have cost a life. I hope you can live with that.'

'Nothing was clear a week ago.'

'If it turns out this girl's the killer they should put you away. Accessory to murder and withholding evidence. What about sex with a minor, can I do you for that? Now listen. I want you to tell me her name and describe to me exactly where she sleeps.'

He leans back, the root of his skull against the glass. 'Jacqueline Chappell. I don't know if it's her real name. Sometimes she is called Alice, or Jack Union. She has lots of names. She sleeps in an underground storeroom at South Kentish Town Tube station.'

'There is no South Kentish Town. Are you trying to –'

'There is. It was closed down eighty years ago. It's on Kentish Town Road, under a shop called Cash Converters –'

'All right. I know it, yes. Red-tiled building, just like Camden station. Christ, it's minutes away.' The policewoman sounds disgusted. As if she can smell the killings, like smog pollution. 'OK. Right. I'm going to call Northern Line Management, for maps and access. As soon as they get to me, I'm going down to find Jacqueline Chappell, or whatever her name is. I want you there too, in case we need to identify her. Inside half an hour, please. Is that all quite clear?'

'Yes.'

As he puts the phone back in its cradle the mouthpiece falls off, trailing wires. The telephone's liquid crystal display goes dead. Casimir steps out of the box, looks left and right. The wet-black stone façade of Waterloo station looms up over the Bull Ring. He puts his head down and begins to run.

The sky over South Kentish Town is grey-orange, London's last evening light reflected up against the rain clouds. Casimir is still half a mile away from the abandoned station when he hears the sirens. An ambulance speeds past him northwards from Camden, its headlights flashing. He starts after it, breaking into a run again.

In front of Al Araf Saunas the pavement is crowded with police and London Transport officials. Casimir stands in the wet street, hands open by his sides, watching the mass of movement and urgent, quiet conversation.

'Mister Kazimierski?'

He looks round into the glare of a flashlight. Beside him is a policeman, his face slack and characterless under the low brim of his hat. Casimir raises one hand to shield his eyes.

'Can you come this way, please.'

The man's quick monotone turns the question into an order. Casimir follows him through the crowd towards the back of the building. Phelps is standing in the open yard entrance, talking to a small black woman, their heads bowed together. From inside the corrugated-metal wall comes the whine and growl of an electric screwdriver. Both women look up as Casimir reaches them.

'You're late.'

'You've found her.'

Phelps shakes her head, frowning, still watching Casimir. 'No. We've been through the whole complex with keys to every room, excavation plans, floor-plans and the lighting turned on. There were three juvenile males down there and a middle-aged homeless couple. None of them looks remotely like Rebecca Saville.'

'She knows the Underground too well. She is here.'

'No. But fortunately for you, it seems she was.' Phelps looks down, sheltering her notebook under its plastic cover. 'Two of the boys saw her tonight. All three maintain they don't know her name, but they described her all right. They also say that she sold them drugs, including a syringe of blue liquid we found in their room. Pentobarbitone. It's a tranquilliser used to put down mad cows. The ambulance crew tell me it's got value as a street drug.'

She glances back up at Casimir, eyes wide and staring. Aggressive. Looks down. 'The older male fell running down a flight of stairs. He's getting medical treatment now, but I'll be talking to him soon. The woman won't say anything, not unless you count "Get off me, I'm the fucking First Lady". This is Margaret Stone, by the way. From Northern Line Management.'

'I'm sorry you've become so involved, Assistant Casimir.'

'Yes.' The manager's hand is cool and dry, even in the rain. He watches her, remembering her voice clearly on the control-room telephone. Low-pitched, very calm. *It is about Rebecca Saville. It is unfortunate.* 'What are you going to do now?'

'The station will be sealed.' She speaks up over the sound of hammering from inside the yard fence, turning away from him as she finishes. Her profile is sharp, the nose aquiline and Asian. 'I have to go. Inspector, I'll need an image of the girl for the posters. A clear photograph of Asher or Saville would help.'

Casimir steps forward. 'What if Alice is still down there?' He is nearly twice the height of the Line Manager. She doesn't look round. Phelps glances up at him and away.

'We've looked. She's not. I'm afraid all I've got here is a photocopied shot of Marion Asher. PC Hill, there's a black folder under the passenger seat in the van, can you get it, please? Fast?'

'Yes, m'm.' The policeman beside Casimir turns away, pushing through towards Castle Road.

Casimir looks round. Through the open corrugated-iron door he can see the entrance to the abandoned station. Two workers in London Transport overalls are bolting a new door into place. Its blue-grey metal surface shines with rain. The wooden door lies off to one side on the decomposing piles of carpet, split almost in two. As Casimir watches, the taller worker leans a two-handed machine against the door. It whines, high-pitched, driving a heavy bolt into the old brick.

He turns back. Phelps and the Line Manager are going through a folder, the policeman a gaunt black figure behind them. Margaret Stone stands back, holding a sheet of photocopied paper.

'Will that do? I can send on a better copy later.' Phelps is handing the folder back to the policeman.

'It's a start.' The Line Manager looks down at the photograph. Casimir comes up beside her, standing close. It is the picture of Marion Asher and the second girl. Leaning forward, laughter caught and frozen. Stone's measured voice is almost inaudible. 'It is a cruel face.'

'I'm sorry?'

The Line Manager looks up at Phelps, unsmiling. 'This will do, thank you. I must go now. Goodbye, Inspector. Assistant.' She walks away towards the alley, small and hunched against the drizzle.

Casimir turns back to Phelps. 'The girl, Alice. She knows the Underground very well. Better than us. There are places she knows which we may not even have mapped –'

'Thank you for your concern, Mister Casimir. That's why I sent twenty-five officers down to look for her. She's not there, and she's not getting back down there either.'

The policewoman looks away towards the crowd, then down at her watch. 'I'd like you to leave now, sir. One of my men will drive you back to your lodging house. If and when I need you again, I'll be in touch. Until then try to live a normal life, yes?'

The police car smells of pine freshener and urine. Casimir makes himself sit back, knees against the side-door and the partition in front. There is no door handle, no window button. He looks out at the city as it goes past, smooth and quick and bright. Rain runs sideways against the car window. As if I am travelling upwards, he thinks. Away from the Underground and Alice. He wonders what he is travelling towards.

He thinks of her laughter, breathless, rippling through her into him. The smell of her wet hair, which is sweet, like her sweat.

The car stops outside the take-away on Lower Marsh. The side door clicks open. One of the policemen in the front seats looks round at Casimir.

'All right? Take a bit of friendly advice, stay in tonight, watch the telly. You won't die of boredom. There's *Blind Date*, you'll like that. Right, off you go.'

Casimir gets out of the car and goes up the lodgers' stairs without looking back. The stairwell bulb is still out and he stands outside his door, gritting his teeth against the dark, feeling for the keyhole, the key. He unlocks the door and reaches inside, batting blindly for the light switch.

The room jumps into visibility, stark in the bare electric illumination. Casimir breathes once, twice, eyes closed. There is a noise from the hallway outside, voices of other lodgers going past and down. One measured, the second roaring drunk. Female. Briefly Casimir thinks of the dog woman and his legs ache suddenly, the body remembering its hurt.

He opens his eyes. On the mussed blankets of the bed is a plate of food, stale white toast and cold fried chicken left unfinished. Casimir walks to the window and opens it, letting in air and the smell of rain. A car goes past up Spur Road, light running along its blue lamé. On the far side of the road someone is putting up posters in the rain, white rectangles trailing away from a single dark figure. Its pale face turns upwards and away.

Casimir goes to the bed, sits down, leans back. After a few minutes he props himself up on one elbow and starts to eat methodically, forcing the oily meat and dry bread down. The newspaper lies crumpled against the foot of the bed and he picks it up and reads, concentrating on the food and his own simple hunger. The headlines, distracting and irrelevant: BLOW HOLE SUICIDE. WEB BOMB FACTORY.

'Mister Casimir?'

He stands up, walks the three steps to the door and unlocks it. Mrs Navratil is waiting in the hall. Her face looks pinched and drawn in the bad light.

'You're becoming rather popular. There was another letter for you.'

'Where is it?'

'I have it. Come up.'

Casimir follows the landlady upstairs. Blue television light fills the doorway of her flat. He steps through. The landlady is bent over beside a tasselled red lampshade. It colours her face like a light bulb seen through skin.

'It came this evening. You haven't shaved.'

'I have been busy.'

'You also smell. You must take better care of yourself. Living on restaurant premises.'

In the middle of the far wall is a massive flat-screened television. A news programme is showing with the sound turned down low, the reader staring out, unsmiling. Casimir thinks of fish in tanks, mouthing oxygen. Video cases are stacked around the television. One lies empty in front of the screen. Dully, Casimir realizes that Navratil is watching her newsreader on video.

The landlady straightens. 'Here it is.' She is holding out a brown envelope. 'Maybe it's from the police. What did they want with you?'

Casimir takes the letter. His address and first name are written in thick pencilled capitals.

'I was helping them with their enquiries.' He holds the letter sideways, to the light. Something shifts inside, tiny and papery. There are stamps above the address but no postmark. 'Who brought this?'

'A delivery man.'

'What did he look like?'

'Fat. Don't bring the police here again, Mister Casimir.'

Navratil turns away towards the television. As Casimir leaves he looks back once. The landlady is still standing, her eyes on the newsreader. Her hands clasped in front of her.

Casimir goes into his own room, locking the door behind him. He opens the letter quickly, not letting himself stop to think. Inside is a folded sheet of white paper. As Casimir unfolds it, a tiny white ball rolls out. He catches it as it begins to fall.

It is a scrawled-up nub of paper, flecked and seamed with red, no larger than a bus ticket bunched up in a pocket. It is almost too small for Casimir's fingers to unpick and he goes over to the bed and sits down, leaning forward, straightening the paper out between his large, blue-white hands. When he has it done he remains bent forward, trying to understand the one line of red text: GET AWAY WITH AN AWAY DAY!

The paper is smooth with magazine ink, torn on three sides, discoloured with age. Under the writing is the edge of a picture, a faded blue line of what could be sky, a fluff of white cloud. Casimir shakes his head. The fragment of page looks to him like an advertisement or article headline. Now nothing is legible except the six words. Like an order, or a warning: GET AWAY.

Casimir drops the paper. Beside him is the white sheet, still folded. He unfolds it on his lap. His throat clicks as he reads, the muscles opening and closing, heart lurching.

### HAVE YOU SEEN THIS CHILD?

Jacqueline Messenger left her foster carer in Tower Hamlets five years ago. Investigations by her carer suggest that Jacqueline has been living homeless in the London area since 1990. Jacqueline Messenger is a tall child with fine features and blue eyes. Anyone with information on Jacqueline Messenger can contact the foster carer at:

Messenger PO Box 191, WC1 8QX.

Under the headline is a black-and-white photograph of a girl. Unsmiling, staring at the camera. To Casimir she looks ten or eleven. Her hair surrounds her face, wildly tangled. The light coming through the hair makes it bright as a corona. In contrast the face is darkened, the gaze unclear in silhouette. He sees that Alice's face has changed as it has grown. It would be hard to recognize her from this child's face. Hard to be sure of what she would grow into.

He stops reading. Walks to the window. Looks out.

Along Spur Road the posters shine, a row of white steps leading up towards the terminus. The poster hanger is gone now, but Casimir remembers him. He has seen him before. A man in black jeans and T-shirt, his face large but smooth, heavy-set and muscular. Not loosely fat. Big in the bone.

As Casimir's eyes adjust he can make out the headlines on

the distant posters. The shape of the words, like those on the page behind him.

The sense of *déjà vu* is sudden and dizzying. Casimir stands still, waiting for it to pass. When it doesn't he leans his arms on the windowsill, head down.

He tries to remember how many times he has seen the poster hanger. He is present in Casimir's memory in the same way Alice once was; as a figure seen many times, a face in the Underground crowds. He remembers him on a platform crowded with commuters, sticking papers up by the telephones, moving away with an odd fluidity. In a side-tunnel, the nails of one hand broken down past the quicks. An Underground oddity; another Rose. Flashes of other memories: hallways, stairwells, back streets. The take-away – he has seen the man inside the lodging house. A figure alone at its corner table, blending into the background, casting the faintest of shadows. As if he can be anywhere.

He steps back from the window. Outside the rain has stopped and a breeze is picking up. The net curtains belly inwards, hollow and white.

*What have I done?* In his thoughts the question has no rising intonation. It is hardly a question at all, more a statement of guilt.

'What have I done.'

Casimir's whisper echoes in the bare room. A rustle of sound along the unpapered walls.

His eyes flicker, staring at nothing, hands opening and closing at his sides. He leaves without closing the door, the room behind him remaining in light, the bulb swung by the wind through the open window.

# 10

# Astrakhan

Along the Volga is where the fish markets are. Really they're just boats but each one is big and square as Gliwice town hall, with white domes and colonnades. Two steps behind my father, I look out of the portholes and see the kebab sellers pulling kindling off the waterfront birch trees, crows belching in the branches above them. Over the market racket I can hear singing. It comes from the mosques on the far river bank. The song shakes over the water. Like heat.

This is Astrakhan. It smells of fish, spilled petrol and broken fruit. The smell is so strong that I feel drunk sick with it for a day. We've been here for two days now, looking for the Iranian.

The fish markets: I keep my lips shut against the flies. We walk together down slick gangplanks and again down unlit steps between decks. Together we go between stalls where salt sprats are weighed in kilos and sturgeon is smoked and cut, broad as logs. Down between rooms where poachers' golden caviare is measured out in small jars. Always down and always together. But we are not together. It's five days since I learned to read my father's eyes.

The second deck has more noise, less light. There are live eels in wooden drawers. Trestles of carp, their gills still working in the hot air. More kinds of fish that I've never seen in Poland. More fish than I've ever seen, so that I'm hungry but too sick to eat with the smell of them.

We are looking for the Iranian. Because there are other things bought and sold on the riverboats, not just fish. We are here for the other things. We walk together, but my father is always two steps ahead. He is scared of me now. When he asks me what's wrong, I say it's nothing. In five days this is what I've said to him: It's nothing. Nothing else. At night when he drinks Russian spirit I can read his eyes.

*

July, the month of holidays. Tonight we leave for Russia, and I learn my dad's business. All afternoon he's in the guest room, watching the football with Slawek and Chorzelski. When he's home this is where he sits, waiting for the next trip. He drinks Scotch or hunters' herb vodka, arms flat out on the armchair's rests, watching daytime TV or nothing at all. Once I was getting ready for school and I went in there and he was asleep with a blanket on him. I never watched him sleeping before. He looked surprised. I breathed soft.

With Slawek and Chorzelski he doesn't bring out the Scotch, though. They drink Lech beer still warm from the corner shop shelves, crackling the empty cans. We can hear them through the wall as we pack, my mother choosing the clothes, me getting them, she folding them into the soft plastic suitcase with the scuffed white corners. Warm clothes for the north, light for the south. Dad is the loudest, barking curses as the TV whines and shouts.

If there's any beer left, my mother will pour it on the balcony flower-pots. It kills the slugs.

I can't think of Astrakhan. When I imagine leaving I go west, not east. Astrakhan is the wrong way. Karol says Russian girls are beautiful at fourteen but old at eighteen. Piotr says there will be an eclipse and not to look at it or I'll go blind. I've seen eclipses before, they're not so great. Dad says that in Astrakhan you can buy ten dollars for a dollar. I listen to them and think of Terespol. Sunlight in Russia, moving across countries towards me.

'What does it feel like?'

'What does what?'

'When you leave Poland. Do you feel anything?'

She looks up from the case, easy and smiling. 'Nothing! Except in your mind. Why, what did you think?'

I go and sit on the bed beside her, looking at my hands. 'I had this dream. Me and Dad were walking into Russia. When I stepped across and my foot touched the ground, it was like pins and needles going up my leg, into my chest. Then I woke up, and I still had the pins and needles in my leg.'

She doesn't take my hand. I know she's still smiling. From outside comes the sound of a klaxon from the steel factories, two long hoots with space between them. We sit side by side, hands in laps.

'I tried to tell him no, but he wanted you to go so much and I got so tired in the end –'

'No, I want to.'

Now I look up at her, to show I really do. At the corners of my mother's eyes are fans of lines from smiling or crying. There are three lines by the left eye, four by the right. I'd like to touch them but I can't do that.

'Can we play a game when we've finished?'

'That'd be fine. What do you want to play?'

'Cards. Pan. Is there any soup?'

'There's borsht and pasties. We can play in the kitchen.'

We shut the case and lock it and go into the kitchen. It's darker on this side of the flat but we're further from the guest room. With the window open you can hardly hear Dad at all, only the ordinary sounds from outside, voices calling voices home. We drink the soup out of teacups and eat the hot pasties off the saucers.

After I've won we clear away together. There's no soap but the water's hot today. The dishes clunk and clank in the water bowl.

'It'll be your birthday when you get back. When your grandfather was thirteen, he grew twenty centimetres in a year. Twenty! And you'll be tall as him. Have you thought about presents?'

'I don't know. You choose for me.'

'No, I'll just pick something horrible. You're big enough to make up your own mind. You can tell me and then forget. I'll keep it secret for you.' Mum talks quietly, not looking up from her hands as she scrubs. 'Do you still keep lists of secrets, Ariel?'

'No.'

I wait for her to say something else but she doesn't, not yet. I'm surprised at her for remembering. It was a long time ago, when we talked about secrets and lists. We were washing potatoes then and her arms were around me. I felt as if I had four hands.

She lifts out the last cup, white with gold patterns. Weighs it in her fingers, the water running off it. Sets it down.

'Ariel, listen to me. Whatever happens in Russia, remember that I love your father. Will you do that?'

I'm standing still, the cloth in my hands. She looks round at me, staring in the kitchen's bad light. 'Why do you love him?'

My mother turns right round and catches hold of my hands. 'Because he loves me. He has taken care of us both. There is good in you that comes from him. Will you remember that for me?'

'Yes.'

'Thank you.' She lets go of my hands, the light going out of her eyes or back into them.

When we leave that night she says nothing to me. She's packing plastic bags of food into the back of the car and I look down and she's still wearing her house slippers. They're light blue, thin on the grass-cracked concrete. I kiss her and she kisses me back and then I get into the car, pressed in with the bags of food. I look out of the rear window to wave but she's already walking to the flats, head bent forward, not turning to watch as we drive away.


We drive north-east, away from home. The evenings are long in July. Outside the car is still lighter than inside. I can see strip fields, each one just a couple of tractor-widths. Rusting combine harvesters, six in a field, still like cows. Birch forest in the distance, whiter than the horizon.

I haven't been alone with Dad since I was small. It isn't the same as it was then. We sit quiet like strangers on trains, until Gliwice is way behind us. Then he turns his head. Not really looking away from the highway, just glancing back quick. I can see his eyes when he talks.

'The roads are clear. We'll be at the border in five hours. What food did we get, then?'

The plastic bags are full of newspaper parcels. Grease-stained, folded tight. I open them carefully, thinking of my mother's hands wrapping them. The highway lights come every few seconds and I hold the parcels up to the side-window. 'Cake. Poppy-seed cake. Sandwiches. I can't see what. Cabbage pasties. And a cooked sausage. And water.'

'What kind of sausage?'

I lift the parcel to my face, smelling the garlic in the warm grease. 'Silesian.'

'Hah! Good.'

'Dad, can I sit in the front?'

'No.'

'I'm old enough. I'm twelve. The law says when I'm twelve I can sit in the front.'

'Yeah, well the law in this car says you sit in the back.'

I close my mouth with the teeth together. Look out. The highway lights have gone here, and Dad swears in the sudden darkness. There are pines close up to the roadside. They flicker past like bicycle spokes. The bitter smell of a rubbish dump blows in through the open window and is gone.

'People won't see you so much back there. OK? What they don't see they don't ask about. And the less they ask, the better for us. Still, there's quiet roads round Astrakhan, nothing to crash into for three thousand kilometres. I could teach you to drive.'

'Really?'

'Sure, why not? It's about time. Anyway, you're supposed to be learning the business.'

'Great! Great, Dad. Thanks.'

East and north-east, past the fat chimneys and long hills of Silesia, on towards Czestochowa. One time Piotr came here to see the Black Madonna with his school and three boys fainted. Now we've got no time to stop. It's hours to Terespol, where Uncle Jan waits in the border-control rooms.

I close my eyes. In the dark I can see my mother alone, walking up ten floors to our flat. The *scuff* of her house slippers on the unlit flights. The creak of the bed as she lies back down.


East of Warsaw the land gets flatter and there are fewer houses. The long ploughed fields go off into the dark, rising or falling away only a little, so the horizon is way off and out of sight anyway, there being so few house lights to mark off the distance. When we come into Terespol it's bright, though. There are floodlights like in a football stadium, high up over the train yards and border roads.

Dad parks by the railway station. There are guards everywhere on the platforms and in the waiting rooms. The trains are painted red and they let off clouds of steam. The smell of burning coal is strong on them, dirty and sweet. It makes me think of home, more than anything I could see or hear.

My father stands by the car, stretching his arms and legs. 'Aargh! That wasn't so bad, was it? Russia tomorrow. When was the last time you saw your uncle?'

'Years ago. I was little.'

'Yeah. Well, you're not so little now. Keep your mouth shut with him. I'm hungry. Get us something, will you?'

We eat two parcels of chopped-egg sandwiches and wash them down with water. Then we go into a station office and Dad asks for Jan. The office man says he's on the trains. We wait ten minutes for my uncle and then he comes out and we drive back to his house. I notice how big it is, his house. Larger than our flat. There's three of us and only one of him.

'Well. You're making good time, Michal. How are you, Casimir, are you well?'

'I'm fine.'

'Fine. Do you drink now?'

'Yes.'

'Then that's fine too.'

He takes off his green-and-gold hat, puts it on the kitchen table. There are four empty vodka bottles lined up beside the back door and Jan brings out a fresh bottle and pours three glasses. With his hat on, my uncle looked the same as years ago. Now I see his hair is gone, all except a white stubble.

'Cheers.'

'Cheers!'

We knock back the vodka. It's cold and thick from the freezer, and I feel it burn my throat and the back of my nose. I swallow fast, so I don't start coughing. My dad sighs and sits down, legs sprawled out under the table.

'Damn, that's good! And next trip'll be even better. I'll only have half the driving to do then. Twice as much to drink. Casimir's learning to drive, did he tell you?'

'No. Big man, eh? When did you start?'

'Not yet. Dad's going to teach me. In Astrakhan.'

My uncle leans forward, pouring again. Two shots, for Dad and himself. I hold hard on to my empty glass. 'Good. Now, there's benzene to shift into the car. Eight cans. Casimir can give me a hand. You'll be wanting to sleep, Michal. You're clear to go across at four.'

Dad looks at his watch. It's already past midnight. 'Casimir, you help your uncle, eh?'

'Yes.'

They both stand at the same time. I didn't know they were going to do that. They even stand up the same way, pushing themselves with their hands on the table, heads down. Brothers. I thought Dad was older, but he looks younger, with his black hair and shaved white skin. His forehead slants out more and his nose is straight; Jan's is smaller and broken to one side. My dad's cheekbones are long, like the face of a dog. They're not really that long but his face feels sharp to look at, like a dog's. If he laughed you'd even see his tongue.

He goes back into the guest room. Through the open door I watch him fall asleep in a hard chair with the TV on. Me and Jan bring the benzene up from his cellar and pack it into the boot of the Polonez. There are blankets too, in case we have to sleep in the car. I stick them under the back seats while Jan checks the water and oil. The car's insides smell of garlic and old cigarettes.

My uncle works with his head down, not talking. He moves like an old man, trudging round the car, then back into the house, not changing his work boots at the door. I follow him down the corridor into the kitchen. He's washing his hands at the sink, hot water steaming as he scrubs. When he's finished I wash my own hands while he gets the vodka out again.

'You want a nightcap?'

'Sure. Thanks.' I sit down at the chipped pink Formica table. We drink without talking for a while. There's a click every time my uncle swallows. It sounds like small bones breaking. I was eight last time I was here. My bones are bigger inside me.

'Your mother, Anna. Is she well?'

I shrug. The vodka settles inside me. Warm in my gut, light in my head. 'She's OK. She forgets things.'

'Your mother's got enough to forget.'

'Like what?'

My own voice comes out high with nerves. I sound like a child asking a question, whining at its parents. But I'm not a child any more. I'm taller than my uncle, taller than my father. The outside of my glass is white with frost. Jan sits back, hands together around his own shot. It must be cold against his palms.

'Nothing you need to know. Ask your mother if you want. She might tell you. If she can remember.'

'I'm asking you.'

He looks up at me. The skin pulls back from his eyes, up into the lines of his forehead. 'What did you say?'

'I said I'm asking you.'

My voice splits on the second word, broken between high and low. Jan looks at his glass. He could be smiling but it's hard to tell. His mouth stays the same, pulled down at the ends. From next door comes the chatter of the television. Snatches of folk music, Russian voices.

'You should respect your elders, Casimir. You know why? Because they know more than you. Knowing things is what puts the grey in their hair. You want grey in your hair, Casimir?'

'Just tell me.'

Jan snaps his head up. His face has changed. It has come alive, staring and smiling. I see he grins like my father, the lips pulled back against the teeth.

'If you like I can tell you all kinds of things. Fuck with me I'll fuck you up, sonny. You just sit there and keep quiet. Drink your big man's drink and then get some sleep. You're leaving in a couple of hours anyway. And where you're going, you'll need the rest.'

My uncle stands up. I sit watching as he clears the bottle and glasses away, rinsing them under the kitchen tap. I close my fists so the nails rest on the fat of my palms, trying to hold the anger inside me. I feel it escape. It trickles out between my fingers, like alcohol.

'I know she's Jewish.' He doesn't answer. My head feels tight and hot. 'I know what happened to Jews in the war. Auschwitz and Sobibor. I learned it in school. It wasn't so different from the Poles. They died too.'

'Jesus Christ.' My uncle talks with his back to me, putting the glasses down hard on the draining board. Water trickles out of them down the grooved wood. First his voice is low, then loud. 'You know where she's from?'

'Kielce.'

'Kielce. Your mother and father and me, we all grew up there. Different schools, same street. Your mother's family were Jews. Jews by blood, not religion. You know what happened in Kielce?'

He turns round. The vodka bottle is still in his hands. I shake my head. The table is between us.

'You wouldn't believe how many Yids there were in Poland then. It was part of everything. Quiet Fridays, I remember that. Men who mended shoes. I never saw real Polish men mending shoes like that. I knew Jews, everybody did. I thought the same about them as everyone; they were different from us. I think they thought the same.

'I was fourteen when the Germans came. Michal was a bit older. There must've been twenty thousand Jews in our town. And when the Germans left there were two. An old man and a little one-eyed girl. They were the last. But that was normal. That's not what I'm going to tell you. Since you've asked.'

He unscrews the top and swigs from the bottle, like a drunk. Staring at me over the bottle's neck. I sit ready. If he comes for me I'll hurt him.

'So the Germans left, and there were all the empty Jewish houses. Nice sideboards, nice wallpaper. People were shocked, of course, but we had our own dead to bury. We got on with life, only with new wallpaper. And then the camps were emptied. A hundred and fifty of our Jews came through alive.'

When he talks, my uncle's voice drags. It sounds as if part of him has died. 'I was walking with Michal and our mother.

We were going to meet father at the repair shop. There was a thin woman standing in the street. You could see the light through her clothes. We came up close and she started to smile at my mother. Her hand was tight on my arm, and it started to shake before she spoke, I don't know if it was anger or fear. She said, "What? Are you still alive? We thought that Hitler had killed all of you." My mother said that. She died six months later, when the Russians were settling in. The woman could have been from our street before the war, but I didn't recognize her. She looked like no one I'd ever seen. Like nothing.'

From somewhere in the house comes the hiss of TV white noise, left on after the last programme. My uncle goes on talking in his hard, slurred voice. My head is still tight but loose, too, thoughts floating in my packed skull.

'So there were the Jews. And then there was your mother. They were always in love, Michal and her. Always together, from when they were very small. Michal believed what our mother believed – that it was better if the Jews had never come to Poland. But Jews and Anna were not the same for him. He was stupid like that, your father – is stupid, I should say. But not as stupid as your mother. She should never have married him.'

'He hid her. In the war, Dad hid her. Didn't he?'

I sound proud of him. My uncle laughs and chokes. Wipes the vodka off his mouth.

'Where? Some people did, but not our mother. No, Anna went to the camps. Buchenwald. Her whole family died there. She was still beautiful when she came back. She didn't talk any more or move much, but there she was all the same. And Michal took her away. He didn't leave a note. In the west they were giving land away, driving out the Germans, but we didn't know he'd gone there for years. He was twenty-two.'

The chair grates back as I stand up. Jan looks up at me, then away. I'm so glad he has to look up at me.

'Is that it? That's nothing. You're so old, Jan, old and –'

'No, that isn't it. Sit down, big man. I haven't finished with you yet.'

I go on standing. Jan chuckles, down in his throat. His voice goes on and on. I want to tell him to stop. It's too late now.

'You are born out of hate, boy. That's what I'm telling you. You're a child of hate. I was going to tell you about the other Jews. Because in the end, given the choice of Jews or wallpaper, people chose wallpaper. Stories started going round – the Jews were killing children, the Jews were making matzo bread with Polish blood. Crazy stories. A boy went missing – he turned up in the next village months later, but it was too late by then. It was July, the holidays, and the heat was getting up. Most of the Yids were living in one house on Planty Avenue. I came cycling down there one day and there was fighting going on. I could hear chanting, *Beat the Jews, Kill the Bloodsuckers*.

'Michal was there. He was hurting them, like the rest. There was blood on him, but not his own. He was like a dog. I couldn't get him away. *Foreigners!* he kept saying, *Bloody foreigners!* There was one man killed holding on to a tree, and I remember a woman too, with blood around her. She was pregnant. I don't know if she was dead. Forty-two of them died, though. She probably was dead, don't you think? The Jews almost all left Poland after that, the ones who were left. All except Anna.

'You see how it is now? Your father hated the Jews, and married a Jew. I think he got it from our mother. Myself, I always thought he hated Anna too. Hated loving her. And now there's you. I wonder if he hates you too.'

Everything goes quiet. We watch each other across the room. Jan has the bottle clutched against his chest. My legs are shaking badly, rattling against the table. I make myself keep on standing.

'You're lying. We would have learned it in school. If that had happened I would know.'

'No. Why would they teach it? No one wants to remember Kielce. If they can, they forget. As if it never happened. What else is forgetting for?'

'You're lying about my dad.' My eyes are hot. I can't tell if I'm crying until Jan starts to smile again.

'You know I'm not.' He leans towards me. 'Because you know him well enough. Don't you? By the time you get back from Astrakhan, you'll know all about him, believe me. Just wait.'

'My mother loves him.'

Jan backs away. He looks bored with me now. 'So try not to fall in love, eh? Your mother was smart, before the war. Not now, though. I can't stand looking at her. She's like a shadow. And now I'm going to get an hour's sleep. You want to sit here and drink, you do that. Good night, nephew.'

I sit alone at the kitchen table. The bottle is there but I don't drink. Sometimes I hear the TV and sometimes not. Once I look round, through the angle of open doors, into the guest room.

My father sits in there with his back to me. Wide shoulders and big head, very still. Beyond him is the TV, its white square and the white noise coming out of it like a sigh: *Haaaah*. I look at my father sleeping for as long as I can. Then it's four o'clock and time to go and I look away.


'Is there any more food?'

'No.'

'Water?'

'No.'

'*Cholera*. I can't stand buying from these cheating Russians. Their faces when they make money off us, I can't stand that. Not that it's real money.'

He laughs without turning. I don't understand why he laughs. I watch the back of his head as he drives. The point of the skull under the thick black hair. Russia goes by around us, its birch stands and waterlands. Silver and black, vertical and horizontal.

'Having dollars here, Casimir, it's like being in a fairy tale. In Poland we're ordinary people, but here – Hey, you could buy a woman. You want to? God knows, you're big enough. In Astrakhan, you can buy a beautiful woman for nothing. The price of that Silesian sausage. Don't let me stop you either. Don't worry about your dad, eh? Casimir?'

There's a pipeline by the roadside, sometimes close and sometimes further away. Its stilts and bridges run down vil-

lage main streets and around town halls. I don't know what
it's for, gas or oil. Yesterday I would have asked my father, but
not today. There are so many questions I want to ask him and
will not ask. I don't want to hear his answers.

'Casimir? You all right back there? What's wrong?'

'Nothing.'

'You've been quiet as the dead since we crossed the border.
What is it, are you scared of Russia?'

A flock of birds is ahead and above us, falling slowly
behind. I crane back and see they're white geese, a big V of
them over the villages and factories. The village houses are
cheap wood, white birch and wet black boards. Nothing
strong in them except the heavy, sloped roofs. Every town has
a statue of Lenin painted silver, and all the statues point north.
Like a warning: *Go back.* The pipeline goes on and on beside
us, south-east towards Astrakhan.

'Jesus, you're not feeling sick, are you? That's all I need.
Eh?'

'Nothing is wrong.'

I look past my father's head. The sun is out. It's the colour of
chalk. There are flax fields all around us now, sloping away to
flat horizons. I turn in my seat, looking out. There are no
houses, no hills, no trees, only the flax flowers. A whole land-
scape blue as irises. My father's head black at the centre of it all.


We come towards Astrakhan at night. It's warm in the dark,
the way Gliwice is only in summer and the first long days of
autumn. For a day there's nothing outside us except rolling
dunes of earth, like a seabed. No trees except along the steep
banks of rivers. I watch the rivers coming, miles away.

The back of the car is full of maps, old books of them with
worn-out covers. I learn all the republics and states from the
Caspian Sea to China: Turkmenistan, Afghanistan. For ten
hours I try and work out if the USSR is bigger than the surface of the moon. Sometimes when I look out there are animals in the dark. I recognize flocks of sheep and small,
muscled horses. There are also tiny deer, no bigger than
horned yellow dogs. Once I wake from sleeping and there

are three camels sitting in the dunes. When I look back to see them again they are already out of sight. I don't know if they were real now.

On the outskirts we stop to piss by the roadside. I pick up handfuls of sandy dirt. Back in the car, I see my fingers are stained pink with its colour.

My father's employer is Iranian. We drive to his office on Kalinina Street but the shop front is locked and empty, grey boxes piled against grey windows. There's no sign to say where the Iranian has gone. My father stands in the street and curses the Iranian, the Russians and their rotting country. Then we get back in the car and drive on to the Hotel Lotos over the city's rivers and tributaries and canals. There's a tourist shop in the hotel lobby and my father buys forty bottles of Löwenbräu. In our room he begins to drink, steadily and in silence, his face full of anger.

Astrakhan is a city of water. The horns of riverboats carry a long way at night. The sound drifts into the hotel room with the mosquitoes. I lie awake listening, ten feet from my father.

It isn't easy to find the Iranian. My father's Russian is good, but no one talks to us. For two and a half days we search, not speaking. When my father looks at me now his pupils are tight with guilt and fear. There is no hate, though. Jan was wrong about that. I walk a few steps behind him, so that I don't have to see his face.

Old women bend down in the streets, splashing dirty water over their boots, washing away the dirt. Everything leans or bends here. There are avenues of ash trees, knotted together above the oil trucks and private cars. Houses which sag down into the mud, the wood of them carved and patterned like icing on wedding cakes. Some are grand like Piotr's house at home, with iron balconies hanging crooked from corners and under French windows. Their metalwork is the green of river water under ice. It must be cold here in winter. You can see it in the buildings.

On the third morning we go to the Volga fish markets. Across the water are golden stands of horsetail, and beyond them, the mosques. There are men singing in the mosques, and the sound of them shakes over the water, like heat. We walk between the stalls and decks, looking for the Iranian. It's five days now since I've spoken to my father.


'Hey! Look at this, look at this. You see this? Fresh sevruga! Try. You'll love it. You want it? Try. You want half a kilo? How much you want?'

'We're looking for someone.'

'A friend? Or business? Where you from?'

'Poland. We're looking for the Iranian.'

'Then why are you wasting my time? You want fish you come to me, you want Iranians, go to Iran. *Bojemoi!* Crazy Poles.'

'I can pay.'

'Listen, I have good Russian sevruga, you see? Fresh Russian sevruga from the bellies of the most beautiful Russian lady sturgeon. What about the young man, now? Maybe he wants to try. He'll like it, I can tell from his face.'

'I can pay in dollars.'

'Is that so. How much?'

'Just tell me where he is.'

When my father speaks Russian he sounds like the Gliwice Militia men, who never smile. I stand behind him, trying to understand them both. The stall-holder spits when he talks and there are cold-sores on his bottom lip. The Russian is not clear like in school. Here it is wet, blistered, thick on the man's tongue.

He leans forward for the money. Under him shine big jars of caviare, tarry black or clouded grey or green, which are the cheap eggs of river carp. I listen hard, catching what I can.

'Thank you. Well then. Go down.'

'Down? I pay you for directions, I want to know which deck and –'

'Just go down, Pole. As far as you can go.' When the stall-holder grins, the moustache pulls back over his lips. His mouth is cracked and red, like the crust of cooked meat. 'The steps are steep down there. Watch your heads.'

At the bottom of the last stairs we come to a long room. There is no door, just a thin man at a table, writing in a fat book. He doesn't look up. His skin is dark. Until Astrakhan, I'd never seen people with dark skin. Only Gypsies. There is no light except on his table.

I wipe my hands on the backs of my trousers. Here there's always dirt on me, I can feel it in my sweat. All day the mosquitoes feed off sturgeon and at night I hear their whine in our cheap hotel room and I sit up in the warm dark, reach out and kill the mosquitoes between my hands. Their blood smells of caviare. Now I wipe my hands and stand waiting.

My father coughs, steps forward. From somewhere in the long room comes the crackle of a cigarette and its glow, away from the table's light. '*Salaam aleicum.*'

'*Wa aleicum es.* You're late. I expected you two days ago.' The man at the table speaks Polish. He has the accent of a newsreader.

'I couldn't find you. Your office –'

'It doesn't matter. Our business isn't until tomorrow. Is this your son?'

The man looks straight at me. His eyes are grey, the colour of sevruga. The cheeks are sunk inwards, as if he has no teeth. When he smiles the teeth are bright and clean and I'm surprised.

'Kazimierz Ariel Kazimierski. You're a man already. Come here. Come, come!'

He waves me over. I feel Dad move beside me, shifting around, uncomfortable or uneasy. How does the man know my middle name? It scares me. I want to look at my dad, to see in his eyes what I should do.

Instead I make myself walk forward, up to the lit table. The man is turning pages. There are rows of numbers and tiny foreign writing. I recognize the writing from home, on the tins of fish in Grandad's old room.

'Do you know what language this is?'

'Arabic.'

'Good! You're a clever young man, aren't you? Cleverer than your father, I think. And quieter. These are my accounts, Kazimierz. Imports, exports. Do you know what we sell here, boy?'

I shake my head. He doesn't look up because he knows I do not know. He goes on turning the thin pages, talking in his easy voice.

'Tomato paste. I bring tomato paste into Russia and your father helps me. Do you know most Russians have never tasted a tomato? Imagine having never cooked with that flavour and colour! My own belief is that the tomato is the basis of all Western cuisines, and many Eastern too. But it's all things Western these Soviets want. Pizza, ketchup, full English breakfasts, chilli in a bowl, hamburger relish and spaghetti bolognese. So, I bring them tomato paste. One day I will have a tomato paste empire, you see? So far I have offices in Brest and Vladivostok, Moscow and here. I like it here best, because I can take the boat home once a month and see my children and sleep with my wife. And from here I will also see the eclipse tomorrow. Do you know what an eclipse is, Kazimierz Ariel?'

'When the moon disappears. I saw one before. It was OK.'

Now he looks up at me. His grey eyes are like his voice. Mild and lazy, as if he is always about to smile. 'Was it? Well, tomorrow is another kind of eclipse. The sun will disappear. I've never seen this myself, but I think you may find it a little more interesting.' The man looks away and down, voice rising. 'Mister Kazimierski, are you ready to work tomorrow?'

'Yes.'

'There will be a shipment fifteen kilometres due south off the coast at three o'clock p.m. You and the boy will go and meet it alone. Your boat is moored at the usual place, and the payment will be there for you when you return. Leave the shipment there. I'll pick it up myself in a day or two. I don't foresee any problems, do you?'

'No.'

'Good.' The man stands up. Stooping, too tall for the ceiling. He shakes my dad's hand but not mine. 'Goodbye, old friend. I'll call you when I need you again.'

'Yes. Thank you, sir. Goodbye.'

We walk back to the stairs. There are no portholes down here on the bottom deck. The walls of the market ship seep river water. My throat is dry and I gulp, trying to make it all right. But it isn't all right, not here. I gulp again and again. My father goes up the stairs first. I follow him close as I can. Each deck we go up, I breathe easier. Up we go, into the market noise and warmth and stench. Up and out into the simple light.

All day it rains and my father waits for tomorrow. He drinks beers from the rattling refrigerator in our hotel room, while the rain comes down over the wooden houses, the canals choked with lotus flowers, the churches and mosques with their golden turrets.

I leave him alone. Even in Astrakhan, it's better to be away from him. I walk for a long time, putting distance between us. It's a hundred kilometres to the sea but I go towards it anyway, past dry docks and factories. There is nothing else to walk towards. The smells of Astrakhan are in my mouth when I swallow. It's like being ill, when you can taste the sickness in your spit. I go as far as I can, down mud streets and over bridges. Then I turn back. The rain is warm on my scalp.

When I look up again I'm at the central market. People are trading or just sheltering under the corrugated-iron roofing. I push in with the crowd. There are stacks of shrivelled rosehips and fresh dates. Bunches of dill and ferny mimosa flowers and lotus, which are pink as the steppes earth. Purple heaps of shredded beetroot and rows of pike-perch, like little green dragons. Bread with caraway, coffee with cardamom, black suspender belts with brass buckles.

I come out between two butchers' stalls. Across the road is the Hotel Lotos. I count up to our room, five six seven floors. The light is still on. My father is there, waiting for me. Beyond and above the hotel there is the sky. Clouds the colour of sevruga. Only at their western foot is a puff of red, where the sun is going down. I remember the Iranian; tomorrow there will be no sun. I try and imagine it and but it's impossible. The flame of a candle after the candle has gone out.

The rain is getting colder. I walk across the road to the hotel. The lifts are working today and I take one up. On our first night they broke down and a Moscow businessman was trapped inside for two hours, hammering on the doors, enraged. The machinery shudders as the lift opens.

My father is at the window of our room, looking out. On the TV is a Russian film. In the film it's a sunny day in black and white. A postman stops his bicycle and falls asleep under the shade of beech trees.

'Did you have a good walk, eh?'

My father stands up and then sits down again. He is trying to smile but the lines of his face work against it. There's a towel on my bed and I dry my face and head with it while he talks.

'I saw you. Across the road in the market. You looked up. He's something else, the Iranian, isn't he? All that tomato crap. He liked you, though. There's a lifetime's work for you here. You could do worse than take up where I leave off. Hey, you want to know the truth of it?'

He comes and sits beside me. 'The truth is complicated. We take things out of the country, not in. There's a chain of people around us. First there are Soviets who sell goods to the Iranian, then we take the goods out of the USSR for him. Then he sells the goods all over the world. If the Soviets could do it themselves they would, but it's against the laws. They can't sell these things to foreigners, the Yanks might notice. So they hire the Iranian, and the Iranian hires us.

'We're perfect for him, you see? He needs foreigners who can walk around here, and not look foreign. Foreigners who look like Russians. Poles, not Iranians. It works like clockwork, you'll see. Years of money. You look wet as a dog. What were you looking for, out there? There are whores in the lobby downstairs, if you want them. I'll go for a walk, eh? Kazio? What do you want me to do?'

'Nothing.'

On the TV the postman is waiting for a rope-ferry. The ferryman is a beautiful woman in shirtsleeves. They watch each other as the traffic drives off the platform, picking up dust.

'Nothing nothing nothing.' He turns back to the window. Outside the rain has eased. 'You used to play a game when you were little, do you remember that? All you ever said was "Why?" Used to drive me mad. Do you remember that radio? When you filled it with – no. I suppose you were too young. Here. I've got something for you.'

I don't look up at him until he comes over and I have to. I see he's wearing a new wristwatch. The face has slipped round but the band is heavy metal, steel and gold.

'The Iranian gave me a new watch, see? Rolex Oyster. So I remember where his new office is, he said. It's a joke. Oyster. Anyway, I want you to have this. Here, put it on, take it.'

He is holding out his old watch, the one with the Lenin face and the radium dial. The strap is worn pale from years against his skin.

'Please, Casimir.'

There is need in his voice. I've never heard that before. I look up and it's there in his face too. He's still holding out the watch and I reach out fast and take it from him, strap it on. There's only one notch-hole. Tomorrow I'll make another, measured for myself.

'There you go. How does it feel?'

It feels good. More than the watch, it feels good to talk again. I look up at him and smile. Everything Jan said must be asked, and I will ask it. But there's time. We still have days together.

'It fits well. Thanks, Dad.'

'Great. Really, I'm glad you like it.' He claps me on the shoulder. My shirt's still wet, warm with my sweat. He wipes his hand dry on his trousers. 'Right, I'm off to bed. We start early tomorrow.'

'Yes.'

'Good night. I'm glad you like it, eh?'

''Night.'

'Sleep well, Casimir. Good night.'


We walk to the boat, towards the sea. First are the high brick buildings of Lenin Street, then the asphalt roads and shop fronts, then mud back streets and slumped-down wooden houses.

In the end there's nothing but shanty town. Chicken runs and dog kennels and hacked-down stumps poke out around the shacks. The back streets get thinner, become tracks. We walk single file, my father ahead like always. Little children play in the lanes. Whenever we come close to them they run ahead and stop again, like hedgerow birds. On our right are the high concrete walls of shipyards and naval docks. The wind hums in their razor wire.

The shanty town opens out on to building sites and a stand of aspens crusted grey with bird shit and lichen. A caterpillar truck moves, way off across cleared land. The river is beside us, wide and green, and overhead the gulls reel out their fishing-line cries. The sandy mud sticks to my boots. Heavy clods of it, until my feet drag and my thighs ache. We stop often, scraping off furls of mud on driftwood and slag concrete.

'How far is it now?'

'Not far. Keep up, will you? We can't be late.'

Dad's voice is hard again, as if last night never happened. I look down at the watch. We've been walking for three hours. The strap's tight, now my blood is running hard. My wrist is bigger than my father's.

In the end we come to a stretch of empty warehouses and depot yards. The ground is black with oil and rust. In the shadow of a broken trailer my father steps too near a nest of mewling grey kittens. The skinny mother spits and runs away from us between wrecked machinery. Nothing else moves here except clouds. Around us are the shapes of derelict cranes and waterfront winches, the sky grey above their giant arms and feet.

My father stops dead ahead of me. I can hear his breath coming fast. I see the whites of his eyes as he looks behind us. 'Right here. This is the place. Christ. It feels like home.'

'There's no boat here. Do we wait –'

When I look back at my father he's already moving, clambering down to the water over the iron counterweight of a toppled crane. Beyond the crane is a lorry cargo hold, its rusted trunk leant twenty metres into the river, doors swung outwards towards the sea.

My father wades in, arms and legs working, pushing out towards the container's doors. The water soaks his blue jeans and green anorak and the cloth clings to his arms in ridges and bubbles.

'Dad! Wait for me –'

He doesn't look back. I go down to the water's edge quickly, pushing between rushes and lotus stalks. The Volga is cold as sea water, muddy where my father has already disturbed the bottom. From up ahead comes a groan of metal as he yanks at the rusty container doors, treading water outside them. I move hard, the water surging against my thighs, waist, up to the heart.

'Dad?'

My feet can't reach the river bed any more. I imagine it in my mind. It feels deep. I swim out and round to the container's high doors and through them, reaching up for the sharp metal, hauling myself into the half-light.

The container is long as a church; long as St Barbary's, by the Strug Estate. At the far end water slaps at the line of floor and wall. Above me the roof is high as two rooms, sheets and pocks of metal eaten away. There's not much light, but the container is full of sound. The small whispers of water in darkness. The slap of shallows in the distance. The echoing clop of waves against the hull of a boat; the bump and creak of its tyre-stays against the walls. I rear back as it strains towards me, the wooden curve of the hull against my outstretched hands.

'Casimir? Where the fuck are you?'

'Here. I'm here.'

My father leans over the boat's side, looking down at me, and he chuckles. The noise travels on in the wrecked chamber, a shaking hiss of sound. 'Mary and Jesus. You look like a dog now, boy. A dog in a sack in a river. Here, step on the tyres, got it? Out you come. Quickly. All right?'

He turns away before I can answer. I stand on the boat's deck, the shirt heavy on my chest. It's hard to find my balance. The boat has benches around its walls, a flat planked floor, a motor with a crooked chimney pipe. The floor is crammed with rope and nets, buckets and life jackets, cans of fuel and long white boxes. I count six while my father checks the motor. They look big in the dark, looming white. I reach out to touch one. The plastic is hard and cool against my fingers.

'Simple as a rowing boat, you see? Just a big rowboat with a motor in. No one'll stop us, but if they do, you sit down and shut up. All right?'

'Yes.'

'Right. Off we go.' He pulls the engine cord and the container fills with its smoke and bellowing noise.

We edge outside, picking up speed. I take a big breath of the wind. It streams against my wet jeans and jacket and I can feel my skin cooling, cold. I look back at my father. Behind him is Astrakhan, the towers of mosques and movement of cranes already small with distance. He sits with one hand on the rudder, legs crossed at the ankles, wet blue shirt sticking to the folds of his belly.

'How long to get there?' I raise my voice over the chatter of the motor.

My father screws up his face into the wind. 'Three hours at least. Two to the coast. Sit back, get some rest. I'll tell you if I want a nap. And stay away from the boxes.'

The corners are round, clamped down with metal. They don't shift as the boat thuds against the hard green backs of waves.

I look round again. My teeth are beginning to chatter and it's hard to talk. 'What's in the boxes?'

The wind and sun have already dried his hair. It flies back from his face, twisted black.

'Dad? What's in them?'

He doesn't hear me. The river widens around us, slow and empty. There are no buildings on the banks now, just broken green where the trees are. A straggling line of sheep, down by the water. Pylons, marching away across the flatlands.

'Dad? What's in the boxes?'

He looks back down at me, face still snarled up into the wind. He could be smiling but it's hard to tell. 'Stay away from them.'

I sit still, not looking at my father. The boxes are close, I could lean forward and open the nearest. It would take almost no movement.

The motor's rhythm goes through the whole boat, settling in my bones. The smell of diesel is like home, sweet and warm. It would be easy to sleep. Easier. The sun is out now, clouds breaking up around it. I lean back against the thrum of the engine and close my eyes.

I wake dizzy with the sun full on my face, my skin tingling with it, already burnt. I can hear my father, his hard voice. Another man, calmer, answering him. What language are they speaking? I hear words of Russian, Polish, Arabic. Other voices and languages I can't understand. A shift and clank of movement, the sound of orders. I recognize orders in any language. Behind it all, the wash and hush of the open sea.

I never knew my father spoke so much Arabic. I open my eyes. The sky is blue with high rib marks of white cloud. In one side of the sun is a chip mark. Small and black, as if the sun were made of glass. It hurts my eyes and I look away.

There's a plane next to us, floating on the sea. I've never seen a plane like this. Only in films. It has us in its shadow. On the wing are two men with dark skin, like the Iranian but with scarves on their hair. Their faces are wrinkled and a deep red-brown, as if the sun has managed to burn even them. Two more stand on the fishing boat. They lift up a white box between them. Eight hands on it, talking in their quiet, urgent tongue.

I look round at my father. He stands above me, talking up to a fifth man. The man wears a Western suit of blue linen. He looks at an open box as he talks, not at my father. Listening to them move through languages is like being a child again, hearing my parents through doors and walls.

'Forty. We agreed . . . less for less.'

'. . . nothing. I just deliver them to you. Talk to the . . .'

'Still, there is this problem. I can find better quality binary systems than this sprayed from the plane, this will leave a smaller footprint. Less deaths, is it not so?'

I pull myself up. The man looks down at me and away without moving his face. His eyes are the colour of dried blood, set into crumpled skin. He goes on talking. As if I'm invisible.

'. . . take them?'

'. . . the VR 55. Only the binary form. The money I will discuss with the Iranian.'

I look into the box. Inside is a plastic tub, transparent as old ice. Inside the tub is white powder. There are labels on the tub, written in Russian: *VR-55, binary chemical 2. CAUTION: HAZARDOUS MATERIAL.* A skull and crossbones. A storage number with many digits.

I think of the flour mill, and my mother's father. I think of the little bottles in the story of Alice: *Drink Me*. Flour and water, and the clack of glass, green and white. Little bottles. If you put them together, you make bread.

The fifth man has a gun in his belt. Oiled black metal, like the chapel grilles in churches. Now he shouts to the other men and they close the last box and take it away. The plane rocks against us and I stumble forward against my father.

'Casimir? Welcome back.'

'What are we doing?'

'Making our delivery. It's just business.'

'You said you would tell me.'

My voice is thick with sleep, as if I've been drinking. My father looks round and high above us, the other man turns away. I can't get my balance. My father turns away. 'Nadir!'

The fifth man raises his hand. The sun is above him, chipped and broken and bright. The wind flaps at the man's thin blue suit. 'Until next time, Mister Kazimierski. And to your son. God go with you. And travel fast. The eclipse has already begun.'

The plane moves away, water boiling up behind it. The wind is colder now. The plane whines faster, lurching up into the air. I start to look up again but my father grabs my face, pulls my head down. '*Kurva!* Do you want to go blind? Don't look up, understand?'

I nod. My jaw hurts where he grabbed it.

'Eh?'

'Yes. I said yes.'

I don't look at him and he swears again, walking back to the engine. The boat rocks and slops under him. He pulls the engine cord and it comes to life, hacking and coughing.

'Come here. Casimir? Get back here. If you're minding the boat, you won't look up. Hold it here. Right.'

He stands beside me as I steer. The sea changes colour around us. First it's shining, you can see down into its clear green-blue. Then the light no longer goes into it. The surface becomes dull, flat as slate, the way water looks in the early evening. I can feel my father standing next to me. Too close. The warmth of his arm in the cold air.

'What was it? The powder.'

'Why? What does it matter? It's done now. We go back and get our pay. Business is business.'

There's no noise around us, only the clatter of the engine. The seagulls have stopped crying. I didn't hear until they were gone. I start to look up but stop. After a time I see the seabirds in the distance, in the low sky, flying towards land.

I laugh. 'Flour and water.'

'What?' My father looks at me as if I am mad. Keen, careful eyes.

'What does the powder do?'

'It kills people.'

'How many?'

'How should I know? Many. Many many many. How many mice dine on a loaf of bread?'

'Why do the Russians sell it?'

'They don't need it any more. They no longer require it. So someone makes money out of it, it's only natural.'

My father bends forward, lighting a cigarette. It's cold enough that I feel the smoke, warmth blown back into my face.

'Two chemicals. You mix them together, like flour and water. And it makes a poison.'

He looks up at me. 'Clever boy.'

'A chemical weapon.'

'Only the best for the best.'

There are shadows growing on the deck now, although light still catches through the gaps of planks above the water-line. I narrow my eyes to see. Through the cracks, light falls on the deck in hundreds of little crescents. The sun is being eaten away.

'How will they die? Does their skin go numb?'

He goes quiet then. We chop across the water. He looks across at me. Fearing me. 'You touched it. When you were little. You remember that?'

'Yes.'

'You've got a good memory. It goes to your nerves, this stuff. One pinch on your skin, one drop, and everything goes numb. When your lungs go numb, you can't breathe any more. Then you die.'

'You should have told me. I will never come here again.'

I don't say it. Only in my head. A shudder of feeling goes through me. It's because of the way the light is going. So fast, as if the world is grinding to a stop. It makes my skin crawl.

'Money for nothing. I told you. We buy things now, to take back to Poland – but it's just cover. Less questions asked. You don't need to tell your mother. Christ, it's getting cold. I could do with a coat now. Still, we've not far to go.'

The light is going faster. Shadows pool out around the ropes, buckets and buoys. I look down. My shadow is growing straight out eastwards from my feet. My teeth are chattering again. I shake when I breathe, the fear gathering in my arms and chest.

'Not too far. Keep on course, that's it. Watch the coast and you'll be fine. Watch the coast and don't look up. Watch it. Casimir?'

There is something happening behind us. I can feel it in the hair on my back and hear it too, a great silence. My father's voice is small beside me. I look round.

A shadow is coming across the sea towards us, racing across the flat water. It is the shadow of the moon. It is as big as Poland. It makes no sound as it swallows us, a cold mouth without language. I look up, head right back on my shoulders. Straight up into the sun's black death mask.

'Casimir? Casimir?'

I look back down for my father, but my father has gone. Beside me stands nothing but an evil man.

# 11

# Care

'I'm a dentist, I know. The range of colours in people's teeth – fabulous. Like eyes.'

'No, they're not.'

'I'm telling you –'

'People don't have green teeth, do they?'

'Not usually, no.'

'Well then. Nothing like eyes.'

He opens his eyes. The northbound train is crowded with evening passengers. In front of Casimir is a wickerwork of limbs and torsos and, framed through that human mass, a couple talking. There is no other sound except the roar of the train. They are dressed for a night out, bright and dark and colourful, the woman sitting forward with her knees together. Casimir watches her nervous energy. He feels it in himself, all his muscles sprung tight. Waiting for action.

At Kentish Town he rises against the train's momentum and pushes through the crowd to the curved Tube doors. Their glass is still crystallized with rain from the city surface, miles south. The drops shiver out into roads as the train decelerates and grinds to a stop. Casimir steps out as the doors begin to open, hauling them apart, the grime staining his hands black.

The station is full of people sheltering from the rain and ticket touts for the Forum concert halls, the sweet public smell of their wet clothes carried down shafts and wells. Casimir takes the escalator in long strides, not breathing fast yet, beginning to run harder as he reaches the street. The pavement is jammed with concert-goers around the all-night take-aways, eaters leaning on the unlit fronts of fish and flower shops, and he runs round the crowds and through them, stumbling once in the gutter as a car blares past. Drinkers yell after him outside the Vulture's Perch and Castle Tavern.

'Oy! 'Kin' 'ell.'

'Slow down, mate! She'll wait if she loves you.'

The alley beside Al Araf Saunas is deserted. Casimir goes quietly anyway, watching for police, Line Management, any of the authorities who could stop him. The door to the yard is closed with a new padlock of layered steel. Casimir leans up close to the corrugated-iron fence. Its wet surface is stained black and yellow and steel-blue, like a wall of mackerel skin.

He closes his hands around the padlock and takes a step backwards. Held up by rotting wooden palings, the metal warps and rattles, rust cracking off it. Casimir has taken four steps when it comes away, crashing and booming towards him across the concrete. He hauls the metal to one side, mouth set with the effort. Looks up at the door of the abandoned station.

There is a figure hunched up beside the door. Indistinct from the piles of rotting carpet and linoleum around it, face turned down so that the hair drips away from the eyes. Casimir doesn't recognize the man until he goes close, up to the mottled white-metal door. The figure's neck is wrapped in pink Elastoplast, its facial features flattened out like a boxer's.

'Bill.' Casimir's voice is deadened by the downpour. He tries again. 'Bill.'

The man looks up. 'Oh, it's you.' His eyes are dull, scrunched up against the rain. Now they go wide and starey. 'Well, you've been living in interesting times, ain't you?'

Casimir squats down next to the older man, catching his breath. He sees there is a tiny dog curled up inside the man's woollen coat, black and tan with attentive black eyes. Rain shines against Casimir's face and he wipes it away with the back of his hand. 'What are you doing here?'

'Waiting for Hilary. This is our emergency rendezvous. Have you met my friend? He's called Snog. Snog the dog, see? It's a joke, you can laugh. Go on, it's good for you.'

'The police had you.'

'Nah.' Bill smiles the word out, his face lit up with something, pride or pleasure. Burnt with it. 'This old Bill's quicker than that Old Bill. The hospital had me, but not for long. Bill has just left the building. I got out through the Place of Rest, down where they take the bodies away in the Black Marias. I know the hospitals, see. I've been there before.'

He leans closer. 'Where is Alice?'

Bill puts out one fist, thumb up. Turns it down. 'She was under the platforms. Creeping around in the crawl-space. They never came out with her. I watched.'

'She is still down there?'

Their faces are inches apart. Now the man leans back from Casimir, whining, his head banging against the old brick wall. The dog looks up at their faces and away, panting into the rain.

'I don't know, I don't know. I didn't want them to find her. But it's all cocked up now she's locked up.' The homeless man begins to rock on his haunches, his voice fast, hissing. 'All locked up underground, it's ironic. It's practically pharaonic, like Rameses, that's what she is, look on my doors, ye Mighty, and despair. Down below the station's bright, but here outside it's black as night – do you remember? Billy Brown of London Town? Back in the war, that was. Back in the blackouts.'

'Quiet now. Try to stay quiet. Will you do that?'

'Yes. Right.'

Casimir leans his hands on his knees, pushes himself upright. There is no guttering on the abandoned station building, and water pours down the wall and the Underground door in slow sheets. The metal doorframe is set flush into the wall. Around it, the brick is scored with unused drill-holes. Casimir reaches out and pushes a finger into one hole, up to the first joint. The soft stone crumbles against his skin. Red, like mincemeat.

'Are you going underground?'

'Yes.'

He feels around the doorframe. There is nothing to get hold of and not all the bricks are rotten. He digs at them, feeling clay collect under his broken nails. Making purchase.

'You should get a move on. Time flies but aeroplanes crash. No, that's not right, is it? Time flies like an arrow but fruit flies like a banana? No, that isn't it either.'

He leans his head forward, resting it on the cold metal. Taking the strain with his shoulders, rolling them back. Air cracks between his teeth as he pulls. Once. Twice.

'Time flies when you're having fun. That's it. Nice to know we're having fun, isn't it?'

The door doesn't move. Casimir begins to swear between his teeth in English, in Polish. Stops himself. He holds the breath inside him, a hard belt of it in his belly. Steadily, he begins to yank at the doorframe. Hauling against it with his arms and feet, like a big animal in a small cage. As if it's him who is trapped underground, not Alice, who lied to him. Who is not Alice at all.

The door warps once, booming like a drum, and immediately there is a squeal of metal as the first bolt comes loose. Casimir works at it with quick, hard tugs. Using his weight, a hundred kilos of muscle and bone forcing itself inside. When both upper bolts are loose Casimir reaches up, pulling the entire doorframe downwards. Inside is the staircase, lit up bright and dull, neon tubes coated with dust.

On his wrist the watchstrap is tight, the veins of his arms swollen with blood. Casimir takes the watch off, folds it carefully into his jacket pocket. Looks up. The homeless man is standing ten feet away. Quiet, well back, the dog still cradled in his arms.

'Well. No hiding from you, is there? What big hands you've got, Granny. Long arm of the lover, that's what you are.'

'Are you coming down?'

'No. No, we'll stay up here, thanks. Got to wait for my other half, my Hilary. Dear Hilary, without her I'm rather ex-Hilarated. Nice to get out of the rain, though, ta. I'll see you when I see you, eh?'

'Goodbye.'

Casimir steps over the flat ramp of the door and goes inside. He takes the stairs at a run. Making long jumps down them, eight or nine steps at a time. He remembers the feeling from childhood; the delight of motion through trees, the sensation of flight.

At the bottom of the spiral stairs he waits, listening to the sound of himself echo away. In the core of the staircase the substation door has been shut. Casimir tries it but the heavy metal is locked and his arms ache to the bone. Two arches lead off into light through the curved walls. Casimir looks down for his own footprints, but the dust has been trampled away. He turns left, into the side-passage with its bricked-up lift doors and wartime graffiti.

The lights are brighter now and Casimir can see pale line-marks on the walls, as if furniture once stood against them. At the passage's dead end he can make out a pile of wooden planks and three sets of bunk-beds, their skeletal frames leant awry.

He stops still. From somewhere in the abandoned station comes the buzz of loose electricity. He can smell it in the air, frazzled and sour. He wonders if the generators are damp with groundwater or simply overloaded, unused to so much activity. There are other sounds too: the cacophony of a car alarm filtered down from the surface, the hush of tunnel air from further underground. Nothing human.

'Alice?' His voice sounds small in the ruined station.

The hush of tunnel air intensifies, gains sound. Its murmur builds to a roar as a train goes through the derelict platforms below. Casimir takes out his wristwatch. It's still before ten, hours until the Underground closes down.

There are four storeroom doors further down the passage, their old wood glossed with strip light. A metal bar has been set across each door, nails drilled into the passage's cracked tiles.

'Alice?'

He comes to the stairs with their luminous wall-stripes. Walks down through the radium light, past the last locked door and the light bulb still swinging on its flex, out into the railway. Silver parallels curve off into the dark, clean and perfect and beautiful.

She is at the far end of the southbound platform, sitting on a pile of Underground signs between high stacks of ironwork litter bins. Casimir is less than a dozen feet away when he sees her. She is smoking a cigarette, leaning back against the platform wall. Her face is still in profile, not turning to look at him.

He sits down beside her, not speaking. The smooth enamelled metal is cold against him. Rat's-tails of unwashed hair fall straight past the curve of Alice's cheekbones. He can't see her eyes or ears, only the downturn of her mouth. From where he sits, it is hard to tell if she breathes.

'Are you hurt?' She doesn't answer, his lone voice whispering away. He tries again. 'I have been looking for you. What are you doing?'

'Waiting to get out.' She takes a drag of the cigarette. The tobacco pops and crackles. Like electricity, he thinks. 'What do you want?'

'I found him. It is a man you knew, a foster carer –'

'I know who he is.'

She looks round at him, forehead pinched between narrow eyes. Casimir remembers the Line Manager. It is a cruel face. He goes on talking.

'The lines shut down in two hours – we could walk to Camden. Or you can leave now, with me. I have removed the entrance door.'

'*I have removed the entrance door.* Christ, you even talk like Arnold Schwarzenegger. You told the police I was here.'

'Yes.'

'You cunt.'

He sees the way her throat and jaw and face move, bringing up the word. Her voice breaks on its harshness and she turns away.

'You knew it was him. The foster carer. You never told me.'

'So? You know now. *Carer!*' She spits the word out, disgusted by it.

'What is his name?'

'What does it matter? All that matters is he doesn't find me. I'll never let him find me.'

He is looking at her hands. The nails have white crescents of calcium deprivation. They are bordered with black dirt under the broken edges. Casimir imagines her at the entrance door, panicked. Scrabbling at the metal, trying not to be heard.

'You thought it was me who killed them. Didn't you? I thought you believed me. You should have. We were lovers.'

'I'm sorry.'

She leans back. Takes a long drag of the cigarette, breathes it out. Casimir sees that her face is wet. He holds himself back. Wanting to touch her, not yet touching.

'You're stupid, Ariel Casimir. You'll never find someone like me again. And that policewoman too, what a mad cow. You know what'd be funny?' She smiles at him but the expression is weak, already fading. 'If they locked me up, he'd never get to me. All the years he's been after me, and then they'd lock me away. Don't you think that's funny?'

'We can tell the police –'

'No!' Her voice rises over his, shrill and strong. Bruised with anger. 'He doesn't even know what I look like, not really. I haven't seen him for years. He used to tell me he wasn't a real dad. He told me lots of times. So it didn't matter what he did to me, that's what he said; because he wasn't real. Still hurt though.'

The cigarette is burnt down to the stub. Alice puts her arm out straight and flicks it. Casimir hears her nails click. The butt sparks off the far wall, trailing down to the catch pit.

'Care! He was careful though. He took care that no one knew. When I was little I was scared of butterflies, I hated summer. Because I thought they'd hurt me. Like butterfly knives. He liked knives. It was all right when it hurt, though. Because what we did was wrong. It was worse when it didn't hurt any more. When it stopped hurting was when I left.'

'There are other places to go. Away from London. I can take you to Poland.'

'And then there were the posters. They were everywhere, it was like –' Her voice is weaker now, and querulous. 'He's crazy. I don't know how he does it. It feels like he's everywhere.'

'He was in Lower Marsh. In the restaurant.'

She looks round at him quickly, as if she had forgotten he was there. It reminds him of Adams, but the supervisor's private voice was quiet, thoughtful. Alice's is different. Cold and clean-cut, like raw meat.

'He sent me a warning. To stay away from you.'

'No. He sent you something to scare you, and then he waited for you to find me. He's clever like that. He'll be here soon.'

She stands and reaches a hand back down and he takes it. There is almost no flesh on the hard bones of her fingers. It is the hand of an old woman and for a moment he feels the urge to pull away.

'It's not your fault. We should go now. Are you coming with me?'

'Yes.' He grins with the effort of standing, the muscles of his thighs and shoulders aching around the joints and bones.

They go together up the green-lit stairs, along the tiled passages, between locked doors. The light bulbs gutter as power spits and hums above them. Alice talks fast, breathless with movement. Close to him, so that their fingers connect and catch, and then they are walking like lovers, hand in hand through the abandoned station.

'How old are you, Casimir? It doesn't matter, though. My grandad was fourteen years older than my nan. She had cataracts, all white. You've got nice eyes. You kept looking at me on that train, and then I saw you in Camden. And he was there already, my carer. I knew you'd help, though. I could see it in your eyes. We can go somewhere, can't we? Poland. What's it like? Casimir? What's Poland like?'

He walks slower, head bent forward as he comes to a standstill.

'What?'

'There is someone here.'

She stops. From ahead and above comes a *scuff* of friction, echoing down the stairwell. A soft clicking of movement, like dominoes falling. The rhythm stops, then begins again, faster and deadened as it approaches. As if the runner is barefoot, racing down the spiral stairs towards them.

In one movement Alice crouches and turns, fast as a sprinter off the blocks. From the stairwell come two claps of sound, almost together; the sound of feet hitting the shaft floor.

Casimir stands quite still, facing the entrance arch. His eyes hurt in the flickering light and he blinks once, twice, clearing them.

No one comes out of the archway. From where he stands Casimir can see a section of stairwell core. Beyond that the second lit archway, leading down. A current of air susurrates through both archways as another train comes closer, along the Tube tunnels.

There are two ways down, he thinks. Panic begins to rise inside him and he forces it back, turning, running on the turn. One of the strip lights has gone dead and he sprints through its band of darkness, down the staircase, out on to the south-bound platform.

'Alice!'

He can see her, way ahead of him and still running, down towards the southern tunnel mouth. The noise of the train is building up now and Casimir's voice is drowned out as he shouts again.

He looks round. A hundred feet back up the platform is the flickering light of a second cross-passage, orange Portastor units piled high around its mock-Tuscan archway. Casimir stares at it as the tunnel air begins to roar around him. But there is no one there – he can see no one, no movement of shadows. Lit up red and grey, a fold of newspaper is blown past him towards Alice. She is at the platform's end wall, kneeling by the tunnel mouth. He runs to her. The newspaper catches at his feet, tearing apart.

'Told you. I told you. He made you come to me.'

'I didn't see him.'

He kneels beside her and she reaches up, kissing him. Hands around his head, feverishly stroking the back of his skull. The train batters by next to them, a flickering arcade of light and faces.

Her mouth tastes of cigarettes, hot and rancid. She breaks the kiss and whispers up at him, mouth to mouth. 'How long until the next train?'

'Not long. Maybe five minutes.'

'I don't care, if he's here. I'm going through to Camden. Will you come with me?'

'Yes.'

'We won't get hurt, will we?'

'No. Stay away from the tracks.'

'Help me down.'

'Wait. Please.'

But she doesn't wait. On the platform's end-wall is an aluminium socket cover and Casimir flips it up and clicks the switch underneath. There is an echo of sound like hands clapped once and lights come on along the curved tunnel wall, strung out towards Camden Town. He can see Alice moving away through the bands of illumination, leaning against the ribbed metal wall.

Casimir climbs down, finding his footing between ballast stones. He enters the tunnel a dozen feet behind Alice. Instinctively, his shoulders hunch forward. The light here feels more temporary than at South Kentish Town, the dark closer and more permanent. For the first time tonight, he is glad to be with Alice. There is no sound except the clatter of their feet on tunnel ballast, their breathing carried off in the tunnel's wind.


'The nearest track is a signal line. The next is the negative current.' His voice echoes oddly, struck off the Tube's metal walls. 'Stay away from both. Even the signal rail has some power. If you fall, keep away from the furthest track. That is the most dangerous. Alice? The furthest track.'

'I heard you the first time. Is he behind us?'

'I don't know.'

'So listen. You're closer. Do you hear anything?'

He slows, head cocked. He can hear nothing but the slight hollowing of air currents as they fill out into the abandoned station, two hundred feet behind them.

'No. There is –'

He stops speaking. From around the tunnel's northern curve comes the clatter of stones on the wet concrete. Only once; then there is quiet again. His mind races, trying to picture causes. But there is nothing animate in the tunnel. Nothing to move or fall, except them.

'I hear him.'

'Oh no.' Alice's voice sounds miserable. Like a child, knowing what is happening, not wanting it, and without the power to change it. Casimir takes hold of the wall's metal ridges and begins to haul himself along. Tunnel stones clack around him as he closes the gap with Alice.

A step away from them the signal rail shines, curving south-west.

'Say something, Ariel. Tell me something nice.'

He tries to think of what to say. The effort of speech and movement takes his breath away. In his head he counts the line-lights, measuring off distance. Twenty-nine, thirty. 'I had a dog. When I was a child. It was called Bison.' Thirty-two, the bulb flickering in its bracket. 'Because in Poland there are great forests full of bison, they are big as Russian tanks and the steam comes off them like the smoke from Russian trains –'

Her laughter comes from deep in her throat and he is glad of it. 'You fucking liar. I bet you never even had a dog. Did you?'

'No.' He is close enough to touch her now. Her hair is pulled over one shoulder and he can see her bare neck under the grimy collar of her jacket. The skin and cloth are sheened with sweat. She doesn't look round.

'I didn't have a dog either. I always wanted one. Something big with real teeth. My carer said I wouldn't look after it but I would have. Then it would have looked after me –'

Alice stops talking. Casimir walks into her as her pace slows, his hands going out against her warm back. 'He's getting closer.'

'No, not him. Don't you hear it?'

He feels it first. Through his feet, a vibration in the tunnel floor. There is a noise behind them, still distant. Pressure building underground.

'It's a train. Isn't it?'

'Yes.' He counts the line-lights. Thirty-nine, forty. 'There is a junction ahead of us. Go as fast as you can.'

'How far is it?'

'A hundred feet. Go faster.'

'Is there room for us? If the train comes first.'

'No.' The train is louder now. It sounds as if earth is moving southwards. Piling towards them through the half-dark.

There is another clatter of stones behind them and a noise that might be human, an echoed *hah* of effort. Alice starts to run. Almost immediately her feet slip on the ballast stones and she stumbles between the nearest two tracks, finds her balance and keeps going.

Casimir picks up speed. The sound of the train is intimately familiar to him, air avalanching before its flat head. Part of him knows how close it is and his mind blanks out, not allowing him to estimate the distance behind them, the distance ahead. The tunnel dream comes to him, very clear. The alcove always beside him. At the last window of the train, Alice's face.

'Where is it?' She is screaming now and as she does so another noise starts up behind them, a braying roar. It is hard to make out as a human sound. Alice cries out again. There is a rhythm to the other voice, violent and reflexive, like sobbing or hysterical laughter. The force of it and the force of the train come barrelling towards them along the metal tunnel walls.

Shadows flicker around Casimir, thrown ahead by the last line-light. Then the junction alcove is beside him. He almost runs past it, so that he has to reach out for Alice, hauling her back under the tangle of cables, holding her into the dark space. Pressing his face into her hair.

The noise reaches them, a deafening rumble. It sounds volcanic, a great force trapped underground. It sweeps on and under them, the ground shuddering like a motorway. A light rain of dust falls on their bent forms from the mare's nest of cables. The roar of air begins to fade southwards, towards Camden Town.

Casimir puts his head back against the alcove wall. Sweat stings his eyes and he blinks it away, breathing hard. After a moment Alice begins to move. Pulling away. Her laughter is high and keen, on the edge of hysteria.

'What was that, what was it, was it a ghost train? There was nothing there, was there? I didn't see it.'

'No. I think it was a postal train.'

She closes her eyes, shivering. 'What's a postal train?'

'There are mail Tubes. Unmanned trains. In some places the tunnels go near ours. I've never been so close to one before.' His hands are shaking and he closes them around her biceps.

Alice opens her eyes. The control is back in them, the pupils dilating, adjusting to the dark space. 'It went underneath us, didn't it?'

He nods. She leans her face against his, forehead to forehead. Whispers to him. 'He would be dead, if it'd been a real train. My carer. And now he's not.' He can feel her breath and the lashes of her eyes as she blinks, almost smiling. Her breath and his steadying together. 'What a shame.'

She kisses him gently. Pulls away, pressing her hand against his lips as she léans out of the alcove, rises to her feet, already starting to run.

Casimir hauls himself up and out. He can see the paleness of Alice's hair, flickering south between line-lights. He opens his mouth to call after her and as he does so, the roaring begins behind him. Gut-deep and angry, rising into a ragged wail. Casimir feels a switch kicked over in his head. The darkness around him, the desperate sound of fear behind him.

He starts to run. On the tenth step his ankle twists, the calf dragging against the signal rail's cold metal. He hears and feels the electricity snapping his leg rigid. Alice is calling from up ahead and he stumbles against the wall and on.

'I can see the end! I see it! Don't look back. Casimir! I can see –'

Still running, he looks back. The carer is less than a hundred yards away. In themselves his movements are not frightening but almost comical, like something in an old film. Sped-up. His T-shirt flaps loose from his jeans. Casimir can see the fish-white flesh of his belly, big but muscular, fat only in the way wrestlers are fat. But so white, like something not used to the light.

And now there is less than fifty yards between them. He moves like Alice, thinks Casimir; the quickness and silence are deceptive. He is surprised at the human face, as if part of him expected something animal. The man stares past Casimir, eyes fixed ahead in their wide-boned cheeks, the roar echoing away around them. There is something in his bunched left hand, the long nails curled around it. Shiny, a vestigial metal finger.

'Casimir!'

He runs harder. Methodical, making himself move. He hears the carer's breathing and laughter bubbles up inside him. The hysteria is not unpleasant but exciting, like the thrill of a childhood game. A hunt in the backwoods, Piotr's laughter echoing away through the stilted forest light. Now he can feel the muscles in his back spasming, expecting pain.

There is a hole in the darkness ahead. He has looked up to see it several times before he takes it in as the tunnel's end.

Beyond it are platform lights. The bright, dark clothes of an evening crowd. The distant glitter of a timetable light-board.

He comes out into bright light. Its clear surface falls across him and he gulps at it, not looking back at the tunnel's mouth. Alice is beside him, kneeling in the thin crowd, and she reaches down and helps him up. There is panicked laughter and whispering around them. The small, clear voices of children.

The human noise seems peripheral, as if part of him is still running. Casimir presses his face against Alice, breathing in the smell of her neck. Against his face, the hardness of her collarbone under the skin.

'Daddy, are they Underground people?'

He opens his eyes. There are two small girls watching him. The same dark irises, dark plaited hair. Their father pulls them back into the gathered platform crowd.

'What's the Underground lady saying, Daddy?'

'The man's got all blood on his feet.'

Casimir feels the wetness on his calves, colder and more painful where the jeans touch the flesh. The wounds there have reopened and he remembers the dog woman, days ago. *Don't hurt my lurching girls.* Alice is talking to him, close and urgent.

'Casimir, come on. Please don't stop now.'

He shakes his head to clear it. Looks round at the tunnel mouth. There is no sign of anyone following. Nothing except the line-lights, bright beads strung out into the dark curve.

'He could come out another way. Could he do that? He could be anywhere. Casimir?'

Over the heads of the crowd he can see a cross-tunnel bridge. It cuts straight and high across the platform's curvature. There are people there, not looking down, hurrying on to other platforms and destinations. Beyond the bridge is a sign in green, EMERGENCY EXIT; beyond that, the control room's passage entrance.

'The control room. We will watch for him.'

Casimir starts towards the passage, Alice just ahead of him, almost running. The crowd moves away from them both. Trying not to touch.

The control-room door is unlocked and Casimir goes straight in, heading for the camera screens. Weaver is by the equipment racks, changing into orange tunnel overalls. A skinny figure in white Y-fronts, his back blotched with wine-stain birthmarks. He looks round, gawping at Alice.

'Who are you? Cass, is she public? You can't have her in here if she's public –'

'Weaver, listen to me.' Casimir leans over the counter, monitor light dulling his face. The four platforms curve away on their separate screens. They are almost empty, a few weekday late-nighters clustered by exits and entrances. 'You must call the police. Tell them – just tell them to come. Weaver?'

The worker is staring at Alice. His face is blotched red and white as he blushes. 'You look just like them. The woman who fell and the other one. What's your name?'

'Alice.'

She has stopped moving. Watching him. Casimir keeps his eyes on the screens.

'Hurry now. Call the police at Kentish Town. The number –'

'Yeah, all right. I know the number.' The trainee's voice is puzzled but light, accepting. There are cellular telephones slung from the equipment rack and he reaches one down, fumbling with the buttons. Alice comes up beside Casimir. She cranes back to see the screens.

'He could go away again. He could wait for us.'

He remembers the carer's face and, more than that, his screaming. A basic, animal sound. On the screens, three of the tunnel mouths are dark. The fourth is beaded with line-lights. A few people still wait there, peering into the half-dark.

'Sir? I can't get through to them, it's busy.'

'Ring 999. Explain to them.'

Casimir's voice is soft with concentration as his eyes go from screen to screen. In his mind he imagines the carer crawling up on to the platforms.

But there is nothing to see. A train comes in, heading south through the City. Pulls away from an emptied platform. Casimir feels his breathing becoming even and slow. The image is so familiar and mundane.

'Cass? What am I explaining again?'

He turns towards Weaver. The trainee flinches away as he grabs the telephone. There is blood on his hands, where they have touched his trousers. His fingers leave tacky print marks on the cell's green-lit buttons as he starts to dial.

Behind him Alice starts to talk. Her voice is quiet, conversational.

'He's still here. Here he is. Come and see.'

Casimir pushes the cellular phone back at Weaver as the line connects. Runs to the counter, eyes jittering between monitors. Alice's voice is soft, as if the carer might hear her through the screens.

'He came out of a different tunnel. He could be anywhere now.'

Casimir doesn't answer. His eyes are settling on one of the cross-tunnel screens. A man runs under the camera's steep angle and goes up the emergency stairwell, out of sight. The camera blurs his movement and the heavy, rounded shoulders, a grey trail fading behind the figure as it disappears up the spiral.

'There.' Her voice is a sigh. As if seeing the carer relieves her of something.

'I saw him.'

'The stairs only go up, don't they? We could catch him.'

'Maybe. I don't think there is another way –' Casimir stops talking, features relaxing.

He goes over to the equipment racks. His work jacket hangs torn down one side and he takes it off and puts on an orange visibility vest. There is a pair of his work boots at the rack's foot. He shucks off his shoes and pulls on the boots, glad of their thick rubber soles. There is a bunch of emergency keys and he takes them too, sliding the cold metal into his pocket.

He turns round, taking in the room. Weaver standing, his thin chest still bare. Alice sitting on the counter, her knees together and her shoulders hunched up; watching him and saying nothing. Casimir wants her to say something. To tell him to take care. Anything will do.

'Weaver. There is someone I have to find.' He reaches out and takes the telephone. 'I know where he is. Stay here with Alice. Don't leave her.'

The trainee stares sideways at Alice, as if she might jump at him, mad as the dog woman. 'What about the police? I can call them again.'

'I don't need them. I can do it myself.' Casimir clips the telephone to his belt. It bangs against his thigh as he walks to the door. A familiar weight, reassuring. 'Watch the screens while I'm gone. Call me if you see him.'

'Casimir.'

He looks back. Alice hasn't moved. There is nothing in her face he understands. 'Take off the vest. You don't want to be seen.'

He stares back at her, not breaking the gaze. Reaches back over his head, pulling off the bright orange material. When she says nothing else he opens the door and goes out without looking back.

It's not long until closing time. He can hear it in the cross-tunnel, the sound of the station hollowing out, the few last footsteps becoming isolated. Casimir turns past locked doors and the dirt-thick grilles of ventilation shafts. The air is cloyed with the smell of cooling kitchens above, Camden restaurants winding down for the night.

There are so many doors, he thinks. He passes them as he reaches the emergency staircase. The walled-up lift portals, the substation entrance. Storerooms and the metal shutters of old cross-passages. So many places to hide. He goes slowly, listening to the station, moving up the metal spiral of cross-hatched steps.

Ten feet up there is another doorway in the shaft wall. Its metal surface has been painted over, not once but many times, the yellowed surface itself scrawled with graffiti four or five layers thick. The mortise lock is covered with paint, up to the keyhole's circular rim.

Casimir tries to imagine how many times he has passed this way, the daily pattern of work making him part of the crowd. It is hard for him to see the deep-shelter door in detail. Familiarity has faded it. He screws up his eyes. Leans close. Looks up.

The painted surface is no longer seamless. Running between the door and its jamb is a fine line, the paint not chipped or cracked but evenly cut through. To Casimir the detail seems odd in its care and violence. He imagines the carer, out of sight, bent forward. His knife opening out like butterfly wings.

He takes the keyring out of his pocket and sorts out the familiar flanged shapes: platform tannoy, crawl-space, surface concourse. He has never been into the deep shelter this way, and he wastes time on three keys before trying a grooved stub of bluish steel. Casimir works it into the mortise lock. Turns it twice, opens the door and steps through.

The smell and the dark hit him together and he raises his hands against them. The deep-shelter air is sour here, as if the trapped dust has fermented over decades. There is no wind on Casimir's face. The bottled-up air hangs around him, pungent as battery acid. He reaches out his hands, feeling along the walls until he finds a panel of light switches.

He flicks them on. At the end of a short corridor is another staircase, spiralling down. Keeled over by the stairwell is a block of machinery, LAMSON PNEUMATIC COMMUNICATION cast into its side.

He walks to the stairwell. The shaft is narrow, and Casimir can see down less than ten feet. But there is a sense of space below. The sound of an Underground train comes through the stone and is carried on into the intervening air. Casimir starts towards the staircase, clumsy with anxiety. One boot clangs against the side of the communication machine.

There is a skittering from below. A rhythm made quiet. The sound of something alive. Casimir follows it down and out, into the deep shelter.

He is standing at the far side the upper hall, thirty feet across from Wanda's red cage-work lift. Casimir's footsteps whisper ahead of him as he starts to walk, northwards, between the shelves and aisles. The neon strip lighting is dead, but Casimir's switch has turned on a series of emergency lights. He recognizes their grille-work brackets, like those in the train tunnels above.

There are other sounds now, softer than those Casimir makes walking. The drip-drop of water falling, far ahead and out of sight. A whirr of ventilation fans, somewhere off in the lengths and turns of the Underground.

Casimir stops by one of the shelves. The wooden frames are familiar now; they are bunk-beds, plain and functional, like those in South Kentish Town. There is space here for thousands of people, he thinks. He goes on under the bars of emergency light.

After some minutes he comes to the end of the archives. Beyond is the empty hall. The line-lights trail off into the distance, clear as a runway. By their illumination Casimir can see stalactites, very white and thin, longer than those in the abandoned station. Storage units, big as truck trailers, their labelled doors locked and dark.

He takes a step away from the archives. There is a difference in the quality of the air here. A greater humidity, a wet coldness and the smell of lime. The environment changing, as if Casimir is swimming out over some oceanic shelf.

The lights help him. It is easier to keep going with the light strung out above him. For a long time he cannot see the chamber's end, and then it looms up abruptly. Casimir reaches a hand out to the flat black concrete. Spurs and surfaces of metal stick out and upwards in three places, as if a massive piece of machinery has been walled up inside. A staircase leads down to the left, light filtering up from the floor below.

It is like being under water, Casimir thinks. Underground and under water are not so different. There is the need to see everything that is hidden, and the desire to get back up to the light. The desire to get out is stronger now. Casimir takes a deep breath, shuddering, glad of the air. Then he goes down the narrow stairs.

The deep shelter's base is more cramped than the hall above, the ground levelled out several feet above the tunnelling machine's original curve. Many of the lights have burnt out, patches of brightness and dark scattered into the distance.

Casimir turns slowly, eyes wide, taking in everything. Under the last spiral of steps is a cavity, narrowed down at its curved end like the volute of a shell. He sinks down to his knees, peering inside.

There is a tiny scuttling in the cavity, insects or tunnel mice, nothing larger. Casimir straightens and begins to walk again. The dust is thicker, matting the concrete under his feet as he moves between shelves.

It is hard to keep track of time. He gropes around for the watch at his wrist, brings it up to his face. But the luminosity is fading. He has been close to the dark for too long. Casimir takes another shuddering breath and goes forward again, eyes wide open.

Without warning he comes to the south end of the shelves. Beyond there is nothing but darkness, the line-lights dead or never installed. Casimir's arm catches a filing box and it falls to the chamber floor. The impact booms dully in the long hall. He kneels down, gathering up spilled papers, marring the hall's thick dust with his movement.

The papers are printed with faded blue shop-till ink. Casimir holds one strip up to the light, then another: '*Asha's World of Booze, 291 Parkway. 17/05/74. Cheque #248285. AC#90887121. Holder: T. T. Cheam. Sun (The) Tuesday, 20 x Skol Lager, 1 Liquorice Allsorts. £6.30.*' '*Ashbery Health Clinic, 2b Pleasant Row. 17/05/74. Cheque #188803. AC#01076458. Holder: D. Falconer. Spinal Massage Treatment. £85.00.*' '*Ashen Entrail Patent Leather Goods –*'

Casimir looks away. Light spills forward from the last line-lights above him, into the dark. There are more storage units ahead of him. Between them, the accumulations of dust are scuffed by movement. Hundreds of feet into the dark is a right angle of light.

He straightens. He can feel the last line-light above him, the slightest warmth of its illumination. Casimir looks up at it, closes his eyes and breathes in. As if he could inhale the light, hold it inside himself. Then he opens his eyes and steps out into the dark.

The shivering begins almost immediately, starting in his legs and creeping up to his arms and chest. After fifty steps Casimir realizes he is still holding his breath. He begins to exhale and then stops himself. He goes on walking. If he looks down he sees nothing, but from the edges of his eyes Casimir can see the dust around him, disturbed ahead of him, a darker path curving towards the right angle of light.

It is clearer now. Casimir can make out the line of a door. He is walking towards the last of the storage units, up against the southern end-wall, as far into the deep shelter as he could go.

It is a dozen steps to the door. Quite distinctly Casimir can feel his heart, its spasmodic movement against his ribs, and the pulse of blood up near his brain. He comes to the door with his hands stretched out, touching the light. Feeling along it as the breath goes out of him.

He stands outside the door while his breathing steadies, one hand by the hinges and one by the handle. There is no sound from inside. Between Casimir's hands is a stencilled sign:

*Portastor #62. Licence #62. Renew 01.01.01*

CARE

He reaches out and opens the door. Steps forward, out of the dark.

There is no one inside. The cabin's walls are bright sheet metal. Light strikes off them from two long-life bulbs. Against the far wall is a red-striped mattress, a metal tool box and two stacks of posters which reach up to the ceiling, white paper pillars. A narrow path is cleared to the bed. The rest of the floor is covered with objects, laid out in neat rows. Reflections glare off tall glass jars, tiny droppers, assemblies of green bottles.

There is a whisper of sound outside. A scutter of feet, moving away. Casimir doesn't turn round. For the moment what is here matters, not the man outside. His foot catches against a stoppered jar and he kneels fast, stilling it before it falls.

The jar is full of a dense, oily dust. It is impacted down into layers of lead-grey and brown, like exotic sands in souvenir glass. The folded texture and colours look almost fungal, Casimir thinks.

There is a label on the far side of the jar. Casimir turns it to see. BEDDING SKIN is printed in old typewriter letters, the Ds bluish and faint.

He puts the jar down, looks up. The room is full of a sweet odour, comforting and intensely familiar. A stack of translucent Tupperware boxes is stacked next to Casimir and he picks up the top one, shakes it. The box is almost weightless, full of a soft flopping sound.

He opens the box. It is packed with Kleenex tissues, pink and white and green, compressed in tightly so that they topple out towards him.

Casimir picks the tissues up. They are all used, the stains clear and dry. In the second box he can see more tissues. Darker stains. A label and date. ACCIDENT BLOOD.

It is hot in the small chamber. The light seems to beat back off the metallic walls in waves. Casimir's breath is becoming harsh and quick.

He looks round him, dazed by the light. Along the left wall is a row of bottles, their necks wound shut with masking tape. It is hard to tell what they hold through the green glass. Beyond them is the mattress, the tool box. A wooden container, polished as a music box.

Casimir steps through to the bed. Reaches down for the box. It is heavy, full of the dense chuff of written papers. Casimir clamps the lid in one hand and the base in the other. Pulls against the tiny lock. There is another label on the base of the box, HEAD, in faded blue.

The lid creaks. Casimir's face is snarled up with effort, eyes fastening on nothing. The objects, the mattress.

He stops. Laid across the mattress are pieces of cloth and clothing. A grey sweatshirt, arms folded. A plain white towel.

The chamber is baked in long-life light. Casimir can feel the sweat on him, trickling down his sides. The towel is folded in four, carefully kept. Casimir puts the box back down, takes the towel. Turns it in both hands. Presses it against his face.

It smells of himself. The odour is acrid, not unpleasant. He remembers Alice's voice: *Like fish blood.* To himself his own sweat smells more mineral; if metal could be smoked it would smell like him. It is familiar as the sounds of the Underground. He thinks of Lower Marsh. The narrow corridors and cheap rented rooms.

He breathes again, closing his eyes. Beyond his own smell is another. Bitter and sweet and lovely, like honey. Alice.

There is an electric buzz of sound, violent in the harsh, bright room. Casimir drops the towel, twisting round, hands finally going to the cellular phone at his belt. He raises it to his face and clicks the line open.

'Yes?'

'Where are you?'

I am in storage, he thinks. In storage with Alice. Laughter rises up in his throat like vomit. He forces it back, throat clicking tight.

'I don't know, I – is that you, Ian Weaver?'

'Sievwright. Where are you? He's here, the guy you – he's right here now!'

He closes his eyes. Holds them shut. 'Sievwright, where is he going? Which screen do you see him on?'

The line crackles with interference, the worker's voice fading in: '. . . the one with the tunnel lights on. Going back where he came from –'

Casimir clicks the cell off. Looks up. In the Underground he knows everything, his mind racing ahead up the shafts and passages. It is two flights to the deep-shelter entrance. Five hundred feet to the tunnel mouth. He knows the way. It isn't far now.

He runs across the room. Bottles and jars scatter around him, crashing together. Outside is the dark but the light is ahead of him now and he runs hard, back towards the deep-shelter stairs. Making it easy for himself, struggling back up towards the light.

At the outer door the telephone catches the wall. Casimir lets it clatter down the emergency stairs as he jumps down to the cross-passage, pushing hard with the muscles of his chest and arms and legs. Leaning into the run as he comes out on to the empty platform.

For an instant the station fades back around him. He can smell the forest, which is also the smell of home. The sap of pines like mint and blood. Voices behind and the squirrel ahead of him, not running. Waiting for him, under the trees. Then he is at the tunnel mouth and he can see the carer ahead of him, or if not the carer then someone, the figure disappearing round the tunnel's curve, the bright beads of line-lights strung out into the warm darkness.

He stops at the platform's edge. Sits down on the white line, reaching out with his feet towards the shining metal tracks. Glances back along the platform. The timetable light-board is a hundred feet away. The arrival time of the next train glitters as the minutes change. Casimir narrows his eyes but they are tired, strained by bad light. He can see only one digit by the train's destination. An eight, or a six, or a three.

'Oy! You can't all be just going in there. That's breaking the law.'

He looks up. Sitting on the last platform bench is an old black man, curls of white hair sticking out under a brown pork-pie hat. Leaning forward, a wooden walking stick across his knees.

'I'm sorry. I have to go.'

'Breaking the law. Tch.' The man goes on frowning, shaking his head. Angry or uncomprehending. Casimir turns away, pushes himself off the platform, and starts forward into the tunnel.

The air here is colder now, the city above cooling towards midnight. From up ahead Casimir can hear the carer. He is no longer moving quietly or even with speed. The chuff of his steps against the gravel is slow and measured, like a spade cutting into stony ground.

Around the first bend the tunnel straightens out. Now Casimir can see the other man. A hundred yards distant, the dark round of his shoulders is sketched into the gloom. He leans a hand on the tunnel wall as he walks and his breathing echoes back down the tunnel. It is monstrous, the breath rattling. Casimir calls out, still moving.

'I see you. I know who you are.'

The other man slows to a halt. He is at the periphery of a line-light's illumination, stark and clear. The face is broad and moon-like. Without expression. He looks through Casimir, as if he sees no one there. After a moment he turns and begins to run again. Not fast but regular, finding his rhythm.

He is limping, Casimir thinks. The carer is hurt. If he is hurt, I can catch him.

He picks up pace, boots crunching against the ballast. Once he thinks he hears another train, a sighing of air, but when he tries to listen it is only the other man. Breathing hard, not so far ahead.

The carer looks back as he runs now, craning round every

few steps. The skin of his face and hands is unnaturally white. Whiter than skin, as if he has been washed in formalin.

'I know what you are. What you want, I mean. Wait, I –'

Talking is no good, he thinks. It takes his breath away. A stitch is forming in his gut, a slow twisting pain. He thinks of Poland again; the birch trees, whiter than the snow. The carer's skin is white as the birch. There is still fifty yards between them when he feels the movement of air against his face. Casimir keeps moving, remembering the postal train.

But there was no wind when the mail Tube passed them. Now he can feel the air pressure; its current, dangerous as electricity. A slight coolness against the line of his nose, as there was eight days ago. Adams beside him on the platform, telling him about the woman who fell.

'Wait – there's a train coming. A train –'

It is closer now, the air building up, acquiring sound. Casimir stoops down. Already there is sound in the tracks. Faint, the whicker of ice warping or water boiling.

'Can you hear me? Listen!'

He is shouting now. Ahead of him, the carer stops. Turns round.

This time he is standing between lights, in a bar of darkness. Casimir cannot see his expression, only the white of his skin. His face, his hands.

There is metal in the carer's right hand. And now there is sound coming from him too, not speech but a chatter of metal, like ticker tape. It takes a moment for Casimir to connect it with the movement of metal. In the carer's hand, the knife opens and closes. Irregular but purposeful, like the spasm of a butterfly in sunlight.

'Come back! We have to go back –'

The sound of the butterfly knife is already being drowned out by the roar of the train. It is faster than the postal train, thinks Casimir. Already it is much too late to turn back.

The sound of the knife stops abruptly. Now there is only the rumble of air. It buffets against Casimir's face and he narrows his eyes. Very still now, watching the other man. Seeing him. In the dark, the carer is smiling. An open-mouthed smile, the jaw thrust out, the bottom teeth a hard crescent.

Like the pike, Casimir thinks. Beside the carer, cables run on along the tunnel walls. In the glare of the next line-light the cables curve up in an arch of grime-black, green and orange plastics. Under the archway is the junction's black hole.

The alcove is less than ten feet behind the carer. The noise in the tracks is more violent now, the train's weight carried down the electrified metal. Casimir shouts into the wind as it builds and thunders.

'You let me follow you.'

The carer smiles again; teeth out, grimacing. He walks backwards two steps, hand brushing along the wall. Now he is standing in the light, the junction alcove beside him. In his fist the knife points towards Casimir. Edge and point on, it is almost invisible.

The wind roars past them both, tugging at their soiled clothes. Casimir can see the other man's face now. He doesn't remember seeing him this still before. He is surprised by the lines of old expression in the man's face. The carer looks like he is flinching away from something, some pain or violence. The feeling is set hard into his features. It is the face of some-one used to losing and loss; the expression of a victim.

From their sockets the eyes stare out at Casimir. Hard and narrow as the face is soft and wide. As if it is his own eyes the man flinches away from. They are Alice's eyes. Blue as blood seen through muscle.

Two hundred feet northwards, the Underground train comes round the tunnel's curve. To Casimir its flat head seems to move with great slowness. There is time to see the driver in the bright cabin, leaning down over the gears. A face in the first carriage, leant back against the dirty window. Blue sparks and fuse-light spat between rails and wheels. Light thrown out across the tunnel's roof, racing across its iron ribs with the quickness of sunlight across fields.

Then the Tube is into the straight, picking up speed. Ahead of it, the carer stands unmoving, a giant black silhouette with the headlights behind it. The Tube's horn blares out, deafening loud, the sound rifled against Casimir's eardrums. He bends away from it, eyes squeezed shut. Reaching out for the tunnel wall with one hand, then with both hands.

The wall cables are under his palms, caked with grime. Above them are the old line-telephone wires. In his mind's eye he sees their parallel lines. The bright, live copper.

He scrabbles upwards. For a second he is hanging off the negative wire, feeling it bend as he hauls upwards. Then he has both wires, their electricity buzzing against his palms. He cries out against the train's roar and brings his hands together above his head. Like a prayer, or a fist.

For a moment there is light everywhere, the entire section of line short-circuiting around Casimir. The train screams down on him. Even in his hands there is light, and a rhythm of pain. Then all the lights go out.

# 12

# Out of Depth

He drives fast, but the sunlight is faster. It goes ahead of us, over the fields and woods. When the birch trees are in darkness the trunks are pale as lightning marks, struck upwards through the black hemispheres of their branches. But when the sun moves on to them the forest is green on top and yellowish underneath, the colour of hair or dry grasses.

The signposts are blue and white, like paintings of July sky. It is ten kilometres to Gliwice. I will be home soon. I will not be home again. How can my mother love my father? How is it that I came to be born?

My father drives without speaking. Around us is the wind, it comes in through the front windows, out through the back. Two front, two back, like blood through a heart. Soon I will see my mother.

The sun moves on to us again and I sit back. When it passes us my muscles harden. It makes me think of Astrakhan, every time. The shadow of the moon, big as a country, coming across the water towards us. The surface of the moon, the surface of Russia. I was calculating them together, but I never finished. I remember my father's expression when he turned to face the moon's shadow. He looked terrified. It was like looking into a mirror. This is the last time I will feel for my father.

He changes down gears at the corner of Aleksandra Fredy Street. Changes to fourth again, picking up speed. I look across at him: his face is curious, as if he is waiting to be hit. I don't understand it. I look away. Out of the side-window I can see the Strug Estate. The blocks stick up, arranged in pairs, like the points of electric plugs.

'Fire.'

His voice surprises me. I look round at him and then follow his eyes, back to the estate. From one of the blocks smoke is rising. A or B Block; not ours, which is further away. It is not like coal smoke, which is brown; this is black and thin. It is a small fire, but the smoke still goes up and up. I am surprised at how far the smoke goes. Miles up it drifts away, east towards Oswiecim.

'Maybe it's your mother. She's been burning duck eggs again.'

I say nothing. Now we turn off Energy Street. The smoke is coming from A Block, and I roll down the window and look out. The afternoon sun catches off the flat windows. Only high up there is one burnt-out window. The glass is all gutted out, the windows dulled two flats above it.

'At least it's not us. At least we're all right, eh?'

We are all right. Not good, not bad. I try to picture my mother's face and it has gone. I put my head right back to see the fire. I count up the floors. Five, six, seven. The sunlight races over and past us.

# 13

# Still

He opens his eyes.

Nothing happens. It is as if his face is paralysed without his mind knowing. As if he is blind. The tunnel dark lies against his face. Somewhere there is the sound of shaking metal and shouting. But he no longer understands this. In the dark he understands nothing at all.

It is something he has been waiting for all his life. And now the darkness is here again, and he is not ready. He is eclipsed. It is as if the life has gone out of him with the light. His legs buckle and he falls although there is nowhere to fall, only a movement through darkness into darkness. Something hits his head and it fills with stars. Their brightness hurts and he is glad of it.

He feels his head with his hands. There is blood, but not so much. The track metal is there, cold and hard, all the power gone out of it. The hammering comes again and the shouting. It could be near and faint, or far and loud. He doesn't know. You know nothing, he thinks.

'Casimir.'

His name comes hissing through the dark. Casimir. It sounds like blood. In the dark, someone is saying his name over and over.

'Casimir Ariel Casimir Ariel –'

A rattle of sound. He closes his eyes again, trying to understand it. It sounds human. He thinks of laughter.

He knows who the voice must belong to, although he has never heard it. For the time being he has no name for it. He reaches down, feet and hands spread, holding on to the track for balance. Sways upwards. Now he is standing in the dark. The balance leaves him and he goes on standing, unable to move. The voice sighs and cries, near or far.

'Ariel Casimir.'

'Here. I am here.'

The words come to him like light. With them, he finds the strength to walk forward. Two, three steps. He closes his eyes again. It is easier with his eyes closed.

On the tenth step he walks into the great flat head of the train. He reels back, arms going out as he falls again. He doesn't cry out. On the tunnel floor he rolls over on to all fours, head down between his shoulders. Teeth together, finding his breath.

'Ariel Casimir.'

There is light in his hands. On the left hand. He raises it towards his face. It is the wristwatch, the only thing of his father's he has kept. The glass is broken and the face is bent inwards, like a bottle top. But the luminosity is still there, shedding its faint limelight.

His eyes adjust. In the pitch-black tunnel, the glow of the watch-face is enough to pick out the whole of Casimir's hand. He presses it against his face, breathing in long sighs, feeling the pulse slow in his wrist, forehead, heart.

'Help me.'

He holds the watch out ahead of him. There is a figure, slumped face-up across the tracks. Casimir moves over, squatting above it.

The carer's face is discoloured, the whole surface bruised dark. The crash has thrown him forward, twisting him in the air as the bones began to break. Ribs have been pushed through his shirt from the strength of the train's impact, Casimir can't see how many. The man's arms are flung out, palms upwards.

'Let me see her.'

'Lie still.'

'I'm sorry. I love her. I'm sorry for all of it.'

The man has been made monstrous with damage. His eyes are crusted with blood and tears but open, staring up into the green light. It reminds Casimir of his father, and he tries to picture him. A weak man, twisted by amorality and a brutal, simple nationalism. There was a photograph, he remembers. He had torn it up, letting it fall from the window, not wanting even to look at it.

He remembers Anna's voice: *There is good in you that comes from him*. He wonders if it is true, and if the opposite is true: he wonders if he can be the monster his father was. Casimir thinks how easy it would be to kill the carer, here underground, where no one can see. To finish it cleanly, for Alice and himself. To make an ending of things and never have to look over his shoulder, back into the dark. He could do it with the strength of one hand.

'Please.'

'Shut up.'

Gently, he touches the man's body. Feeling for damage, drawing back. The hammering and shouting come again, somewhere behind him. He ignores it. Holds the carer's eyes with his own, steadying them.

'I'm sorry. Can I say sorry to you?'

'No. Not to me.'

'Take me to her.'

'Quiet now.'

He reaches under the man's waist and head. Lifts him in one movement, head and spine held as still as he can manage. He waits for a few seconds, making sure of his footing. Then he starts to walk. Away from the train, southwards towards the station. He measures the steps out, cradling the carer.

'I'm dying.' The man sighs. Turns his head forwards. 'It hurts. You wouldn't believe how much.'

His feet crunch against the ballast stones. He moves with care. A parent or an undertaker. He remembers how strong his father was, and wonders whether Michal would have used his strength for this. Casimir thinks that perhaps he would.

He thinks of how old his father is. It occurs to him that there is still time to go back to him, in Poland. He wonders if the old man will ask him for forgiveness, and if he is the one to give it.

It takes a long time to round the tunnel's curve. Now Casimir can see the light of the tunnel mouth. A tiny white oval, it becomes imperceptibly larger with each step. He keeps his eyes on it. He tries to remember where he is coming out. London or Poland. The deep forest or Astrakhan.

'Can I see her?'

'Yes.'

The tracks shine beside him, catching the distant light. Against the carer's body, the palms of his hands ache and burn. The dark is still around him and behind him, but ahead of him there is light.

'Are you taking me to her?'

'Yes. Lie still.'

Now he can see Alice in the tunnel mouth. The light is behind her. He walks towards it, not looking back.

*With thanks*

For their help: the Figurski family in Warsaw, the London Wiener
Library, the London Polish and Nigerian Embassies, the London
Polish and Jewish Museums, the London *Jewish Chronicle*, the
Astrakhan Kremlin staff, Jerry Murray at Goodge Street deep shelter,
and London Transport staff at Belsize Park, Green Park, Down
Street, British Museum, Camden Town and South Kentish Town. For
rhythm: Charles Perry, 'Portrait of a Young Man Drowning'. For
financial assistance: the Harper-Wood Studentship for Literature,
administered by St John's College, Cambridge University.